Mrs.
Sinden

Mrs. Sinden

Thomas Richards

GLOBAL
COLLECTIVE
PUBLISHERS

Published by Global Collective Publishers, LLC
16 North Bryn Mawr Avenue, #1355
Bryn Mawr, Pennsylvania 19010 USA
www.globalcollectivepublishers.com

Hardback ISBN: 978-1-954021-97-6
eBook ISBN: 978-1-957831-00-8

This is a work of fiction and all characters and incidents described in this book are the product of the author's imagination. Any resemblance to actual persons, living or dead, is entirely coincidental.

Thomas Richards asserts the moral right to be identified as the author of this work.

Front cover photo credit: © RMN-Grand Palais / Art Resource, NY

For B.A. Thilakawathie

Where but to think is to be full of sorrow.

—KEATS

1

april 2003

THEY HAD BEEN LEFT ALONE on the Peak for ten days. Jessica Sinden did not like to think about why. But this morning there had been a call. Elaine was sorry. She could do no more. The authorities knew about Philip. The world around her—the Chinese part of it, because most of the expatriates were gone, fled to who knew where—was starting to stir.

For the longest time China had seemed inert, like one of the noble gases, serene and unreacting in that mandarin way she so admired. But when the government at last began to take actions against the disease, Jessica began to be alarmed. Actions were things to be taken against other people. She was a being unto herself, and just wanted to take a bath with Philip and open up the window by her bed to hear the rain. The occasional peal of thunder might come and go, but nothing more than that need affect her. The world should do its dirty work somewhere else. Somewhere downslope, beyond that hairpin curve off May Road, which led to that unlucky tall white building with the coffin-shaped windows, always the first thing she saw coming off the Peak. Philip would report to the hospital in his own time. In *her* own time.

The day was getting gusty. They were on the terrace facing the South China Sea. Lifting her eyes over the rim of her white coffee cup, Jessica saw the green of the ocean graying, and the seagulls, flying high, bending inland.

Looking down, Jessica caught sight of some blood stippling Philip's collar. Dipping her napkin in a glass of water, she began to dab it, trying, as best she could, to think of the dots as red sequins on his shirt, or as little pink tulips on the collar of one of Poppy's blouses.

"It's only water," she said. "But it gets blood out."

Then she squeezed some of the water out of the napkin and began to blot his collar more deeply with the crumpled points of the white napkin, which turned a very light pink.

Jessica could hear the wind in the trees. Philip had left the sliding door open. Jessica looked across the living room at the dining room table, an English one a little too long for the room, its boards scrubbed and knotty, where Edward used to study his medical books many years ago when they were first married. The table was from another life that had once been hers: the life of a British matron in Hong Kong, once (oh once!) a crown colony, a doctor's wife with three children, one dead, but two still living and sent to Discovery Bay for safety. And she, Mrs. Jessica Sinden, reduced to hiding out in her own home, tending to her sick American lover.

Philip coughed. He tried to make it slight, raising a handkerchief to his lips.

But when he took it away from his mouth there was blood on it.

He coughed again. A little more came out, mixed with phlegm like red tapioca.

For just a moment, Jessica thought of trying to act as though everything was just the same. She was used to doing this with Poppy. Last month Poppy spilled water on the cover of a big art book about the Limoges enamels. She threw a dishrag over the book, dabbing it carefully, while Poppy fled into her room. She knew not to slam the door. Her mother would not have it. She closed it quietly, as though everything was just the same.

"Dear God," said Jessica, making herself look down at the handkerchief. This was not water on a book.

"What are you going to tell Poppy and Tristan?" Philip asked, catching the drift of her thought. "They've been calling, you know. They're afraid you might have it, too."

"I can't tell them anything. You know that."

"And Edward?"

"I haven't heard from him for days." She paused. "I mean, I had no idea he'd be going into the *center* of it. My God, the First Peoples Hospital in Foshan! You know they're saying even the doctors there are dying."

Jessica closed her eyes and shook her head, trying to expel the image. This morning there had also been a second call. A voice, clipped and toneless, told her to expect visitors. The voice could have come from Government Hill. Or it could have come from Queen Mary. She tried to ask about the visitors. But the voice only said they were coming for her own good.

They went inside for a warm bath. Jessica let Philip undress her. He went in first, then she nestled between his legs. Listening to him trying to breathe, she took his hand and pressed it against her breast. The window was open a crack. It looked over the pergola in her little side garden. Mina was tightening the restraints on some of her weak yellow orchids. Another maid passed by, greeting her in Tagalog. Jessica listened to their conversation, picking out a word or two. She was beginning to feel a little short of air.

2

january 2003

THE HELENA MAY did not have private dining rooms, which was just as well. What the club had was little private bedrooms, one of which Jessica retained in a little adjoining outbuilding next to the tram. The cars passed by from time to time, but the cables and gears between the tracks ground away all night. She would have to let him in through the front foyer on Garden Road, which passed through the main dining room. It was best that he was coming at a crowded time, and early in January, when there were a few men around. The management frowned on assignations. Some of the boarders at the women's club were rather more long-term than the Helena May would have wished for. Many were separations pending divorce. The women there were mostly very unhappy. The two of them would have to be very quiet.

Usually she planned things just so. But after today's walk with the dogs she had turned to Philip and said, very flatly, to meet her at the Helena May for dinner, and issued him a time. She did not have much time to think it through. Simply repairing directly to the bedroom would not do. She knew all the waiters and most of the members. She only ate here with her daughter Poppy or her best friend Elaine Kwan, so there would be talk when she brought him in. She told Benson she wanted one of the best tables, which, at the Helena May, were also the most conspicuous, the ones nearest the sofa and the piano. It was not a question of concealment. She knew better than to sneak around. It was a question of getting people on her side. She would need to show him off to the ladies of the club, but without appearing to.

For she did not just want one evening with him here. She wanted to make the Helena May their place as it had always been her place, her home away from home, and this called for a rallying of the membership. Everyone from Benson, the head waiter, to the least of the cooks and maids, would have to know of her liaison with the American, and approve. With complete approval, too, would come complete discretion. It all hinged on this, their first night together. Philip would have to know what to do and when to do it. Though she already had a high opinion of him, she wondered if he was up to it. The degree of scrutiny would be something out of Mayfair, and not, well, wherever he was from, north of New York somewhere, the Hudson River, or perhaps it was Hudson's Bay, she could never remember which.

He was on time. Benson sat them just under the portrait of Helena May, next to the window-sill with the geraniums on it. It was an Edwardian photograph, blurry in that strange way they had, indistinct except around the eyes, where her wrinkles were sharply accentuated. Being a lady of her time, she sported them like chevrons of rank. Helena May had come here as the wife of a governor. She found that the men running the colony were very busy and ignored their wives. The poor women had almost nothing to do. They lolled around their mansions all day, bored. Helena May did not much care what women did, but she wanted them, at the very least, to be busy. An admirable aim, she thought, thinking of Poppy. She was so often not busy.

The tablecloth was soft with the light of early evening. Jessica tapped her menu against it. She knew she frightened people. Did she frighten him? Philip seemed so at his ease as he turned the pages of the menu. He was dressed in his usual quietly rumpled way, neat but so nearly dowdy he fit right in. The dining room of the Helena May was to him like his own private conservatory. He somehow knew that, other than Benson, the head waiter, whom he treated as an invisible attendant spirit, the ladies of the club would be the ones to scrutinize him that night. It was for them that he seemed so very natural, very much unposed, as though he were sitting on a long window seat, the sun breaking into little amber shards of light around him. In that light, he was ever so slightly austere. He had a way, too, of looking at the menu, of pointing his finger at just the right entrée, and saying, at the end of the meal, how excellent the Black Bullace Plums had been. Jessica knew just how much this bit of horticulture would appeal to the membership of the club, just as it did to her. Black Bullace Plums, the bitter native variety, celebrated in that most British of treatises, *The Plums of England*. And the other women in the room noted too his formality, his slight stiffness, his reserve. Magnificent. With nothing other than his hardiness and that of the wild plum, Philip Nye had won them over.

"How did you know—" Jessica started to ask him, as, finishing dinner, they left the dining room and headed for the back stairs.

"Poppy told me to expect an invitation."

"She did?" she asked. "To come here?"

"Yes. Here."

She folded her arms. "So she's taken your side, has she?"

Philip pretended not to hear the light tease in her voice, saying, "She said Tristan wanted to know everything."

"Tristan would. And Poppy will tell her. And then she will do what she always does."

"What is that?"

"Take whatever side is *not* mine."

"Your husband's?"

"Oh, no. Edward will take my side. He's very honorable about these sorts of things."

They had come down the back stairs to a rear door. It led across a small garden to a modern outbuilding, modest, but white and well-built, a bit like what you saw in Switzerland. Crossing the little garden made her ever-so-slightly animated, and, nearly trilling, she started telling him about the dinners she used to go to at the Helena May. How meticulously Benson would wind the back staircase railing with light thin wildflowers—

dahlia and dancing ladies and yellowbell. How the dinners in the garden would have little intermissions where the middle-aged women would come to the bathrooms upstairs, just on the second floor landing, talking and pushing more makeup into the creases of their wrinkles; how all the bedrooms in the Helena May, including the ones in the outbuilding, had been done in pastels, the light pale colors of shells, with fluffy white sequin coverlets on them.

"Well, we're here," said Jessica.

She opened the door then closed and locked it behind them.

"So we are."

He looked around. It was a simple room you had to look at closely to see its quiet luxury. It had a trim German bed, a little lower than the ones he was used to, but also a Louis XVI writing table and a small make-up table. All the lights had dimmers.

"Shall I undress?" asked Jessica.

He smiled patiently, sitting on the bed.

"May I watch?"

"Well!" she exhaled.

"I'd like to know where you put your things, Jessica."

"I can't see it matters to *you.*"

"It matters to you." Philip knew how much she liked to see things put in their places. And how irritated she was at forever picking up all the little slinky things Poppy dropped on the living room floor.

Her eyes widened, and she began to tear up.

Jessica had on a light cotton top. Crossing her arms and gripping the lower hem, she pulled it over her head with a snap. Underneath she had on a thin silk blouse.

Then she started unbuttoning her blouse, talking as she went. "I button it up," she began, "all the way to the collar. I used to wear my blouse unbuttoned but now the freckles have become rather mottled with time." She took off her blouse, holding it by the collar and smoothing out the wrinkles with the flat of one hand. Her arms were thin and sinewy, her bra, no larger than a girl's training bra. "I don't like wearing too many clothes," she continued, "but I like being covered."

"You must like the women here," Philip said.

"Yes, the Chinese women. They are marvels of modesty. They manage to cover themselves completely even in the most punishing heat. Elaine says it's because Chinese skin yellows so easily in the sun. Well, mine burns. She's often taken me to Shanghai Tang to be fitted. We wear the same size, you know, even though I'm taller than she is, relatively speaking, of course, for southern China." She lifted one foot, then the other, out of her skirt, a very long skirt that just brushed her ankles, then laid it out on the bed next to him, quartering it in even sections.

"I fold it thusly," she said.

She slid open a drawer on the dresser, running a finger along its bottom. "Good," she said, finding no dust on it. "You may ask, why I am using a drawer in what is, after all, a kind of public locker. Elaine would not think of it. But I like to make a home of wherever I happen to be. I sometimes put odds and ends in there. Little things, you know, bits of dried hibiscus, a rock Poppy gave me. In the best London hotels you almost never see those awful what-do-you-call-thems—"

"Folding luggage racks," Philip put in, loving how unselfconsciously, already, Jessica spoke to him, standing before him for the very first time stripped to her bra and panties.

"An American term, probably. And so ugly, too, like the name of that luggage company. Samsonite. It's such a beautiful myth, the story of Samson and Delilah, and then to make a kind of plastic out of it. Really it's too much. Not that I am up to the standard of Delilah."

She turned to him, putting her hands behind her back, unhooking her bra, then sliding it down her arms.

Her breasts were very small. They sagged slightly like pouches.

"They had, well, a specific gravity once, but there's still some buoyancy left in them. I'll never regret breast-feeding my children, though. There were times when I felt rather more love for them than I do now, and that was one of them."

Then she hooked her thumbs to her panties and pulled them to the floor.

Jessica Sinden stood naked in front of him. Philip took her in. Her breasts were arched with a slight sag, her nipples wrinkled and tight. Her legs had not more than a dab of hair between them, light like her eyebrows. Her belly sagged a little. Then, slowly, she turned around. Along her spine was a line of diagonal scars in a hatch pattern. Parts of the pattern were dimpled. Others were puckered, the skin contracted into small folds.

Seeing him notice her scars, and not avert his eyes, she said, "I hope you don't mind these too much."

"No," he said. "Scars make sense to me."

"They do?"

"You wouldn't be here without them, would you?"

She did a double-take, her eyes moving rapidly back and forth, taking in the whole of his face.

"You couldn't have said anything more perfect," she said.

"I didn't know," he told her.

"I rather thought you didn't."

"How—many?"

"Four operations in total."

He sat on the side of the bed. She walked over to him and placed the flat of his hand on her back, pressing her chin on his head. He felt the deep hard firmness of the scars.

"They're all right, Jessica," he said.

"They are?"

"Yes. They are."

"Good," she said. "Because there may be more coming."

He paused for a moment, seeming to consider some scruple, then asked: "May I ask for what?"

Jessica appreciated his hesitancy in asking. It was not something she spoke about easily, even to Edward, who was a doctor.

"Meningitis," she said.

"I thought that was—"

"An old disease. It is. I had it as a girl. But it never quite goes away, you know. I have this tear in the dura around my spine." She pressed one of her scars. "The last one was—here. They keep trying to fix it, but it's like trying to sew wet kleenex."

"I'm sorry, Jessica. Can they ever fix it, finally?"

"I don't know. I'm used to hoping. But I'm afraid it can't be fixed. Not all the damage, at least."

He lowered his head.

"No need to be sad," she said. "I'm not. I think of them as, well, a kind of Cesarean, only on my back."

Her voice had a brave edge. She caught sight of her scars in the mirror over the dresser. Then she looked back at him expectantly. He felt her modesty even as he took in her nakedness.

She moved to the window to check on the curtain. She rustled it, opening it a bit, then snapped it shut with a tug of her wrist. "There's an avocado tree outside this window," she said, turning and bumping into him. She hadn't heard him come up behind her, and as he took her in his arms, she felt the firmness of his skin and the light beat of his pulse. He was present to her in some pulmonary way that was new to her. They almost seemed to be breathing together.

"Right in the garden," Jessica went on. "Sometimes avocados drop onto the roof and roll into the gutter then drop off into the fountain. With a *plop*—just like that. I love the sound. *Plop!* It's so loud you can hear it over the falling water of the fountain."

"So this has been your room before?"

"No, well, yes. I mean, I have retained it for some time."

"But you've never slept here, have you?"

She blinked at him. "How did you know?"

"I didn't. It just doesn't smell like you."

Jessica grimaced. "You mean I have a *smell*?"

"Don't worry," he assured her. "It's very light. Like a mist."

"A mist," she repeated. She took a couple of breaths. "A mist, you say?" Then she started to cry, very lightly.

"I'm not sure anyone has ever seen me this way. A mist you called it."

She swallowed a sob.

"You don't have to say anything," she added. "Not everything has to be responded to."

Philip nodded.

"I'm so used to ordering people around. Mina. Poppy. Tristan. Even Edward. I suppose it's terribly off-putting."

Philip put his hand between her legs for the first time. "Jessica, I wanted to make love to you the first time I saw you."

She folded her bra over her arm, looking at the bra, not him. "I know." "You did?"

"One can always tell," she said, wiping her nose.

"The way I looked at you in the salon—"

"No, not looked. And it was not what you said either, but how you said it. The presumption in your voice. You spoke to me as though we'd already had sex and had just, well, uncoupled, in bed, afterwards."

'Oh Jessica," Philip said, touching her face.

'I feel so much," she said. "I'm scared."

"By me?"

"No. Not you. By us. I've always felt so alone. And now all I want is to be near you."

She squeezed his hand so tightly the color went out of it.

"It's just that I'm used to knowing what's ahead. My life has always been so—tidy."

Jessica slipped out of her sandals and tiptoed to the dresser, placing her bra and panties carefully next to her skirt and blouse, then tapped the drawer shut.

'Like this drawer. Look at it. Everything in its place."

'It's not so bad, Jessica."

Oh, it was much worse, she explained. Her closets were all little libraries. Even in the bathroom it was *A, B, C, D, E.* Alembics, Bitters, Calamines, Diuretics, Emetics. She did not like throwing away anything that could be saturated with chemicals, starved for air, and locked away in some cabinet.

She paused. "I'm just warning you Philip."

"You don't have to. I like these things about you."

"You do?"

A little bolder now, she turned and opened the narrow closet and ran her hand over a row of wooden hangers.

"There were wire hangers here but I took them out. They were so *unsightly.*"

Philip started to smile.

"And I put a few things in there too," she said. "Some sweaters and a dress. No skirts, though. I have just this one. You can see I'm a bit too thin in the hips to hold them up."

"I already feel like I'm home," said Philip.

Jessica's voice broke. "I—I do, too."

Philip reached out to her, taking her by the thighs. She moved stiffly towards him.

Then he pulled her down over him.

"Wait," she said firmly. "Let me."

Philip held his breath in anticipation as she unbuttoned his shirt and pushed down his pants. Jessica saw light-colored hair under his arms, and the hair on his chest, a darker brown patched with white. She touched his belly and slipped her hand under the band of his cotton briefs. Philip arched his back, pressing his head against the wooden headboard. Jessica slipped under the covers and rolled over on her side, facing him, her eyes open.

⌒

They left their room early the next morning.

Breakfast was light. Philip had toast, while Jessica quartered an orange. The water in the glasses was warm from the tap.

They had emptied themselves into one another and then there were no words. There was a curious piece of art on the wall above their table. It showed a Chinese warrior riding a horse, where you clearly saw the distress of the horse. They ate quietly under it, returning to the ordinary pulse of time.

A few women came and went. They could not help staring at Philip Nye. But he saw how quickly their eyes moved to her, always lingering on her. There was something apprehensive about it. It was not curiosity—but fear.

Jessica said last night she frightened people. She said it so lightly that he had been inclined to brush it off. But this was not light. She also said, *I'm just warning you.* Philip tried to remember what he had been told about Jessica. His ex-wife Roma said she had three children. But she talked only about two, Poppy and Tristan.

3

july 1, 1997

JESSICA FOUND Felicity's body on the day Britain handed Hong Kong over to the Chinese.

They were late for the ceremony. Edward was already down at the Consulate with Tristan and Poppy. Felicity was in her room. Jessica wanted her to come look at a dress she thought was suitable. Felicity wanted to go in a peasant dress and flip-flops. Jessica was sorry they ended up in a quarrel last night, but protocol was protocol. Hadn't she learned anything at Oxford? They would be sitting one row behind the Governor. Her daughter simply had no sense of occasion.

Felicity's door was locked. The transom was partly blocked by stacks of old books. Jessica tried standing on a stool. She saw only a sliver of the ceiling. Felicity had taken down the light and disconnected all the wires. The open ends of the wire were carefully covered with black electrical tape.

Jessica heard a creaking; she tried forcing the door; it stayed where it was.

"I want you to open this door right now," she said in a pressured whisper. "I have a dress ready for you." Adding, "An *appropriate* dress."

Jessica heard a rustling, then it stopped.

"I have a key, you know. And I will use it if I have to."

She waited another minute. Then she reached wearily into her fanny pack and took out a single key.

She turned the lock and opened the door.

Felicity was hanging from the ceiling in her pajamas and a dirty red Christmas sweater—dead at the end of a rope—swaying slightly in the still air.

Oh dear God *that sweater*—

Jessica tried to brace herself against the door frame.

Felicity's eyes were open, plangent green eyes like her own—and yet she wasn't there behind them, sullenly following her movements around the room the way she usually did. Her eyes were glassy and remote.

Then—the tape broke. The body thumped to the carpet. Her daughter twitched a little, then was still.

The air went out of Jessica's lungs. She stumbled and fell to her knees. She reached around to right herself but everything solid seemed far away. She tried to recover her breath. She could barely open her mouth. Slackening, she pressed her cheek against the floor and closed her eyes.

She called Felicity's name. She didn't know if her voice could be heard. She could not hear it.

Some time passed. She needed to open her eyes. She did not want to. But necessity called. She forced them open and saw Felicity's face. One side of her mouth tilted away from the other. She almost reached out for her daughter—to right her face the way she might adjust a collar or button a sleeve.

A little air more came into her lungs. She tried to keep her eyes on a distant point, a cotton tree in the back yard, flowering red, its fibers floating in the wind.

What now? she kept asking. What *now*?

But there was no answer. Jessica looked at the clock on the side table. She was due at the Consulate. Edward was waiting with Poppy and Tristan. She would have to do something.

She lifted herself up and crawled toward Felicity. Then she steadied her hand and took out a tissue from her fanny pack and laid it over her daughter's face. It draped just over her cheeks. There, good. She smoothed it down before she began, trembling, to untie the rope around her neck. She took out a box of talc and powdered her neck until the shiny flesh under the rope was chalky and dry. She put the rope in a bag. Felicity must not be found as she found her, her neck coiled in a noose, the sweater from that terrible Christmas wrapped around her torso. There would be pictures; publicity; an inquest. A child dead by accident would be about the child. A child dead by suicide would be about her.

"You still have two more," she imagined her husband saying when he found out. But Edward would say nothing, knowing, somehow, that the saying of nothing would be swirling around them for the rest of their lives, pulling them like an undertow deeper into the cold dense water where they had always lived.

Jessica attached the ends of her glasses to her ears while she started to called the police. The action was involuntary. Authorities were required, weren't they? But she put the phone down.

Today was the Handover. The body would have to be found afterwards.

The ceremony was not for three hours. Edward was already down at the Consulate on Des Voeux Road with the Governor. He would need to be told. Tristan would not. Poppy she would not tell, but then again, she might already know, for it was just like Felicity to send her sister a note, asking where the key was to where her mother kept that sweater, and just like Poppy to decide not to interfere. In that way she was like her mother. If her sister wanted to go into a locked room and take out something her mother had never been able to throw away (could she, at twelve, have imagined what one sweater meant to her?) who was she to say that she couldn't? They all had their suspicions about Felicity falling out of the car—supposedly by accident. Their mother kept the reindeer sweater she was wearing that Christmas—in a box filed under *F*. It was there to be seen, though everyone in the house, including Edward, was afraid to look at it, thinking, fearing, that even after all these years, it might still be chalky with her blood.

Maybe Poppy showed her where the key was to keep her out of her room. Poppy liked her room, and didn't want it ruined by whatever Felicity was planning to do.

Tidying up came easily to Jessica Sinden. It was the placing of things back into order. Well, not back. Forward into an order that should have been. Kneeling next to her daughter, running her fingers though her hair (still so tousled, even in death!) she thought of how Felicity taught her the word "proleptic." It was not part of her vocabulary until she came back from Oxford, after writing that Special Paper of hers on the rhetoric of sixteenth-century verse, saying,

"Mother, you're so proleptic."

The word meant anticipating the worst, and acting to forestall it. Well, the worst had happened—and for the second time. The first was when she threw herself out of the car in England. And it was no time to stop being proleptic. Anticipating the worst meant the worst was always about to happen. Even when it seemed to have fully arrived, as now, her lovely bright girl buckled into death, it was never far off, waiting for the worst to worsen.

She glanced at her watch. Ten-thirty; she was due at the Consulate at one-fifteen. Felicity would have to be found after the ceremony. The Governor conferred a great honor in placing them in the first ranks of the British dignitaries at the moment of the great handing-over to the Chinese. The second row, but the first rank.

Would the police now not be British? Would she really have to hand her daughter's body over to the *Chinese*?

A shudder consumed Jessica. Everything always had to be so arranged. Even death was an arrangement, in fact, as she had experienced it, it was nothing but arrangements, little ones, one after another. Even Felicity had to have made her arrangements. She wished she could have been there. Not to stop her, though she would have: but to know. She let out a soft howl, breathing shallowly, her throat constricted with pain, feeling an inrush of smells, damp laundry, a stale mattress, old onions in the kitchen—everything mildewing that she always meant to throw away—knowing that Felicity was far beyond reach of her power to make sense of anything ever again.

Perhaps understanding would come later; perhaps not. She threw her body a final, fearful glance. She was close to her, but her face was upside down, unrecognizable, a frowning mask, like a grotesque on the wall of a theater. Like the last time, she had done something to her. Her final act had been a curse on her, the second of two. She put her hand on her forehead. It felt cool, cold even, and yet she would not have known, feeling it, that she was really dead. Felicity always slept so cold. She needed three space heaters to keep her room warm at Jesus College. Felicity loved Oxford but hated winter. She could feel her windpipe freezing. And she had long thin fingers that chilled so easily! She used to like riding the top of a red bus on Kensington High Street London because it was warmer up there. She took attic rooms at Jesus because someone told her they were hot and stuffy. She was such a Hong Kong girl at heart.

Before she left for Central, Jessica took a last look around the upstairs room. The window overlooking the garden, the desk with a framed photograph of Judy Royce-Chapman. Felicity used to touch it gently whenever she came in. How did she get in? That upstairs room was always locked.

Poppy. Poppy must have let her in.

She knew nothing, that girl. She would take it up with her later, if she even remembered giving Felicity the key.

———

Jessica walked down a long corridor made of marble, then up some stairs with portraits of past Governors on the walls. *Sir Alexander Grantham, 1947–1957.* Edward's father had known him, slightly. What would Sir Alex think of this now? Out of the window on the stairs she could see the marshals organizing the ranks of the parade, a portly group with faces like the waxy leaves of the jade plants in her garden, one wearing reading glasses, another leaning on a cane, another so old he seemed blind and deaf. And then she was on a landing, a bright open atrium, so un-British in its lack of intimacy, where there were lots of doors with numbers on them. Her husband was going to be there too, behind one of those doors, with the Governor and twenty or thirty other people she never liked seeing but had come to think of as necessary to her life on the Peak. She opened her bag and took out the note she would hand to Edward, ready to give it to him at the first chance.

He would open it and read:

Felicity is dead. We must go on.

Jessica caught sight of herself in a long mirror. She touched her head. Her hair was tied back in a rubber band. A rubber band! It seemed incomprehensible to be wearing such a thing, here at the Consulate under the scattered light of chandeliers. She tugged at it, snapping the band, running her fingers through her hair and smoothing it down behind her ears.

A door opened. People were inside. There was nowhere for her to sit except on a row of chairs lining a far wall as in a ballroom. When Edward saw her, his eyes narrowed and he turned back to listen to the Governor, who was saying something about how much he liked egg tarts, asking if they had been to that little place on Hollywood Road. She was early. Her husband did not like that she was early. Timing was everything in a ceremony, and Dr. Sinden did not like how unceremonial his own wife's arrival was. She was due to arrive later at the head of a delegation of women from the Helena May. He would then cross the room to welcome them to the Consulate, and present them to the Governor.

The time came for tea. One servant gave them cups, while another poured.

Jessica hated the sound of water being poured into a cup. The close gurgling, a suffocating sound, and often, at a restaurant or café, a hand other than hers passing close to her face, the near press of servitude. Mina she kept in a room detached from the flat, entered only through a drafty storage area, a mudroom filled with wood and tools, entering and leaving unseen. Mina poured drinks in the kitchen and served them on a tray; she saw to that. Mina was probably in Causeway Bay on her day off, watching the handover on the giant television at Times Square. Jessica wished she could see it in black and white. Back when color television was new, black and white was for servants. She still made Mina wear black pants and a white smock. Even Benson, the head waiter at the Helena May, wore black and white. It was right and proper—*meet*, to use an old word she liked, though she never used it with anyone, because no one knew it any more.

The people moved around the room, talking of nothing. Jessica saw her chance. She folded her note to Edward and put it on the saucer like a calling card, holding it down with her thumb. Then she made her way across to room to Edward, saying,

"I brought you tea."

Edward did not drink tea, but he took the cup, first noticing, with mild surprise, what she was wearing: a gray skirt and gray socks. His wife was still in her house clothes. The folded note sprang open up a little when she released it with her thumb. Seeing it, Edward quickly pressed the note into his palm. He nodded lightly and moved off.

She turned away. She must not look at him opening the note. His grief would be private, just as hers was and would always be, the images hers and hers alone, Felicity's mouth still moist, her hands (oh why her hands?) a little bruised, her shoulder blades stuck out from under her bunched body, the rope like a second plait of hair coiled around her neck.

For a moment she thought of reaching out and touching her husband's hand. She started to move her hand, but she withdrew it.

She thought, this is more than we can stand. She wanted to say, not now, Edward, *not now*.

Edward's hand was trembling. His eyes scanned the polished floor. She sensed his disorientation. He had not been warned. Edward liked being warned. He took pleasure in warnings. He warned his patients, warned Poppy about crossing her mother, warned Tristan about his various girlfriends. He didn't know where to go or how to be. Maybe he was thinking they should go back to their flat on the Peak and sit in it, keeping vigil. But for what or for whom? They tried never to have guests, just Jessica's one friend, Elaine Kwan. Edward was now looking through the enormous room with the ceiling molded into squares and chandeliers like dripping gold wax. Men and women stood about in groups, all holding their cups of tea, as though waiting, staggered, to catch the wax dripping on them from above.

Jessica was sitting on a chair backed against the wall. She moved her hands as though she was knitting. She hated knitting. When Edward saw her, she stopped moving her hands and held them to her breast, smoothing down the crinkled linen of her blouse. She found herself thinking about a Nativity Play Felicity did at school in a drafty old auditorium in Kowloon Tong not long after she cancelled her deposit on her place at Wycombe Abbey, where she was the Angel Gabriel. In the play they called her the Angel Gabriela (for it was a very modern school), and she wore a white washcloth on her head. Her little brother, Tristan, was the first Shepherd.

The Angel Gabriela said, "Behold the child."

The First Shepherd said, "Is this *the* child?"

Then the Angel Gabriela noticed the three chairs lined up for the three wise men, who would come in later. She sat down in one of them.

The Angel Gabriela said, "I feel tired."

So true; Felicity was born tired. She nestled under Jessica's neck in the lying-in hospital. Poppy whinnied. Tristan sneezed. Only Felicity had this deep exhaustion about her, a reluctance to exist, as though she had been born into this world from another that lay behind it somewhere, and was still out there, waiting for her to return. And yet Felicity had been just the child she wanted, an old soul who played the piano with the softest touch she ever heard (Tristan played with his feet, while Poppy, who knew Mozart, pretended she didn't and played chopsticks). Her birth was an epiphany after six years of marriage to Edward. For her, she was always the child nuzzled under her neck with swaying small hands. She had a night light in her room. When she was five she went in to check on her. She was on the floor reading under the small light. She stroked her hair and told her she could read in bed. Only when she closed the door, moving back to her bedroom through the dark house, did she have the thought: *my God she taught herself how to read.* Only later did she see she was reading the book upside down.

Double doors opened. A herald seemed to summon them. Jessica seemed to hear trumpets, a summoning that was more of a long-delayed reckoning than a summons. Her children were outside. She felt herself hardening. She covered her knees with her skirt, stood up, smoothed it down, saying, under her breath, Felicity, and again, *Felicity*, adding,

You did this. You did this. You did this.

Her head felt cold. She wondered if Felicity had begun to smell. Her face was already waxy. The flat was warm. She always turned the air conditioning off when she was not there. Had she turned it off? Had she remembered to draw the curtains?

She approached her husband, passing stiff pinkish faces in the room, faces that hardened even further when they saw her. One that didn't was Elaine's, but no, she could not talk to her now.

A telephone in a small room nearby began to ring. Jessica watched an adjutant slipping away to answer it. Was the call about Felicity? Was she being summoned, even here? She once told Felicity that pain was everywhere, even in the bright light of ballrooms. Felicity had asked her to describe the pain in her back. She wished said something else, something less universal, even though, closing her eyes and trying to steady herself, she felt the truth of it.

"Edward?"

"Yes, I'm here."

"Tell Poppy we will go through the entire ceremony, exactly as planned, without deviation."

Edward sighed, hearing the words, which were hard and clear. He was relieved, as he often was, that she had made a decision for both of them. He would never know how, seeing their daughter, she took a napkin from a table and held it to her mouth, praying that there was a heaven and hoping that it would be warm there.

"Does she have the flag?"

"I don't know."

"We shouldn't have given it to her. If you see her, take it from her. I will give it to her when the time comes for her to hand it to the Governor." Adding, "They may ask why they can't come home. Make up something. Like quarantine. That's unlikely enough."

When the time comes. Well, it had. They moved outside to a platform. Poppy and Tristan were sitting in their assigned seats. One seat was empty. Tristan looked angrily at it. Felicity is always late, her son was thinking, and she's just the one to get away with it. It was as if he knew that Felicity was the one her mother liked best.

They assumed their positions. The ceremony began.

She heard, from the dais, some words, British words:

Tonight's celebration will be tinged for some with sadness. So it will be for my family and myself and for others who like us will soon depart from this shore. I am the 28th governor. The last governor.

And in antiphony, the Chinese response:

The national flag of the People's Republic of China and the regional flag of the Hong Kong Special Administrative Region of the People's Republic of China have now solemnly risen over this land. July 1, 1997 will go down in the annals of history as a day that merits eternal memory.

The words echoed over Victoria Bay. A few spotlights passed over its surface, making the water look blue and clean. But it was brown and muddy. Jessica sometimes had the feeling that the bay was muck waiting to swallow up the city at any minute. Best to live, as she did, on the Peak, where one could admire the water at a distance, pretending it was clean.

And she heard, *The return of Hong Kong to the motherland after going through more than one century of vicissitudes.*

The Sinden family stood in a row, listening. They had been among these vicissitudes. Jessica saw Prince Charles standing uneasily near a row of old smiling mandarins. The Chinese also seemed to conduct government as a family business. A row of officials stood in uneasy likeness, as though related. Her friend Elaine was now one of them, having married Simpson Kwan, who was related to someone, who was related to someone else, and so on until the chain reached Tung Chee-hwa. Such a glut of relations, an expanding universe of them. She tried to turn her head to what remained of her family, Edward, Poppy and Tristan. Edward was implacable. Poppy was tense and compulsively alert. Tristan's eyes were brown and gentle, the weak eyes of a doe. And on an awning above them, in gold and red letters, the bad English that was now everywhere:

SINCERE WELCOME TO OUR SHINING CHINESE GARRISON

The Sinden family stood in a row close together. The platform was high up and she could look down on the world. Jessica did not know—she forgot her watch—at what precise moment Hong Kong reverted to the Chinese. She had meant to count it down, but now Felicity had taken away time. A hush was in the air. A row of grenadiers stood at attention. A band somewhere started to play, but nobody was listening. The people were all watching the sky. Thousands of faces were turned upwards as though for an annunciation. Something was coming—some sign—but all Jessica could feel was her glasses pinching the backs of her ears and the bits of graying hair that had been released by the snap of that awful green rubber band. Poppy was holding the stamps the General Post Office had issued just last month, pairs of stamps with flags crossed like swords and the severed heads of leaders in profile, Queen Elizabeth and Tung Chee-hwa. Jessica's head was bowed, but Poppy was looking up, first at her and then at her father. Something was wrong. Felicity was not here. Tristan, as usual, saw and thought nothing, glancing, blinking, at his sister, wondering what she was thinking, for she was surely thinking something, observing it with that strange feeling of exaltation Poppy had when something occurred to her that had never occurred to her before.

"Mama, I'm not as sad as I should be," said Poppy. "You and Papa. You look as though someone has died."

"Not some*one*," said Simpson Kwan, overhearing her and turning around from the first row. "Some*thing*." He looked at the Sindens. "I had no idea you felt so strongly about the end of British rule."

"I don't," said Jessica.

Simpson, who knew Jessica Sinden through her close friendship with his wife Elaine, sensed she had just said something true, though in what way, he did not know.

So he turned back to his wife.

At last the fireworks came. They were so disappointing. With the lights of the city turned down, Jessica was staring mostly into the dark. The city before her was a rolling panorama of skyscrapers, some as high as the mountains behind them, blue in places, brown in others. Above them were little hanging points of light, but they kept flickering out. She stared, trying to hold onto the moment of the brightness, but by the time she saw it, the flash was gone. Poppy squinted at them, too, but with determination: Jessica would not be surprised if she came to her, wanting to have a Chinese fireworks tattoo on her thigh. Something indelible to frighten her mother, more than that CLOSED sign on her bedroom door, its windows half papered with black construction paper and inside, clothes piled in cardboard boxes all over the floor, and next to her bed, a side table with two candles burning on saucers. Poppy was sloppy, but somehow she expected her mess to amount to something. Not like Felicity, who—

Another line of red dropped, shuddering, through the sky. Then there were more flashes, balls of them, then lots of dropping sparks, more pin-pricks that never seemed to reach the ground. This time she tried to cover her ears. An area of the park between the bleachers and the bay had been fenced off with chicken wire. Men moving in the shadows set them off; from there the fireworks hissed into the sky, disappearing before bursting with pops and crackles. The display was curiously unimpressive. Below them, the skyline of Hong Kong never darkened, for tonight the lights in all the buildings were turned on even though they were all empty. Jessica imagined the fireworks rocking the skyscrapers, but they seemed unrockable.

Tristan was shifting in his seat. He seemed bored with the fireworks. He knew so little, saw so little, that boy. How many times had she showed him the plants of her garden, chanterelles, bullaces, fennel roots, and wild garlic, all ordered from Thompson & Morgan in Suffolk, but he had shown no interest. Not like Felicity, who in the side garden once said,

"Look at these poor gillyvors, Mother. They've been dry for days. Doesn't it make you think of Cardinal Woolsey in the play, I forget which one, saying,

This is the state of man: today he puts forth
The tender leaves of hopes, tomorrow blossoms;
The third day comes a frost, a killing frost.

"There is no frost in Hong Kong, Felicity," Jessica told her daughter.

But Felicity had been right. Like those fireworks, like those twigs, everything seemed to disappear, there it was, one moment, vivid and crisp, and the next left you blinking because nothing was there at all besides traces of smoke and a few falling sparks. As a girl, Jessica thought there would be rules to life. She was not sure what they were, but suspected that various adults other than her father knew them but for some reason had simply decided not to pass them on in any way that made sense to her. The world was organized in some places, but there were a thousand places where it wasn't. The parade that came grinding by was organized. It had rules. It was factory-made, probably somewhere in southern China. Jessica watched without interest as a corps of men in band uniforms beating cymbals passed by. A wall of girls, walking in stiff unison, with pale lemon flowers pinned just under their shoulders, followed by boys dressed as cowboys in chaps. Rows of men in black satin pajamas embroidered with Chinese characters. A large tank filled with tiny diaphanous fish. The air was heavy with flowers, so many different kinds that they gave the parade a thick funeral sweetness. A contingent came by carrying small boxes, an offering perhaps, but to Jessica they seemed to be bearing the ashes of the British Empire. The boxes were enameled, that cheap Chinese kind, not the perdurable cloisonné of her reliquary at home. The parade was a cheap funeral in bad taste. At its end there were armored cars, coming from the Chinese garrison stationed discreetly in Mong Kok. It was just below Lion Rock, near a hill scattered with those ancestral tombs. The road did not seem wide enough for all of them. The dead always took up so much space in Hong Kong. There was simply no room for them. They had to go into the cemeteries every few years and clear them out to make room for the newly dead. She wondered where they dumped them all. Felicity would be spared this. She would lie near Judy Royce-Chapman on a Sussex down.

She talked to Edward just that morning before they left.

He asked, "Do you want to go back to England after the Handover?"

"We're here because of you, Edward."

"No, we're here because of you." Adding, "Ultimately, because of what your father did to you."

Jessica did not contest the statement.

"But can we stay here?" she pressed him.

"I am willing to see it through."

She did not know what the *it* was, but Edward was not the kind of man to ask. He would not ask anything, and so would never know how, finding her, she backed out of the room, took an embroidered pillow from the couch in the hallway and stabbed it with scissors until the down fell out in clumps. He would never know, too, how carefully she cleaned it up afterwards; how she vacuumed; how she washed her hands and dried them. She had a sudden ache thinking of all the years ahead of her with Edward. An empty future life, with two young Sindens left, the least of them, she was afraid.

Then the parade was over. The two young Sindens she turned over to Elaine, with instructions to take them to Stanley for the night. She and her husband then quietly slipped away into the crowd. They seemed to follow it wherever it led, through Victoria Park, past shops, cafés, and cinemas, bright and buoyant though nearly empty because everyone had taken to the streets. Jessica found herself walking down Great Jones Street, where a long capering dragon still took up most of the street, a dragon that was all spine, its crooked meninges propped up by sticks—so like her own back, held together with staples and pins! She had no idea where she was walking to. She was glad for the commotion and the litter and the bland street lights, each with its beige corona. She made her way on Lockhart Road through some red and white confetti, stooping to put a handful in her pocket. She passed a man dragging home a large portrait of Sun Yat-Sen, and some teenagers from a marching band carrying scuffed white tubas that seemed bigger than they were. A few women followed in long dresses of dull blue silk. Elaine Kwan gave one of these to Poppy for her eleventh birthday, but Poppy never wore it because she said the emblem on the back reminded her of the watermark on her mother's stationary, a cursive *JBS* where all the serifs wound together into a knot. It was just like Poppy to complain until Jessica went into the closet and gave her a smock which belonged to Felicity. Poppy took such comfort in wearing her older sister's clothes, though when Felicity was home from Oxford, she would have none of it. Felicity had been away at Jesus two years, which Poppy considered to be an awfully long time.

Her husband followed her at a respectful distance. He would leave her alone until they reached the car, though it was in the opposite direction. There was no one to help her. His wife was impossibly alone. She was moving stiffly, holding her shoulders back, shaking her head slowly, saying something to herself. When they got home he would call the police. She said to tell them that the way she arranged her was the way they found her. Felicity's sweater she had buried. The rope was hidden. Her note was still in her pocket.

Mother, I feel so alone.

4

september 3, 1997

JESSICA DREADED the Inquest, but as she found out much later, Elaine certainly did not.

The spectators crowded in. There were far more people than chairs, so some people had to stand, some already a little faint after the heat of an early September afternoon in the city. The judge's voice could hardly be heard above the shuffling. Elaine Kwan, pert in her new outfit from Shanghai Tang, had never seen such a crowd of the Hong Kong well-to-do, at least the ones she would speak to. The suicide of Felicity Sinden was a family matter that had somehow turned their lives inside out, and here they were for the Inquest in the old Court of Final Appeal, decked out in all their finery in a paneled room with high windows and polished brass plates, facing a judge who looked like an old doll propped up in a chair. The judge, a cousin of Simpson's, cleared his throat and said:

"Please. Be seated."

It was a shame the Sloane Shaws, near relatives of Sir Run Run, could not come. Pity that inquests couldn't be catered, especially in such a fine neoclassical structure, the granite and red brick courthouse, by far the classiest building on Government Hill. Elaine had gone to some trouble to move the hearing here, rather than holding it in that bland white block of a courthouse on Queensway in Admiralty, and a bit of finger food would be welcome, pineapple wrapped in prosciutto or melon balls and strawberries. She smiled to herself, wishing she'd saved a choice seat for Simpson, who would look forward to seeing his cousin Dickson in his fluffy white wig of justice that made him look like a duck. The duck of justice, Elaine thought, knowing full well what was about to happen and putting the phrase on mental file for her to share with her friend afterwards. Dickson, at least, knew how to keep a civil tongue in public while he was ducking justice. Not like Elaine, who never minded giving cynical little snorts and saying something cutting, even about Jessica herself, who today was wearing blowzy blue linen slacks she'd never been fond of.

Elaine opened her purse and took out a small plastic bag, and opening it, broke a cracker in half, and ate it.

Dickson Kwan began:

"The judiciary of Hong Kong has long prided itself on its independence and transparency."

Hah! Elaine Kwan knew all about what her husband called polarized transparency, seemingly clear as glass but actually filtering out all but one direction of light. Simpson considered the idea of transparency to be the perfect expedient: perfectly clear and completely filtered, both at the same time, a very Hong Kong solution to the problem of justice, she might add. Dickson was apparently one of its apologists. Elaine smiled, knowing what she knew. She wished Jessica knew too, but she was under strict orders not to let anything on about this particular duck of justice.

In any case her friend would know soon enough. Dickson Kwan stood and rapped the gavel three times. He didn't need to, but after all it was the symbol of his trade, like a stethoscope around the neck of a doctor. A toy horn with a quacking sound would be more like it. And predictably, there were whispers among those in the know. They amounted almost to a light hiss.

Dickson Kwan continued:

"Order, please."

The room became very still.

"I said, Order."

The stillness deepened. Sitting next to her lawyer, Wilson Kwan (another cousin), Jessica Sinden did something she almost never did. She took Edward's hand. She wished she could talk to him alone on their patio overlooking the South China Sea. They were closer, yes, but this was the worst moment of her life. Not her own death, but the public crying of her daughter's death to the world. Her breath began to mist up her glasses, which she wore, not because she really needed them, but to keep everyone at one remove from her eyes. It didn't work. She was tired of living. Not as tired as Felicity, but she was tired of making the effort. Edward could somehow still smile and talk. She could talk but not smile, and then only just barely. Poppy and Tristan were waiting at home to be talked to, though thankfully not smiled at. Jessica thought of the empty room next to theirs, the handsome green-eyed girl who would never sleep there again, reading late into the night by flashlight with a sheet pulled over her head, her long lemon hair draped over the pillow behind her. An image lingered in her mind: about how Felicity had been at the sink that last day in June, rinsing glasses before loading them into the dishwasher. She always left the water running, but not that day. The spigot was turned tightly off.

Jessica yearned to disappear, to be dead and forgotten.

"I did this," she'd said quietly to her husband that morning over breakfast on the patio.

"I was afraid you might say that," said Edward.

"I don't want to go back, ever."

Edward knew to take *back* in different ways. Back was home and then into whatever future was about to come up on them, but back also was the past, and not just one part of it, but the deep channel that had led to this moment. Dr. Sinden remembered teaching Felicity how to drive. How he was afraid to be in the passenger seat with her at the wheel. How before she even pulled out of the garage she gunned the engine so hard that it stalled. It came to him that Felicity viewed the car as a machine for taking chances with. She had three accidents her first week out, all mirror in themselves, but taken together, quite a premonition. Bad luck, he said at the time, but his wife hated chance. As a doctor, he learned to make his peace with it, treating people who sometimes got better, and sometimes didn't. But Felicity was reckless. She would do something without knowing what would happen afterwards. Like the time she put a flounder wrapped in foil in the microwave oven. The foil cracked and sparked, the kitchen started to fill with smoke, but when he came in, Felicity was just standing there, fascinated by what she had done. It was as though for her actions had no consequences. They were just—actions.

"We could stay down at the Helena May for a while, you know," he started to tell his wife, putting down his coffee.

"No."

"Why not?"

"I think—I don't know—someone has to help *me*."

Help *her*? Edward knew his own limitations. Edward could do things for her but he did not have the remotest idea how to help her in any palpable way. Her mind had always been far from his, as though her thoughts were clouds, billowing in the high distance. He was more down to earth. He often found things funny and strange. Not that he smiled much, except, perhaps, to himself. That much they certainly had in common. Other people often found them to be a sour pair. When they first met, he used to say small kind things to her after making love. She always said, *Edward, Stop.* He never considered himself romantic; working in hospitals inoculated him against that; but over time he became extremely plain in his speech with Jessica. She hated any form of hyperbole, almost mandating it:

"Plain speech, Edward. Plain speech."

It was a pity, really. There had once been more in him than there was now. Life with Jessica had slowly made him into a dry vessel. He felt himself rubbing his chin even though he had shaved just a few hours ago. His wife did not like even the trace of a beard on his face. That morning, as always, she sat at the foot of the bed, facing the wall, while he dressed.

Only once he had covered his arms and legs, glazed as they were with light brown hair, would she turn, pull open the heavy curtains, and speak to him. He was the first, and probably the only person she had slept with. There was hardly a *with* there, for she always slept at the other edge of the bed, facing away from him. As a child she had been told what to do and think by that mad father of hers, a Methodist preacher of the old school, who, arms raised to heaven, maintained a grim grip on his Bible and its lessons. Whitfield Bright lived in a kind of solitude, dreamy and wild; read the Book of Revelation over and over; went out to Hyde Park Corner every day, distributing booklets and proclaiming the destruction of a great city, his gaunt daughter by his side. He used to wear a blue linen suit when he was preaching, standing on a box near the Marble Arch, bawling on a gray February day about the Four Last Things, Death, Judgment, Hell, and Heaven—though never once a word about heaven, so Jessica always thought of them as the Three Last Things.

I will lay waste your cities and you will become a desolation. Then you will know that I am the LORD.

Edward knew she no longer believed a word of it. Her father died of a stroke when she was twelve. After that, her in-laws on her mother's side, high church Anglicans who had always considered poor Whit to be as mad as a hatter, spirited her away to Wycombe Abbey, to be reeducated in an anodyne Anglicanism (another story, bad enough in itself, for it led to another death), but in those years in Hyde Park, her father brought her up to believe that the judgment of God was perfect in its severity. He used to cut her hair himself, and the thin girl with the choppy short hair was always to be seen standing next to him near Hyde Park Corner, handing out tracts with names like *A Way Forward in the Darkness*, *Going On in an Irremediably Corrupt World*, and Edward's personal favorite, *Making Your Desperation Serve the Lord.*

Edward considered that it was something of a surprise for Jessica to wake up each morning and see that she was still there and not being spirited away for punishment by her father's grim God. Sometimes he wondered if she ever let herself yearn for the love of God. Probably not: hers was a Methodism reduced to habit and instinct, and he was certain she was not aware of it at all, just that she, for some reason never quite clear to her, had been expelled into a world where she felt herself to be a scavenger. He remembered how she gave her babies baths, rubbing them with sponges as though flaying them with a scourge. And how she reproached Poppy for grabbing a sugar donut from that petrified display of sweets under a bell jar in the kitchen. The sweets of life were there to be looked at, not tasted. Hell no longer existed for her, but the renunciation of all pleasure did.

Dr. Sinden found himself thinking about what he could possibly say to his wife about Felicity. They had been married for thirty-one years. They had three children. All their small talk was about their children. How can someone make small talk about a child when the child is dead? It seemed as though there was even more to talk about now, a lot of things he'd like to know about Felicity, questions he never dreamed of asking before she killed herself. Did she ever love someone? Was there a friend that mattered, even a dead one like his wife's childhood friend, Judy? But the only ties his wife kept up were on the Sinden side of the family. They visited his relatives in London, but never hers. She had been the one who wanted him to take the job in Hong Kong because she liked the snapping sound of cutting every conceivable tie to her father, dead but somehow alive in her, who told her that beautiful churches were sins against God, that fashionable clothing courted God's wrath, and that most of the people lying in graveyards were irrevocably damned. My father never taught me anything, she used to say, except to pray and to fear.

Dr. Sinden looked at his wife over the breakfast table. Her face was drawn. Her body made a stiff right angle in the chair. He wondered if she was ever happy. What was it she had told him? That things came at her with blunt force, and her life was a recoiling.

"How do you know that?" Dr. Sinden used to ask his wife. "Our life is very quiet."

But then he considered: *his* life was very quiet. Hers was calm only on the outside. He had seen pictures of her father, tall and rumpled, his hair a little shaggy. In one, he was leaning over and kissing the top of Jessica's head, as though to stop the beating inside it.

"I'd get up and leave but I have nowhere to go," Jessica continued saying over breakfast. "This—*this*—will always follow me."

"Maybe you'd better go home, Jessica," he said now. "If only for a bit."

"Perhaps you should take me to the cemetery."

Edward did not know what to make of this. Did she want him to take her back to England? Felicity was already buried south of London near her old friend Judy. Was she saying her life was over?

"No more deaths, Jessica. One in the family is enough."

He took in her lined white face, her neat brown hair, just beginning to gray around her ears, the tense precision of her taut mouth and stiff posture.

"You're much stronger than you think you are."

"I know," she said, wiping her eyes. "But there are times I don't want to be."

"Don't say that. Your strength has to be enough for the rest of us."

She lifted her eyes.

"Edward—can you do something for me?"

Edward fixed his gaze on his wife. "Yes. What?"

"Don't think things will be better after a while. I am responsible for my actions and nothing will change that. But strength is beside the point. Strength will change nothing."

Jessica sat on the very edge of her chair, feeling the truth of what she had just said. Edward did not have strength, but stamina. Poppy squandered her strength, and Tristan, like her own father, would drink it away until perhaps one day he would, also like her father, find God. Yes, she was the strong one.

And this was the time for it now. Jessica had been in the courthouse building maybe twice in the twenty-seven years she had lived in Hong Kong. Once, when Edward testified, about what she couldn't remember, and another time, to arrange to extend Mina's contract from two years to six, not because she liked Mina, but because looking for a maid was such an awful bother. She supposed she'd done stupid things. Trying to ship Felicity off to Wycombe Abbey, where she herself had been so miserable; laughing at Tristan for his weak efforts to cut back on his drinking and walking into the living room to separate him from his various girlfriends as soon as they became tangled on the sofa; imposing a lengthy penance on Poppy after she ran over the neighbor's cat. But at least there had been some justification (if that was the right word for it, and perhaps it was not) behind them.

Jessica squirmed in her seat next to her husband. The chair seemed to stick to her back, which was always weak at times like this. Poppy tried to give her some herbs to calm her nerves before they left the Peak for Central. She wouldn't drink the tea, but her wrists still smelled of rosemary and tarragon. The Chinese believed the herbs brought them luck, and in matters of superstition, Poppy always sided with the Chinese. That morning Jessica relented, letting her daughter anoint her wrists with herbal extracts she bought in a store in Causeway Bay.

"But what if people notice?" Jessica asked her.

Poppy laughed lightly. "No one's going to notice, Mama."

At least her remaining daughter had not lost her sense of humor. Edward still had his, telling her the herbs would be good for the garden party they were about to go to. Garden party! Some kind of Chinese-run commission was about to stand in judgment of her. Her father once preached a sermon about judgment to the brethren at chapel. He said it came to this: that if all would come to the altar, and say some certain words, they should be released. She used to pull her dress over her knees wondering what those certain words were, and what she should be released into should she say them. She still could not imagine that words had anything to do with anything. People said all sorts of things; they lied with impunity; and yet somehow life went on. Maybe that was what her father meant by release: an expulsion into something. She certainly had lived a life of expulsions, from Judy expelled into death, to her own expulsion from England into the colonies, which was what they used to call them back when they called things by their real names.

She tried to think of another time, when they were all together, the five of them. But *together* was such a hard word to apply to the Sindens. Like that time they were walking on the beach below Pat Sin Leng. Soft waves were rolling in. The sun slipped behind the clouds, scattering its light. The Sindens were also scattered. Poppy was at one end of the beach gathering shells. Tristan was off at the other, building a row of sand castles as though they were tract houses. Edward was reading a newspaper on the grassy rise of a hill. She was walking with Felicity, but not for long. "Bet you can't follow me where *I* wanna go. See if you can catch me!" her daughter cried suddenly, breaking away from her toward the sea, her feet slapping the waves. Jessica was not inclined to run after her until Felicity said, "Mama if you don't want to play, well I'll *make* you!" and started running off into the water, flopping out into the shallows and pulling herself out to sea with long strokes. Jessica, knowing that this was one of those beaches in Hong Kong that looked like a beach but wasn't really swimmable because of the rip tides, almost jumped after her into the incoming waves, grabbing the strap of her swimsuit bottom so hard she almost stripped it off. Felicity squealed, but not with delight; she was like her mother; nothing was play, even though she sometimes used the word. If she hadn't stopped her, she might really have gone so far out into the water that even she, a strong swimmer, would not be able follow her out to bring her back.

"I wouldn't care if I never came back," Felicity told her later on the beach.

"Don't say that," said Jessica.

Somehow, with this play-that-was-not-play, Felicity decided she wanted to retire from the world and be a monk. She made her mother move her old Limoges reliquary—the one with the two bickering angels, as Felicity put it—into her room, and she started making up her own monastic rule, calling herself a *girl monk* (but not a nun, because that was not a made-up thing and would have entailed unforeseen obligations,

always a danger in the Sinden household). She had been taking Latin
and somewhere she had come across *The Rule of St. Benedict*, at least the
part where he said monks needed to be reading for hours every day. She
sensed that there was some kind of life to be lived outside the Sinden
household, and she was determined to find it in books. She walled herself
in with them. Jessica knew Felicity set herself against her because she had
once done the same thing against her own rule-saturated father. By the
time she was a teenager, Jessica sensed her father would tear her apart if
she didn't root him and his religion out of her life, and now she had to
watch as her daughter took to doing the same thing. Except here there
was no religion left to root out, just *her*. As a girl, Jessica stopped reading
anything intently so she could stop reading the Bible, a book whose
terrible final meaning was clear only to her father, and Felicity, sensing
that her mother was suspicious of reading, took to reading everything
in sight. And she had her father's horrible medieval taste in books, too.
If Jessica knew her daughter was reading in her room, and that reading
was not required as homework, she would try to interrupt her and set
her to some make-work job that was suddenly urgent, like sweeping the
car port or arranging magazines on the shelves (magazines were safe,
end-stopped reading, and the ones she saved were ten years old anyway,
like her marmite).

But she read anyway. And God, the things she read! How she found
Chaucer's *Troilus and Criseyde*, Jessica did not know, but the things she
pulled out of it were beyond belief. Like that one line:

Te he, Te he, quod she.

"It's tee-hee, Mama. A medieval tee-hee!" Jessica never knew if Chaucer
actually wrote this, but it became Felicity's favorite line, and she used
it for everything it was worth, saying it in Middle English every time:
tay-hey-tay-hey-kwode-shay. Jessica tried telling her daughter that surely
there had to be another line from Chaucer worth quoting, but she had

never read Chaucer and could not see why anyone would want to. She just had this one daughter stamping around the house, chortling,

"Te he! Te he! quod she."

Jessica felt a little better, later, when she went to Oxford to read Middle English, but truly, Felicity always seemed like an aimless reader to her. Her favorite book was, unaccountably, William Harvey's *The Circulation of the Blood*. She wrote all over that book and carried it everywhere for a while. Jessica had no idea how she found it. But unlike Poppy, who was always finding things that were lying around and piling them in her room, Felicity found things that were nowhere to be seen except by her. Jessica supposed that was what they did in the Bodleian at Oxford, looking at things most people could easily have done without. She certainly could have done without William Harvey:

In the dead body, I have found the left ventricle of the heart to hold upwards of two ounces of blood.

Hearing this, Edward turned his head and commented, dryly, that some day she might make an excellent pathologist. But Felicity never had any interest in anyone's anatomy but her own. Jessica once tried hiding the book in her jewelry box, but Felicity always managed to find it, giving her a look that amounted almost to pity: for she believed that her mother would never be well versed in matters of the heart.

The hearing would be over in less than an hour. Elaine had called her earlier in the week to say she'd found out that her cousin Dickson would be presiding. Jessica heard the precise lie in the *found out*, confirmed by her lightly fluttering invitation to take her out to lunch afterwards in Lan Kwai Fong. But still it came as a surprise:

"I will be brief. I have reviewed the police reports. An accident on Mount Kellett Road took place on the morning of July 1, 1997. The body seems to have been moved, but that does not alter the facts. Lacking further evidence, this case is closed."

Accident: the word reverberated through the room. Jessica's eyes met Elaine's. Elaine was capable of surprising Jessica as much as Jessica was of surprising her. A month ago, Elaine came to the flat announcing, "I'm going to do something you're really going to like," adding, "You don't have to say anything. I just want you to know." And it was true: she took Felicity's death and made it all about *her*. A Kwan represented her, a Kwan sat in judgement, calling it an accident, and more Kwans, Simpson and Elaine, were sitting in the back row of the gallery, directing the action. She made it so that, years later, *she* would the the object of talk, and not Jessica Sinden. It was justice by substitution. Elaine Kwan would always be known by what she had done for her friend. Jessica felt a slow stream of admiration pass through the room. Now this, it seemed to say, *this*, is true friendship.

Jessica felt something stirring within her: a capacity, perhaps, or maybe it was only a yearning. Elaine Kwan had shown her what one person could do for another, and she resolved that the lesson not be lost on her.

Only much later did she manage to tell her friend:

"There's something I don't understand."

"What?" Elaine asked her.

"I mean, how did you do it?"

Indirection was not only Elaine's style, but her way of life, so she bristled at the directness of her friend's question.

"Well!" she said. "Somebody has to preside over these things."

She said it as though the hearing had been afternoon tea rather than an inquest. Then Elaine said:

"Do you really want me to talk about it?"

"No," said Jessica. "It's just that I don't know what to say."

"Then say nothing." Adding, "Saying nothing is always appropriate."

"Edward says I shouldn't butt in. He said it went as well as it could. He said it would be a mistake to know too much."

"For *you*, yes," qualified Elaine.

"But what about all those other people?"

"I—invited them." She cleared her throat. "Jessica, there can be no secrets among equals. I was, you know, if you need to know, the hostess of the inquest."

They sat in silence for a few moments.

"I don't mean that this should matter very much to you," Elaine went on, "but I think it's good for them to see that things aren't necessarily as they seem. They will know that there is something to know, but what I have done was to make them perfectly at ease with *not* knowing it."

"Won't they want to know more?"

"It's a form of managed curiosity. They will know that there is more, but they will also understand that the *more* is in the hands of someone they can trust."

"You mean Dickson?"

"Oh, no, not him. No," she said. "I mean *me*."

The hearing was almost at an end. The judge stood up. They had only been there for ten minutes but it was clear the inquest was at an end. His words had been plain.

This case is closed.

She'd imagined far worse. There was that old school exercise book she found near Felicity's body. Always ready to consider authorities as all-seeing, Jessica feared being called to the stand and asked:

"Madam, do you recognize this?"

"Yes. It is my daughter's school notebook."

"There's no name on it."

"Oh, it was hers, all right. Felicity liked to draw with a blunt pencil."

The notebook laid being laid open in front of her, she would then be asked:

"So what are these?"

"Drawings."

"Could you be more specific?"

"She was playing hangman."

"And the girl with the blonde hair, hanging there in the gallows?"

"That was in yellow crayon."

"Her identity, Mrs. Sinden. Her identity."

"That would be Felicity."

"But Mrs. Sinden, your daughter actually took the game of hangman a bit further, didn't she? She not only showed herself being hanged, but she showed the hangman himself."

"The hang-woman *herself*," Jessica would certainly say.

"And the hang-woman was—you."

"Yes. Clearly. Me."

It could have gone this way, but it hadn't. Elaine had spared her this, though if she had been able to think it through just at that moment, she had already spared herself this particular line of questioning by burning the notebook down to ashes.

The judge turned and left, closing the door behind him. Then Edward was leading her out of the courthouse. She felt the pressure of eyes resting on her.

The Sindens crossed the street and walked into Chater Garden. No one was coming toward them yet. Jessica was afraid she might have to run out of there. Reaching a small fountain, she dropped her handbag in relief and stood looking at her husband. She didn't remember exactly what the judge had said, but she knew he had told her that they could go back to their lives. She would never have to admit to the world how she buried Felicity's sweater and burned her note along with her notebook. The thought of all the other lies that would need guarding and watching did not occur to her yet, though it would come to her soon enough. Felicity's death had made her life into an open secret. The sense that everyone around her would always be curious about the so-called accident but would never ask already made her feel so tired that she wanted to lie down in the middle of the plaza and sleep.

5

november 2002

THE FIRST TIME Jessica met Philip was in a fog. The second time her hair was full of goo.

Having her hair done was never to Jessica's taste. It was, unfortunately, public and protracted, and there were no private rooms here in the salon as there were at Matilda Hospital on the Peak, where Edward was a doctor working with infectious diseases, which could come out of China at nearly any time of the year. She saw how long it took the girl to bleach the color out of the gray until the strands of her hair were as clear as cells. And that was even before she could begin to dribble on the color, a dirty sort of brown. Sitting there in the open, twisted like a hospital patient under a bed sheet, it was all she could do to look straight ahead without catching anyone's eye in the corner of a mirror. She was rooted to the spot. A light portière might at least have been drawn between her and the other clients in the salon. Even the common Chinese hospitals did that. Jessica Sinden need not have been seen in public with her hair washed out to an egg stream, very like those stringy translucent frog filaments you saw dripping from trees every spring along Plantation Road. It was so reminiscent of the worst of nature.

So *egg-stream*. Jessica had to smile. It was just one of those silly puns Edward was so fond of. But a pun, he always reminded her, was always very much of a moment, and once that moment had passed, the fun of it was gone. She would never be able to reconstruct it for him. For

Jessica Sinden knew that things had their time and their place. After the British had handed Hong Kong back to—whoever they were, anyway—she had been the one, had she not, to say that the moment of Kipling's "Recessional" had come at last to China. But her husband had reminded her that, though Felicity was dead and buried, Poppy and Tristan were still in school here and it would not be seemly for the members of the Ascendancy, for so they thought of themselves, to be seen to panic. She had not panicked that day, but tidied up. The Governor may go, Edward said, and so may the Garrison, but the rest of us can stay on, if only to sound the trumpets after them. She had often wondered what he meant by that, sounding the trumpets after them. Certainly not a retreat, nor a surrender. Her twenty-seven years in Hong Kong should have more majesty than that.

Looking in the mirror, Jessica held her eyes steadily on her face. The salon was the one place where she let herself closely examine her own appearance. Such short hair! She, who used to wear her hair so long. She, who had so loved putting it up and taking it down. Her body had been alive with feeling then, before Felicity's accident. The inquest, mercifully, had called it that, and perhaps it was, in God's eye, a kind of accident. Who was she to say that it wasn't? She remembered the smell of diesel engines idling at the scene later that day in July and the way so many police cars came so quickly to their flat on the Peak, as though for a funeral cortège. Her hair turned gray afterwards. To her surprise, she came to like having a taut face in all its pinkness set off against such stark white hair. And for the longest time, in her mid-fifties, that seemed to be who she was, the woman with the dead girl, dead at twenty by accident (or so they said), who startled people like an apparition whenever she turned around, so like a wraith was she! Edward was the one who wanted her to tend to her two remaining children. She tried to. She learned to take an interest in the little differences between them—Tristan's drawings and trophies, Poppy's certificates and her collection of the skulls of small birds. She liked showing them the stars and the planets, the crook in Orion's belt or the pink lady that was Venus. But something inside her stayed dead, and never that far off, circling her at night like the moon, the earth's own dead girl.

"Jessica?"

Jessica gave a start, pulled out of her own thoughts. Her first name. Nobody but Edward used it.

"Jessica?" the voice said again pleasantly. "I thought that was you. Funny to see you here, of all places."

It was the new American from Vivian Court. The one with the dog. They had met, but then again, she had taken great care not to introduce herself.

"I say," said Jessica.

"Say what?" asked the American.

Jessica said nothing, feeling her face flush and hoping he would go away soon, but no, he was well settled in the very next chair. Michael, who owned S/Z, was personally jabbing at his hair too, which was actually a little longer than hers. She kept her hair quite short, not because she liked it that way, but because she colored it now that her skin was thin and her face was drawn.

"You don't have to say anything, really," he said to her. "It's nice to see you."

Nice to see *her*? Jessica stiffened as his eyes passed over her. She swore he looked her up and down in just that way a man does when he is interested in a woman. But she wasn't sure. Men examined her so clinically now, as though to see, from mere curiosity, what was left of her. Just a thin woman with veins in her forehead. She saw the way they turned away after looking, with that same twinge of pity one had after inspecting a mummy in a museum. She had met the American once, perhaps twice before, a matter only of dogs because he, like her, had an Italian greyhound, not show-grade, like hers, but perfectly tractable as a pet. He, like her, too, liked to walk it on Peel Rise in the late afternoon, when the fog thickened around the Peak, padding the city and reducing the other walkers to vague awkward shapes stumbling in the mist.

The mist was pure December. The Chinese on the Peak, who lived up here because it was fashionable and expensive, actually hated the high montane weather with its dense chills. December and January were the most Chineseless months of the year, with many of them well away before their new year, though this year a few lingered because of some new flu rumored to be sweeping the southern provinces of the Mainland. Jessica Sinden often preferred to forget in what proximity she lived to the Chinese. They were polite people, to be sure, and like her, rich, but their taste in varnish was excessive. There was little restraint in their decorative sensibilities. You never saw a faded oriental rug, the red having aged to a nice dull ocher, in a Chinese home. Their homes had a certain flashiness that gave you headaches. The night before she had been at a dinner party at Elaine Kwan's, just down Mount Kellett Road. Elaine fancied herself a Londoner, keeping a townhouse in Sloane Square, but she was really just an old Chinese lady with her chinoiserie, just as she herself was really, when all was said and done, just an old British matron with her knick-knacks. The two of them connected on that level. They were both future dowagers with a proprietary interest in the remnants of a society currently crumbling around them. They certainly both disliked the same things. Old poverty. New wealth. Garishness in art, and incivility in politics. Disdain was such a comfortable bond. They had it for each other, too, residually at least, but together they had it for nearly anyone who wasn't able to live on the Peak.

Elaine also had a dead daughter she never talked about. But Ivy was there, just as Felicity was, and Elaine, unlike Jessica Sinden, was not above believing in ghosts.

Thankfully, a sharp break in slope ringed the Peak, setting it apart a high tower in the clouds. Jessica was glad for it. The Peak really was a world unto itself, part of a continent where, after all, they buried people or hills. The old colonists had managed to get up here before the Chinese did, claiming a mountain-top as something other than a graveyard that was nevertheless a world apart, the supernal realm of Hong Kong. No one who lived on May Road, in itself a perfectly acceptable address but the last of the Mid-Levels before the big switchback up, could possibly make the claim that they lived on the Peak. Up here things were different, in a carefully disinviting way. Most of the houses, though they were valued in the millions of dollars, were to all appearances very derelict. The old stone mansions had been torn down long ago, leaving, under grass and moss, only bare traces of their foundations. The new ones were little boxes that appeared to have been pieced together out of bathroom tile. The buildings had height without hauteur, grandness without grandeur, and, more to the point, China without the Chinese. The Hollisters of the Hollister chain of hotels lived up here. Conrad had a pied-à-terre in Vivian Court, named after his mother, Vivian Hollister, who still lived on the top floor, partly in the manner of Camilla Parker-Bowles, mellowed by a patina of old scandal, and partly in the manner of Howard Hughes, that madman in the attic of American wealth. So did Michelle Liu, who had been a Bond girl in one of the lesser Fleming films, gratuitous in its way but still a fine testament to the spirit of the old Empire, especially up here where, unlike Shimla in India, nothing at all looked British.

That day on Peel Rise, she had been barely conscious of his face. He was certainly somewhat younger than she was. He came with a strong step out of the fog just as she was rounding the corner to Tin Wan, coming down an easy gradient where the path widened out a bit before its final drop down. It was an odd crook on the path that turned toward Aberdeen harbor, the last place in Hong Kong filled with junks and sampans, not much freight there any more under their canopies, just empty wicker baskets and flowers grown in packing cases for that big tourist trap, the Floating Restaurant, docked nearby, plus a few old triangular fishing nets hung up just for show. There were always fishermen there, though Jessica did not know why. She never saw anything longer than her finger come out of that harbor.

The dogs were two of a kind and they sniffed one another out readily. She was uncomfortably conscious of perspiring in his presence. She liked moving her body when she thought no one was looking. Walking Bovary was a kind of dancing for her, or as close to dancing as Jessica allowed herself. She always felt light on her feet, following Bovary. He must have seen that, because his first words to her were,

"You seem to be flying."

"Swimming is more like it, in this fog," she said to him. Naturally shy, she often talked to people in the fog because the mist reduced their faces to grayscale, and she was fairly sure they could not see her. Other dog owners were often good for short, safe conversations. She knew only the names of their dogs. She liked keeping it that way.

Another man brushed by in the mist. Short, Chinese, he turned his neck to catch sight of the two dogs, odd creatures after all, all ribs and legs like parts of a chicken. Then he disappeared, like the city itself, swallowed up by fog.

Through the mist, she could barely see the man with the dog. He dropped to his knees and cradled his greyhound protectively, a small young blue gone prematurely gray in the snout.

"I know your dog," he said in a mild American accent, looking up at her.

"You do?"

"Through your maid, Mina. She often walks here."

"Mina knows so many people," said Jessica, leaving off the second part of her thought, habitual with her, the *that-I-never-would*.

The American didn't hear the omission. "She's the salt of the earth," he added.

Jessica could not make out whether he meant plain and common, or, alternatively, vital and essential. Certainly not both. Americans, in her experience, never said two things at once.

"She's great with Bovary," he continued. "The other day I saw her let her off the leash, you know, in that little park next to the old bunker over by High West."

Jessica hesitated. "You mean she—released her?"

"Ah," he said, "I see you didn't know."

Jessica sighed; such intrusiveness. Perhaps, after all, he did not know about the dog poisonings over on Kennedy Road. Surely every caution was justified. But she would not be the one to tell him.

"She didn't run away," he continued. "She just ran around a bit, that's all."

"I should think she didn't," she said, regretting the lie almost instantly, because she always thought she would.

He continued. "I'm sorry. I see you disapprove. I don't want to get Mina in trouble. You're rather stern with her, aren't you?"

Jessica thought at first, that is absolutely none of your business, but then again, there was something about this man she liked, not his directness—all Americans had that—but his sudden intimacy with her. It was a kind of transparency that had an edge of interrogation to it. So she said, quietly, almost against her better judgment,

"I am."

"I know you are. And it's habitual, isn't it?"

She almost walked away, hearing this. But something about the sight of this one man did something to her, took away her power to say no. She felt a vein beating in her forehead, a shortness of breath, an unfamiliar heat welling in her body.

"Quite," she managed to say, adding, "And rather severe too, I suppose."

"And yet you don't really feel yourself to be like that, do you? The way Mina probably thinks you are?"

"I try to be—fair."

"And in your own terms you probably are. Mina told me you are one of the only employers left on the Peak who gives an annual bonus."

"She told you that?"

"She also told me it was appallingly small. Not even enough to buy a few trinkets at Causeway Bay." He paused. "I think I saw you there with her once."

Causeway Bay! Yes, it could have been her, but Jessica had never become accustomed to the awful march of people there. She pictured herself walking in clipped steps along the wide, crowded sidewalk on Hennessy Road, her handbag clutched under her arm, her hands jammed in her pockets, her head turned away from anyone who might recognize her. She hated jostling among the men in tight suits (the size of girls, really!) and the women in close-fitting blouses and skirts (clean cats, these, tiny but never undernourished), her eyes skimming over the alleys where shopkeepers drooped over their counters, slurping noodle soup and selling strange hairy plants. Jessica always tried to keep her trips to Causeway Bay to a minimum, so he must have seen her there on one of her periodic trips with Mina to the Sogo on Great George Street in search of German-grade linens, so hard to find here new, for, as much as she liked tracking down good values at rummage sales, used linens would simply not do.

"Yes," she said to him slowly. "Quite possibly. I was there. And with Mina." Adding, for the record, "As for that bonus, she knows I don't report it."

"I don't think she has any sense of the tax laws here. For her, you are the law."

"Well!" said Jessica, with a certain self-satisfaction.

"Well, indeed," said the American.

That was what they had said then. In that fog she could not make out any of the expressions on his face, not like here in the Salon, under the hard halogen light. For a moment, his eyes seemed to linger on her breasts. They were small but he seemed to like them. Not all men did; some looked away disdainfully when they saw how small they were. She felt a little tingling up her spine. She had to smile. If he heard that, Edward he would wonder if her meninges were acting up again, and offer to get them tested at his Tropical Diseases Clinic. He tried to be helpful in this way. He took that residency in infectious diseases at University College London because she had one.

Jessica folded her hands. The skin on her wrists felt loose. She wondered if he noticed her noticing signs of her age. Felicity had been like this. She once told her her skin looked like pink rayon. Like so many things Felicity said, it was impossible to construe her own attitude from it. She may or may not have found her hands repelling. It was only, simply, true, for looking down at her hands, they did, even now, look *just* like pink rayon.

She glanced at the man. He averted his eyes from the mirror in front of him, then closed them. Like her, he seemed to avoid his own image. She tried to catch sight of his face in the mirror.

"Some gel in your hair, sir?" Michael asked him.

He opened his eyes and blinked.

"No, no."

Again Jessica had the thought: he seemed to not be part of the real world. Something about him seemed shielded from work and obligation. Maybe he shielded himself, or maybe he had someone or something who did the shielding for him, a wife, perhaps, or an inheritance. He seemed to be dozing a little in his chair, his arms folded, and his fingers resting against his arms. He didn't have a wedding band on. He opened his eyes from time to time, trying to look at her without seeming to.

"I'm sorry," he said at last. "I didn't mean to make you feel uncomfortable."

She adjusted her smock, twisting her finger around its collar until it pinched her neck.

"Jessica?"

"Yes?" she said, almost in spite of herself.

He seemed to stop to reflect. "I like the way you say *yes*. It's so sibilant."

She wanted to turn away but she couldn't make herself. There was something about him. That cant of his shoulders, Handsome in a Hanseatic way, as her father had been at the pulpit. Tall and blonde and rectilinear, his hair the color of hay, his eyes the dark blue of high altitude. Already he seemed to be seeing her through all the roles of her life, as a girl almost breaking into dance with her dog on Peel Rise, as a housewife stern with her maid, and here she was, a middle-aged woman having her hair colored, a cloak thrown over her shoulders, her wrists hanging over the arm of the seat, her fingers moving and her head covered with brown paste. It was unsettling and very new. For a moment, as on Peel Rise, she felt like just walking away from him. She might tell him more things, or he might be the kind of man who would find them out for himself. It was so easy for her to avoid people when she wanted to. The Peak was high but there was not a lot of open land there, though she could always retreat to her small side yard. It was a very dear place, with a weathered bench, a fountain, and a pergola.

Still, Jessica frowned, as though to put him on notice that she was inclined the let the conversation drop.

But then Michael came back.

"Well!" said Michael, hair dryer in hand. "I see you two are becoming acquainted. I always like that, you know. You know what the *South China Morning Post* said about us? That *S/Z* is oh-so-cutting-edge, but such a friendly place, too."

Turning to Jessica, he did not see her wince, continuing:

"Oh *Jessica*, I so wanted to tell you about this new little place that just opened. It's called Grisaille. It's on a side street near the Helena May. I thought of it because I know you're a member there. It sells iron work, and I mean *old* old ironwork. I saw a Gothic grille there that that would go nicely with that old reliquary of yours you told me about. It reminds me of the one in the Met in New York, you know, in that little alcove off of the big tapestry room."

"I know that piece," said the American. "It's French. Twelfth century."

He turned to her. "It's near that big reliquary with the two angels. The one that used to be at Leiden, in Holland."

"You know it?" she asked him, surprised.

"Oh, yes. I love old Limoges."

Limoges: the word went off in her head. This man—he can't have known what that word meant to her. The reliquary that came down in the Sinden family, given to some past Sinden centuries ago by a minor official of James I—*her* reliquary.

"I've got an idea," Michael was saying. "Why don't you and Philip go there together after we're finished here?" He was looking at Jessica, but now he turned to Philip, whose name she heard for the first time. "It also has some old Hong Kong ironwork, very early industrial revolution, painted iron doors from the old Canton factories in the Delta. Some of them look like nothing's changed since eighteen-something. All the original paint, fittings, everything. It might be interesting."

"Possibly," said Jessica, as Michael wandered off again.

"Really we don't have to go that far," said Philip. "There's a little place near here. It's called Riposte. I know the chef there. It's a fancy French restaurant but they serve coffee in the afternoons."

"You know Gilles?"

"Well, not exactly. My ex-wife does. But I've met him a couple of times. Why don't we go? It sounds like fun. And if we feel like it, we could go to Grisaille afterwards."

Go—coffee—fun. The words seemed to hit her separately. This man, he wanted to see her. Her. Mrs. Jessica Sinden.

And she clearly heard how his wife was his *ex*-wife.

"I—"

She hesitated. Her face contracted, turning pink.

"Please say yes."

"Okay, then," she repeated, mouthing it, but not quite meaning it.

~

Risposte was only a few doors down.

"I can't stay for long," Jessica said abruptly just after they came in, sliding into a chair.

Her eyes quivered, looking at him.

"I don't want to be here either," he said quietly. "I'd rather we were alone."

"But you asked me here."

"I think it was Michael, not me."

"I can go, you know."

"I know," Philip said.

"But I won't," she said. "I can't. Even though I want to. I keep telling myself this is going to be a disaster, but then I feel that even if it is, it won't matter. It will be my disaster."

"*Our* disaster."

"Our," said Jessica. "You're already using that word."

Philip knew to wait and listen.

"I never use it," she started to explain. "Not even with my husband. I say *the* children, not our children. *The* house, not our house."

Her face was small and pale. She frowned a little.

"And I don't like taking chances," she said, her eyes raking his face. "It's not in me to do something unless I think it can be done."

Philip heard the *and*. Jessica Sinden was already setting conditions. It did not bother him that she was. His life, at fifty-two, had seemed conditional for a long time, and Jessica Sinden seemed well at peace with conditions. It gave her such an odd appeal. She had manners without charm, poise without grace, slimness without elegance. He had no doubt that in some basic way she had failed at being feminine. She was probably not much older than he was; just past fifty-five was his guess.

"Do you mind my telling you this?" she asked him.

"That you feel constrained? No."

"I hope you would also be frank with me."

A woman about her age passed by with a cup of coffee. Jessica dropped her eyes, sliding her chair to be closer to the wall.

"You know her?"

"Possibly," said Jessica. "But I have trouble remembering faces."

"And yet you've been here—"

"These twenty-seven years." She took in air through her teeth. "I might know her husband. Or perhaps it's Edward who knows him. I'm not sure."

She took out a pen from a little fanny pack she wore around her waist. Then she wrote out her name and number on a napkin. Thin lines of ink reached into the paper from each letter.

"I'm giving you my phone number," she said, folding it and giving it to him. "I'd like you to call me. Would you do that?"

"Yes," Philip said. He'd hoped they would go to Grisaille together to look at the old ironwork, but heard clearly how she was nearing her limit.

"If I'm alone I can talk," she said to him.

He opened it. She had written, *Mrs. Jessica Sinden,* and a number.

"I'm going somewhere tonight. But I'd like you to call, say around ten. Will you?"

He was afraid she would leave at any moment, but she didn't. When they left Riposte, turning onto Arbuthnot Road, he expected her at any second to say a sudden goodbye and pivot away from him as fast as her legs would take her. But she didn't. When he pointed to an old woodcut in a shop, he brushed her arm with the back of his hand. Her green eyes darted from side to side and she moved away a little. But then, as they continued walking and talking—talking about what, he didn't know and couldn't remember from moment to moment—she started moving in closer and closer. At one corner, where they waited for a light to change, she seemed almost to rest her head on his shoulder. Philip sensed that if he gave any sign that he was aware of what she was doing, she would instantly recoil. So he crossed the street and they kept walking.

At last they came to the Foreign Correspondents' Club. Jessica did not say goodbye.

"I'll call," she said, and swerving around the pointed corner of the building, she was gone.

She did call, and they talked until four in the morning. Being in public was hard for her. She was shy as well as reserved. Even in the Helena May, where she said she had been a member these twenty years, she felt she was in a girls' locker room, showering with everybody else, trying to keep her eyes to herself even though they were all watching her. She had made her peace with the women there, but on terms she considered unfavorable to her, for they all knew who she was, and what she had done. She would prefer, at least for now, to meet only to walk the dogs. Philip could join her for three walks a day, just after meals. Wylie would be welcome to sup with Bovary.

The first and third walks were rather perfunctory and public. The second, the afternoon walk, was really a long hike deep into the country parks. Then they could talk.

6

december 2002

POPPY SINDEN met Philip Nye after her little victory over her mother.

That morning in December Poppy knew she had it in her to stand up to her mother. The last time she tried to talk to her about going into acupuncture, it had not gone well. Her mother did not regard it as medicine, nor even as a legitimate profession. Poppy tried to tell her that the University of Hong Kong had an excellent reputation in it, but she would not listen.

"It's rated seventeenth in the world, Mama."

"In what?" her mother asked her. "And by whom?"

Poppy did not know. She had read it somewhere, and the number seventeen just stuck in her head. Maybe it was one of their lucky numbers here in China. They had so many. Eight was good, four was bad. It was like trying not to step on cracks on the sidewalk. When they bought this flat it had grates on the doors. When her mother had them taken down because they were ugly, one of the Chinese workers told her they were to keep out ghosts. She said they seemed rather too porous for that, then instructed him to remove the solid brass hinges, which she might be able to reuse someday, and threw the doors away.

Only people who believe in ghosts see them, her mother told her later. It was very much something she would say because it completely bypassed the question of the existence of ghosts. For her mother, you either saw ghosts because you willed yourself to believe in them, or not. Whether or not they were actually there was irrelevant.

Perhaps Felicity was a ghost somewhere. She wished she could see her. Poppy tried to remember her. She often held himself so still she could barely see her breathing. Was she a tired ghost? Felicity was always one for sleeping without moving. When she was little she used to go in her bedroom and bounce on her bed. Felicity did not stir. She would open her eyes without blinking, and say, Ah, you're here, always adding *here* because here is where she was and she always seemed somewhat surprised to be wherever she was, watching everything moving around her.

Mama used to read her letters from Oxford. Poppy remembered snippets.

Today it's so cold in here I have to filter my breath with my fingers. It makes me aware that my breath smells, a slightly stale smell of flat coffee and dissolved yeast. Is that my smell? Really it reeks of decomposition.

And:

There are workers here at college, doing menial jobs, but they seem to work in the morning only, doing things like piling stones or filling cracks in the walls. Jesus is an edifice that is always on the verge of crumbling. Aren't edifices always like that? Beauty and dereliction are very near.

Her mother used to called them *Letters from Jesus*, as though they had been dictated in heaven and were being read here on earth. Poppy used to feel that it was a violation of privacy for her mother to read these letters out loud. She knew how Felicity felt about singing. Like her mother, she felt that all singing should properly be private. That it was an intimate act, a lullaby or a declaration of love. But she had a fine alto voice and was put in the choir at Jesus College. She said she tried not to listen to the voices but to the echo of them in the fine 17th-century chapel. There was a little window there showing the Parable of the Sower. Felicity liked it, the surplice of the college hanging around her neck, because it made her able to imagine the words of her song falling on stone.

"I expect you noticed, Poppy," her mother also said, "that Felicity has developed new habits at Jesus. She goes to sleep late and wakes early. She knows she can't afford to miss too much time."

Poppy found that ominous, even then. Perhaps Felicity sensed she did not have much time left. But Poppy also heard how her mother wanted to believe that Felicity was beginning to make better use of her waking hours. It simply never occurred to her mother that her daughter couldn't sleep, possibly because she couldn't.

Poppy lay in wait for her mother that morning. Well, perhaps not lay. If she was doing nothing it would put her mother in a bad mood. She circled the dining table looking for something to appear to do. It did not matter to her mother if she were doing anything necessary or important or vital. She considered her a lazy, inert creature who did well in school only due to genetic happenstance. Her mother actually despised her genes. They made her so intelligent that she could afford to be slipshod. Poppy had difficulty concentrating, not because she couldn't, but because she always could. She never had to try. She did better than anyone in school else just by keeping a seat warm. Warmth: now there was an idea. She drifted into the kitchen to boil some water. She could tell her mother she was sterilizing, well, something or other. Or making her own lunch, but no, that was Mina's job, and it would make the poor maid look lazy instead of her. Better to be killing germs.

Her mother made no noise coming in. She never did. She was thin and light-footed. Felicity, too, had been noiseless like his mother. Poppy became aware of her only because Bovary darted by, going from the kitchen to the sofa and pillows in the living room. Making a run for it. She did not know how any living thing could survive her mother. Bovary would now sleep for hours. She wished she could sleep too, but if she did, she would hear her mother's light insistent rapping on her door just as she was drifting off.

"I did not hear you come in, Mama," she said to her, not turning around.

"I always hear you," said Jessica. "I wish for once you would be quieter about," here looking more closely at the pot boiling on the stove, "well, whatever it is you think you are doing."

Poppy heard the *think you are doing* and winced. Possibly this was not the best time to bring up the program. But it had taken her a week to steel up her courage to ask her. There was no turning back now.

"I was—going to boil rags."

"Where are the rags?" asked Jessica, who knew very well she did not keep them.

"To sterilize them," said Poppy, pretending not to hear her.

Usually this was the point at which things became worse. Her mother would tease out her lie and force a confession. It was always the same. She was avoiding real work. She was lazy. She would cry, or pretend to. Then she would offer excuses, never quite apologizing, her mother drilling her with that look that said, *Now don't give me the old answer the Truth this time Poppy.* Then Poppy would ask Mina for dinner in her room, and she would not see her mother until the next morning or the morning after (neglecting before she went out to do her hair, which got her mother's goat more than anything), at which point there would be no mention, ever, of what had transpired between them.

And even worse. Almost any incident could provoke one of her mother's slavish rituals. She would have to grovel, but in the right way. The last time, when she had run over a neighbor's cat, the composition of what her mother called "A Note of Apology, on Vellum," had taken up the better part of an afternoon. *I'm sorry* would not do. Oh, what was it? *Dear Mrs. Neighbor: My gardener has just told me that I ran over your cat whilst backing out of the driveway yesterday. I am aghast at my carelessness. I want you to know I have taken the special step of enrolling in a driver's academy to ensure that such a thing will never happen again. Although I know I cannot compensate for the poor dear creature you have lost, I can only ask you to accept my contrite apologies. Always sincerely yours, Poppy Sinden.* And what was worse, it was not to be just slipped under her door and forgotten. Poppy was also expected to join in the period of mourning, stopping by

Mrs. Neighbor's from time to time, inquiring after her feelings, bringing little gifts. After a decent interval of time (how her mother calculated this, she never knew, but she seemed to have an inner ear for it) Poppy could then go back to avoiding her, which, like her mother, she was very good at. The slightest approaching shadow on the terrace, coming from outside of course, would send one or the other of them scurrying inside, where they quickly occupied opposite areas of the flat, never mentioning it, as usual.

Poppy was looking over her mother, wonder how bad this was going to get, when her mother said, "Rags? Well, then. I shall try to find some for you."

Poppy almost erupted in tears. "Thank you, Mama!"

"In the meantime, why don't you come and sit with me?"

Sit with her? Her mother never sat with anyone. She was far too restless for that.

"Yes, Mama."

Poppy meekly followed her into the living room. Her mother sat on the sofa next to Bovary, who rolled over on her back, stretching her legs into the air.

Now was her chance. Poppy blurted out: "Mama, I went to the acupuncturist again."

"For your wrist?" she asked.

"It really helped."

Poppy had developed carpal tunnel in her right wrist from typing too much at school, because she always did everything at the last minute, typing for hours at a time.

"Computers have a dictation function nowadays," said Jessica, who favored technology when it speeded up working, thus making even more work possible. "And it works quite well."

"I prefer using my hands."

Her mother seemed to think for a moment, then said, "Yes. I like using mine too."

Her tone was mild and benign, almost introspective. It was now or never.

'Mama, acupuncture is really gaining ground in the West. Did you know that most health plans now accept it as a form of treatment?"

'How does it work, though?" asked Jessica, ever the empiricist.

'I don't think they know," she replied, honestly enough. "But they know that it does."

"But how, Poppy?" Jessica pressed.

"I think the needles just do it, well, on their own. And they plug in something to the wall, to make them buzz and pop."

Buzz and pop? Her mother frowned. Anything effortless was suspicious. Labor was what ran the world. The world would simply cease to be if people stopped grimly laboring at whatever they were doing. Mama always seemed to be making a renunciation, but of what, Poppy was never sure, except that, having done it, she went back to work. Work had for her the rhythm of breathing, something involuntary, something you were born with, something if you stopped doing, you died. Her mother believed in work, not happiness, and certainly not her happiness, nor even her father's. After all, her husband performed nearly the same sequence of actions almost every day as an surgeon in his tropical diseases clinic at Matilda. He would surely have to make at least some effort to overcome tedium, and in that stamina, her mother saw a sort of heroism.

"The needles come in sterile packages," Poppy continued, beginning to feel a hopelessness about it all.

"Chinese packages?"

"Some things do come from China, Mama," said Poppy, knowing to what lengths her mother went to eat tomatoes from Holland, oranges from Florida, and lettuces from France. Only root vegetables, suitably shielded by a foot of topsoil from whatever blights were raging there across the border, currently some sort of flu but really it might be anything, were permissible. But Poppy could not remember seeing a Chinese potato on their table. Not even one. Did the Chinese even have potatoes?

"Do the packages have Chinese writing on them?" she heard her mother saying.

"They speak and write it there, Mama."

"Ah," said her mother, with a certain note of regret.

It was a family point of pride not to learn Chinese. Perhaps if Mandarin, not Cantonese, had been the language of Hong Kong, her mother might have felt differently. She liked things mandarin, particularly those red-buttoned caps the top grade of civil servants in the old Chinese mandarinate wore. Poppy thought of getting her one as a Christmas present, but was torn about getting her the whole cap, or just the buttons. Her mother was very discreet about her alarming preference for the color red. Perhaps it was because the Chinese considered it the color of happiness, for she knew how her mother felt about happiness.

"Well, then. Is it your settled wish?"

Poppy's mind raced to make sense of this question. It was something new in her mother's armamentarium. The image of settling was of something slumped in the mud. But it begged the question of dislodging it. For the first time, Poppy heard an ever-so-slight inclination in her just to let things be. It was possible that her mother was willing to let her lay slumped in the mud of her own making. But Poppy was not sure. Her mother's tone was different. And her mother knew how attuned she was to any slight modification in her voice. She never did this with Tristan, whom she considered incapable of subtlety. She had to have intended it. It was almost too much to ask for.

"I asked," Jessica repeated, "if is it your settled wish?"

"I heard you Mama. I was not being dense."

"Heaven forfend," she said, for she had picked up this expression from Elaine Kwan. The two of them often trafficked in expressions of high disdain.

"As I understand it, then," Poppy began slowly, drawling out the *then*, with its drift toward a conclusion, "you may be willing to allow me to enroll at the University's School of Acupuncture."

"I may be," said Jessica.

Poppy brightened, but with caution. Her mother would not want to give her permission, but would want it to be inferred. She wanted to say it without saying it. In a household where everything went without saying, everything went unsaid. It drove Tristan mad. It drove Felicity to Oxford, where, trying to escape her mother by spending all her time reading in the Bodleian, she morphed right back into her, winning some kind of prize at Jesus for interpreting the obscure allegories of medieval mystery plays.

'Say that it became,' Poppy began, "an object of consideration."

'That it could become," said her mother, in her balanced way.

"Would not a trial period be appropriate?" she ventured.

Her mother widened her eyes with approval. Poppy would be both doing it, and not doing it.

"It would have to be—"

"Yes, yes, Mama, limited in duration," Poppy said, feeling herself getting a little giddy, but trying, as best she could, to contain her excitement at the way the conversation was going.

"And your living arrangements would be—"

"Strictly the same," said Poppy, using one of her mother's favorite words, *strict*.

"Even so." Her mother frowned. "You don't have to pander to me, Poppy. And I wish you wouldn't burble so."

"I'm sorry, Mama," said Poppy, trying to solemnize herself.

"You should be. Because I am quite willing to allow a grace period."

Poppy caught on right away to her mother's substitution of *grace* for *trial* period.

"Yes, yes, a grace period," echoed Poppy.

"A period in which, shall we say, no penalties would apply."

Penalties? Poppy opened her eyes a little wider than usual. Severe as she was, her mother often surprised her with entirely new dimensions of her severity.

"If, after, say, nine months of trying, if you found that it was unsuitable—"

Poppy heard how she could not bring herself to say *training*. That was too much for her. *Trying* was more abject. And she also heard clearly how unsuitable meant unsuitable to *her*.

"The relationship could be terminated with no further discussion on our part."

Poppy hoped there would be another clause, beginning, say, *but if it were suitable*, but, on second thought, that was almost too much to ask.

"That would be an excellent arrangement, Mama," said Poppy.

"Good," said her mother. "To mark our little compact, I suggest a plate of marmite."

"Shall I get it for us, Mama?"

"Yes," said her mother. "But Mina said we have run out of Carr's Crackers." She paused. "I thought we had a package."

She reached for her fanny pack and car keys.

"I'll be back in a few minutes."

Poppy knew that package. It had expired in October of 1992. She was the one who had thrown it away.

⸻

Philip Nye parked and went around back. He had never been in the front entrance of Jessica's flat. Dogs came in through the rear, and so did he.

Philip circled round past her small garden. The beds was smooth and dark. Jessica liked violets and those were doing well, as was a small meadow of asphodel. Some of the more sensitive vegetables, lettuce and baby carrots and small new potatoes, stood in rows under a sheet flapping lightly in the wind.

The door to the kitchen was open. Poppy was sitting on a stool, leaning on the counter, propped up on one elbow. She was trying to adjust the channel on a radio, which crackled with static.

"There's such bad reception on the Peak," she said, seeing him in the doorway. "You'd think with all these stupid antennas everywhere—"

"Maybe they're just for show," said Philip.

Poppy laughed lightly, much as her mother did. She wore jeans and a white woven blouse.

"You're Philip Nye, aren't you?"

"Yes."

"Hello," she said, holding out her hand to him. "I'm Poppy. I live here—sort of."

"Sort of?" he asked, looking her over.

Poppy had that blond pinkness her mother must have had at one time, but with deep lines around her eyes. Life with her mother had probably etched them in.

Poppy went on. "Well, Mama wants to give me a comforter but I use a sleeping bag on my bed." She swiped her long flaxen hair to one side. "Because, really, I'm just camping out."

"Do you have a tent?" Philip asked.

She blinked at him unfamiliarly. So unlike her father he was. So game for her little conceits!

"You know, I've actually thought of it. A pup tent in my bedroom. I once proposed it to Mama."

Philip laughed, nodding lightly.

"She said I was more than welcome to camp in her garden."

"The one on the side?"

"Yes. As long as I did not roil the grass."

"Roil the grass?" Philip smiled more broadly. Such a Jessica expression!

"Well," he asked her, "did you roil it?"

"So far I have kept off from it. Mama does not want me to disturb the fertilizer."

"Well, you probably shouldn't sleep in that stuff anyway."

"Why, I don't think Mama would view it that way. She would say, 'In the garden, Poppy, the fertilizer has first priority.'"

"I'd be curious to see it," Philip said.

"Actually," said Poppy, passing over it, a bit emboldened simply by his attention to her. "I was just thinking." She watched as he reached in his pants pocket and took out a gold pocket watch, checking the time, then checking it against the clock in the kitchen because it was clear he didn't trust it, then rewinding it. There was something about him she just didn't get. He was a little old-fashioned, yet he wasn't conservative like her father. He was formal yet casual, sad yet content. In his khaki suit Philip Nye seemed dressed for work, yet she couldn't for the life of her imagine what. And then there were those heavy hiking boots with their red laces. But she put it aside and said:

"Can I try some needles on you?"

"Needles?"

"Acupuncture needles. I don't know quite where they go yet. But I won't put them in that far, I promise."

"Just not too far," said Philip.

"You don't need to worry. I've been sticking them all over myself and they don't seem to do anything bad. See?"

She held out her arm, which had needles up and down it like nails in a board. Some were bent over.

"You don't even feel them once they're in," she added.

"You don't?" said Philip, beginning to regret agreeing to this.

"Only every once in a while, though, they do seem to get stuck."

"Stuck? What do you mean, stuck?"

"They don't seem to be going in that far under the skin then it seems to get gooey down there and they go pretty far in and then I have to use a special tool, to get them out."

She reached for a pair of pliers, not seeing Philip wince at the sight of them.

"It didn't come in the kit but it works pretty well."

She took up the pliers, picking up a stray needle from the table, which snapped in half when she gripped the handle too hard.

"And once the needles are out," Poppy continued, "I have to dispose of them properly."

She pointed to a straw waste basket, on which she taped a notecard lettered STERILE NEEDLE DISPOSAL.

"See? I already have an office set up." She tapped her side pocket. "And I have the needles right here!"

Philip squinted doubtfully at the thin pack of needles, bent like a warm stick of gum.

"Oh, they straighten out just fine," she reassured him. "You'll see."

"Okay," said Philip, rolling up his sleeve just a little. "Let's get started."

"Oh come on," said Poppy, "it has to be up more than that."

He pulled his sleeve back as far as it would go. Poppy put a few needles in his forearm, but so lightly and shallowly that most of them fell out. There were long ones and short ones but she did not know the difference yet. She also said there were thick ones that seemed rather scary to her. When she graduated and set up her practice in Central she would definitely keep them under lock and key. She already had an office picked out Did Philip know the Tun Wo building on the corner of Jubilee and Queen's Road Central? It had such nice potted plants in the lobby. The elevators were lined with teak, though she was thinking of bamboo for her office. Bamboo floors, plants, even a bamboo ceiling. Her mother considered bamboo a rather untoward plant. It grew pruriently. Mama prefers orchids, which, you know, you have to grow in traction. But they die so easily, Poppy added, with a slight note of triumph.

Philip heard a key scratching at the lock in the back door. Likely, thankfully, Jessica coming home.

Poppy heard it too. She was coming back with crackers.

"Mama!" she cried out. "Mama! I have found a stray!"

"Not another one of your pets," said her mother from the kitchen.

"No, I think he's yours."

Jessica put down her box of Carr's Crackers on the kitchen counter, striding into the living room.

"Poppy I said *no more pets*—"

Then she saw him.

"Philip!"

"Hello, Jessica."

Her eyes went straight to his arm, pin-cushioned with acupuncture needles.

"Ah! I see you've met Poppy."

"Mama," Poppy said, tearing open a sterile dressing, "I think I'm going to try putting one in his neck."

"Don't you dare!" scolded her mother.

"It says in this booklet here it helps your brain. There's a nerve that leads up there and the needle jiggles it."

"Jiggles it?" Jessica rolled her eyes, for Poppy often followed out thoughts that were based on precious little.

Poppy fumbled with a needle or two, not really sure how many she had in her hands.

"Philip," she said, folding her arms, "if you elect to keep sitting here, I'm afraid I can assume absolutely no responsibility for what this child may do to you."

He heard how she said *child*, not girl, or even, young woman, which, at eighteen or so, she certainly was.

"I'll think I'll take my chances," he said, trying to be cheerful, but sounding anxious, too.

"Good!" chortled Poppy. "Let's get started."

Philip frowned, holding himself quite still. He had hoped she was nearly done with him. He stole a look at Poppy, who had stuck a finger in her mouth, looking around as though she was missing something.

7

december 2002

Tristan Sinden met Philip Nye after his mother gave him a good grilling about Aspidistra.

That afternoon she was waiting for him in the dining room. A fire was going in the fireplace. They had one of the few real fireplaces in Hong Kong and she was very proud of it. Even in December it made the room uncomfortably hot.

Thankfully, the fire had died down a bit by the time he came out from his bedroom. His mother was frugal with wood and sat next to the fire, poking it from time to time, as though to remind the flames that they did not quite measure up. Her eyes lit up when the gutted logs crumbled into embers. It seemed to confirm her opinion of the fire.

"Mother, I think I could find a few more logs if you like."

"These are the last of them."

Untrue; there was half a cord out back. But for her everything was the last of everything. The last of the canned tomatoes, the marmalades, the treacles, the marmite. Even her children were remnants to her, though of what, he did not know. Certainly not herself. She saw very little of herself in them.

"Mother, I have been invited to dinner at my girlfriend's."

"The one with the Orwellian name?" asked Jessica.

Orwellian, for Tristan, meant *1984*. But his mother's tastes in reading were rather more recondite than that. She meant *Keep the Aspidistra Flying*.

"Really, Mother, she's not that bad."

"Her mother is rather more handsome, or was, once. You said Aspidistra lives with her."

"It's a lovely modern flat."

Jessica winced. He did not know if it was at the word *modern*, the word *flat*, or at his use of the word *lovely*. She had long since stopped correcting him. She did not see him as worth it.

"Something you say to your clients, I suppose?"

"It's my job. To take them places. To talk them up a bit."

"But do you have to use your name?"

"What? I don't get it."

"I have been in Central, the western addition, where they are selling off all the old Chinese buildings. Near that small botanical garden."

"And?"

"And I saw a number of signs with your name on it. *The Thorpe Group, Realtors. Tristan Sinden.*"

"I'm the listing agent, Mother."

"But your name is mine. I do not like seeing it used flagrantly."

"It's only normal practice. You see it everywhere."

"Just what I mean. The name Sinden—"

Tristan feared his mother was going to launch into one of her genealogical disquisitions, based as they were on her idea that there were a finite number of good old names, and that they always risked being driven from currency by becoming bad new ones, by a kind of Gresham's law of naming, really.

"I didn't put them up," said Tristan, reddening, "and I can't take them down. I'd lose my job."

"That will not be necessary." Jessica unfolded a small map of Central. "I took the trouble of marking the ones that are, well, offensively visible."

Tristan frowned and started to stand up. "That's what you wanted to talk to me about?"

"Not at all. I wanted to talk to you about Aspidistra."

Tristan sighed and sank into his chair. He tried to think of what to tell her. The normal valence of words never worked with his mother. "Girlfriend" she regarded as an oxymoron of "girl" and "friend." "Dating" was something you did with a die, stamping something with today's date in red block letters. "Sweetheart" sounded to her like sweetbread, the thymus gland of a pig. So he tried:

"I'm pretty sure I love her."

"I do not doubt that you are, just as you say you are, *pretty sure*. But does she love you?"

"Of course she does."

"How do you know that?"

"Because when I say, I love you, she says it back."

"Then she pecks at you," said Jessica, barely concealing her distaste. "I've seen it."

"You mean she kisses me?"

"Yes, in a kind of light liturgical way. The way a priest kisses the host."

"So you're afraid that she might be religious?"

"Her religious aspirations do not interest me. Only her financial ones do."

"I don't know anything about her money."

"There's not much to know. She doesn't have any."

"It just doesn't come up much. We talk about other things."

"I saw it when you brought her over on one of her little inspection tours of our household."

"Inspection tours?" sighed Tristan. "Mother, really."

"I am sure you did not see them that way. But she did. She was taking an inventory."

"I don't think she's that crude."

"No, she's far more cunning than that. She wants the best of what we have. Did you hear what she asked me?"

"No. What?"

"She asked if the little medieval casket I have, you know, the one that used to be a reliquary—"

"Yes. The one from Leiden with the two angels on it."

The one, he never added, that he was always afraid to open, thinking, knowing his mother, that it might just have real ashes and bones in it—Felicity's, for starters.

"She asked if it was real Limoges, or just a later Flemish imitation in cloisonné."

Tristan sniffed with a hint of pride. "She knows her stuff, doesn't she, Mother?"

"She knows our stuff, Tristan. Other than that I don't know what she knows."

His mother went on to say that Aspidistra's mother, Jill, had taken to writing her little notes on monogrammed stationary. The notes were very goody-goody but also rather flowery, and in his mother's opinion, they overused adverbs. *Completely, totally,* plus some she had never heard before. *Majorly.* She said she was majorly happy that her daughter had met such a nice boy as Tristan. What did she think he was, some kind of brevet?

Tristan then heard a light knocking at the back door. The maid's entrance, but it was not Mina's blunt knock but the delicate rapping of a middle knuckle. His mother pricked up her ears when she heard it.

"Are you expecting someone?" he asked.

"No," said his mother, "or rather, yes. Quite possibly."

"Your American?"

"He has a name, Tristan."

"The man with the dog?"

"The dog, Tristan, is an Italian Greyhound. A blue of fine bloodline. So I would rather you have said, *the dog with the man.*"

When he came in, the back way as he did, she did not introduce him. Her son already knew who he was. That was enough. Social grace was beyond her, though social obligation was not. His mother regarded introductions as superfluous. Any addition to acquaintance was a new grave in an old and stately churchyard. Not just anyone could be let it in. There was only a little space left, and the newer graves were jarring in the quiet and overgrown enclosure. She would only introduce him to people she already knew, as though they were already dead and buried in her mind, safely settled in the graveyard of her acquaintance, and even then, it was to say, *You remember*, not politely, but pedantically, as though Tristan were not capable, on his own, of even the simplest act of recall.

Tristan looked over Philip Nye in a desultory way. Americans gave one so little to look over. Their accents gave nothing away, and they dressed so carelessly. His suit was a light khaki bag of a thing, and a bit soiled, too, as though he lived rather than worked in it. His shirt was rumpled and hanging outside his pants. He also had on a pair of Italian hiking boots with bright red laces.

Tristan tried to put together what he knew about him. He lived with his ex-wife somewhere on the Peak. Their arrangement was beyond peculiar. They had separate bedrooms. Aspidistra said they sometimes slept in the same bed because of the dog. Because of the dog! She also said they both concluded a divorce with a complete separation would be too hard on their sensitive little Italian greyhound.

Tristan watched as his mother leaned forward to untwist one of Philip's shirt sleeves, picking at a few stray threads while she was at it.

"Philip. There."

She tugged at his sleeve and patted it. Strange how he seemed to like that his mother was grooming him. She was also looking down again at his hiking boots with the red laces, smiling. Smiling! His mother liked bright red things, like the crimson tips of the angel's wings on the Limoges piece Philip Nye just noticing on a table in the corner.

"The wings of the angels come through very well," he started to say, looking over the reliquary. "Something about the pigment they used. What was it?"

"A kind of umber," she said.

"Yes, from Cyprus."

"Have you seen—" asked his mother.

"Awful places," he said.

"Are they—"

"I'm pretty sure."

"Did they—"

"I think they did."

"It makes me feel—"

"I know. Me too. "

"They were like that with dogs too, you know."

"I can't even think about it, Jessica."

Tristan strained to listen. The more they said, the less he was able to follow what they were saying. They sped up, too, when they talked. Tristan had seen the old Roman mines in Cyprus, the ones where slaves were chained to dig a hole until they died, so he knew, approximately, what they were talking about. But he had to check himself to make sure he was seeing what he was actually seeing. His mother was actively engaged with another person. She was by no means animated; she never was. But what he said had a way of opening her up. Remarkable. He would have to tell Poppy about it.

"You know, Jessica," Philip was saying as he arranged a little nest out of blankets and pillows for his greyhound, whose name was Wylie. "I think I'd like to try some of that marmite I've heard so much about."

"The marmite?" said Jessica, wincing out a smile.

"You said you wondered why nobody ate it, when it's still good."

"It is," she pronounced.

"So I'll have some then. How do you usually serve it?"

"Spread on crackers."

"Then I'll have—" And here he paused. "What do you think?"

Tristan could see his mother making her calculations. She was saving her marmite. As against what, he did not know. The Four Horsemen of the Apocalypse, perhaps. The oldest wads of it must have been at least ten years old. The caps were gummed on the jars. Sometimes she needed a pliers to remove them. But still: it might last a little longer. And there would be other guests, other requests for her marmite. She should be sparing.

"Would two crackers be too much?" he asked lightly.

Tristan's eyes widened. Two was just right. A third was, well, a mite excessive.

"I'm sure I can find that much," she said. "If not, I shall open a new jar."

A new jar? Tristan's eyes almost jumped out of his head. The contents of his mother's kitchen cabinets were as ancient as mausoleums. New additions were definitely frowned upon, until they had the requisite patina of age and decomposition.

"Why, thanks," returned Philip. "And—"

"One for Wylie, of course."

"That'd be great."

His mother went off to the kitchen to get some marmite for him and his dog. Tristan was struck by Philip's affinity for his mother. She had a fetish for serving guests food that had expired about ten years ago, but was, in her opinion at least, still perfectly good, even if it stung the throat a little going down. Poppy even had a verb for it. To marmite them.

He turned to him now, twisting his chair as well as his torso.

"You look wiped out, Tristan."

"Mother can have that effect."

"The others are trying to get out of here as fast as they can. I guess that leaves you."

Tristan saw the truth of it as soon as he said it. His mother had a certain amount of applied force. With Poppy going, or at least wanting to, and Felicity dead, it was all directed at him.

"It's almost measurable," said Philip.

"Even so," said Tristan, finding himself, despite his own instilled reticence, wanting to talk to him, though still holding back.

"You don't have to say anything," he said. "I think I know what she told you."

"You do?"

"Stopping doing whatever you are doing, and doing what she wants you to do instead. Especially with Aspidistra."

"You know about—"

"Not much. But I can hear how she says the name. Asper–dist–rah."

Just like, he went on to explain, her name was a peculiar compound of the two words *asperity* and *distress*.

"Yes," said Tristan, almost involuntarily. "You know her?"

"Kind of. She used to walk our dog."

"Ah," said Tristan.

"She didn't like him," Philip continued, "and she wasn't any good with him. I think she took the job because her mother wanted her to."

That sounded like Aspidistra. Tristan felt her mother behind all the questions she had been asking him recently about his family's holdings. She would crease her forehead, trying to recall exactly what her mother had wanted her to ask. Tristan was sure Aspidistra knew nothing whatsoever about Limoges. Jill must have wanted her to find out something about this American. If he had means they were very mysterious. He had been at Harvard. His ex-wife had some kind of large and important financial job in Hong Kong. She had gone to Harvard Business School, which Tristan supposed to be on something like the Palatine Hill of Harvard. He had some sort of lesser degree in classics, genteel in an elegantly shabby way, which is what his mother had once called Felicity's degree in English from Jesus. If Harvard really was some kind of American system of royalty, Jill Benning would want to see about insinuating her daughter into it.

Philip returned to looking over at the reliquary. He tilted his head slightly, saying, "There are three of these, you know. The Met has one and the Prado has the other. I like your mother's best. It looks worn, as something old should. The other ones in the museums are so—polished."

Right then and there, Tristan had the idea that his mother should divorce his father, marry this American, and go live in their little reliquary together. Life without his mother: he and Poppy could open a bottle of Chianti and watch foreign films and order take-out every night of the week. Or he could host a rugby party for the Hong Kong Sevens, coming up in April, and empty his mind of everything but gin, Eddie Jones, and his beloved Ba-bas, the British Barbarians.

But another marriage? No, better still if she remained unmarried. One of those Roman Catholic annulments would be perfect for her. Pity the Church of England had never adopted the practice. For Jessica Sinden it would be not at all hypocritical to say that a marriage of thirty-five years had never taken place; it would be hypocritical to say that it had. Having always been alone, a high lone raptor of a woman, it was not casuistry to say that she had never entered into a marriage. Whatever marriage was, and that Tristan was not sure of, having contemplated the prospect of a life with Aspidistra, his mother was not capable of it.

Philip Nye seemed nice enough. But for the life of him, Tristan could not see what he saw in his mother. She had once been thin and pretty. Now she was thin and desiccated. *Jessicated*, he heard his father once say in his punning way, referring to one or the other of the Peak's crinkly dowagers, but also using it once, even more pointedly, on a trip to Italy, referring to the silt of some saint in a glass box. She was anything but companionable. You could almost feel the air stinging her throat as she talked.

He had once seen her kill a cobra. It had come out of a culvert on Homestead Road and had coiled up, ready to strike Bovary. But she struck first. She was carrying one of his old cricket bats and swung fast, flattening its head. The snake's body dropped, twitching, and she kicked it aside lightly as they passed, saying, "Those round bats. The American ones. They are rather more nimble than yours, I think, unless I take to drilling holes in the flat of this one to make it into a paddle. I should like to try one once."

Some weeks later she took delivery of a package with an Adirondack bat in it. It was called a Louisville Slugger.

8

january 2003

THESE LITTLE JAUNTS of Jessica's did not sit well with Elaine Kwan. They could afford to live on the Peak, so she did not see why they should spend so much time scouring the Mid-Levels for bargains. Bargains! Elaine Kwan was a woman who prided herself at never looking at a price tag. Jessica was a bit of a vulture when it came to these sales. She would monitor the *South China Morning Post* for tidings of divorce, accident, death in the family, then sweep down on households to pick through the ruins. She was generous with the spoils. When Elaine opened her friend's present on her fifty-ninth birthday, she recognized the Mont Blanc pen. She had been there on Conduit Road when Jessica paid three dollars for it.

They took turns. One Sunday it was rummage sales, the next, Lane Crawford. This Sunday it was Elaine's turn to be miserable. Normally, this time of year, she would be in China for the New Year. But this time she canceled her trip, fearing whatever flu they were talking about this year. Today Jessica had put together a full list for the afternoon. Robinson Road, Mosque Junction, Chancery Lane.

"I wish you'd ask Philip to come," Elaine said as the car dropped down into the City after the hairpin turn on Magazine Gap Road. Sometimes her ears popped at this point. Jessica's never did, or if they did, she never complained about it.

"Your ears?" asked Jessica.

"Sometimes I think I should never come down," said Elaine Kwan.

"It would be a loss," said Jessica, who never could hear hyperbole, "though perhaps not a tragic one."

Elaine settled back into her seat. They passed the famously unlucky building on Stubbs Road, the one with the coffin-shaped windows. Elaine always winced passing it, but Jessica hardly noticed it. She was always so focused in pursuit of bargains. It was there in the way she reviewed the listings she had circled in the paper. She looked at them as though, if she stared at them hard enough, she could see what they were hiding from her.

"Philip is not fond of shopping," said Jessica.

Elaine knew her well enough not to be surprised that she considered this "shopping."

"Even so," she said.

For Elaine Kwan wanted to see Jessica's American for herself. Harvard always made for such a good calling card. She had rarely been disappointed in the Americans who had gone there. They so often had a formal reserve, which expressed, for Elaine, both a deep reticence, an unwillingness to disclose anything untoward, and an abiding sense of reservation, a clear harboring of doubts about others. Elaine liked people who kept their qualifications to themselves, and assumed that Philip had the discretion not to press Jessica about Felicity. All the Harvard people she had met were examples of *noblesse oblige*, though in a democratic vein, one she had come, with certain reservations, to admire, being herself a mild exponent of democracy, a form of government which, if she could only have it without any lessening in her way of living, why, then, she was certainly in favor of.

The first visit was not a success. The occupants were long gone from their flat on Robinson Road, and the price tags were large and hurt Elaine's eyes. All numbers ought properly to be inscrutable.

The second visit was to Chancery Lane. The building was promising. An old Chinese block of flats had been redone by a young architect. The ground floor, which had its own garden, had been let out to Jeremy

Wallace, president of Wilberforce Holdings, who had run off with a woman from Chengdu. His wife was having the sale. Mostly his things, which meant his wife would be selling them for nearly nothing just to get even.

Elaine never liked hearing these stories. The objects should be consigned to an auction house. But after Jessica reminded her that Elaine would never allow herself to be seen in one, she stopped complaining, though she insinuated she might go, if only Jessica were to bring her American along.

Elaine stole a look at Jessica Sinden. That, of all people, she should fall in love. Elaine would have done it differently of course. She would never have allowed herself to be seen with her lover. Tristan said she walked around with dogs and talked all sorts of clipped nonsense with him. He must be giving her something she liked. Her words had an uplift Elaine had never heard in them before. She seemed light on her feet, too, fresh, eyes open, wide awake.

Her lightness made Elaine feel old and heavy. Sad that love was so untransferable. Even if she met the man she would understand very little of what Jessica felt for him.

But one thing she felt sure of. Philip Nye had exquisite taste. So she asked her friend about that.

"You said he has a good eye," she began.

"Yes. He does."

"Have you ever seen where he lives?"

"No. Just pictures. His ex-wife gives him money so he can buy whatever he wants, but he's oddly frugal. He looks and looks, and is usually let down. I've seen this before. Great lovers of beauty spend most of their time being disappointed by ugliness. But every once in a while, he finds something. And then, price is not an object."

"I am relieved to hear it," said Elaine, entering the flat. Her eyes passed over the wall-to-wall carpeting, veneered furniture, and badly framed prints of Impressionist paintings. Sliding doors opened to a little garden in back, tiered with dusty, drooping flowers. "I can't imagine him finding anything here."

"He loves me," said Jessica, "but I think he finds my taste deficient in certain ways."

"I *would* like to meet him, then. Have you told him about me?"

Jessica tightened her lips, which is what she did when a polite lie was called for.

"I see," said Elaine Kwan, always humored by her friend Jessica's need for veracity. "You need to break him in first."

"Yes. Poppy and Tristan have only just met him."

"What about Edward?"

"He has told me he approves of our walks. Though what he really knows about what I do is always a little unclear to me. Really I prefer it that way. Being lightly separate."

"That's a nice way of putting it. I so wish Simpson would adopt your attitude."

"But he won't, will he?"

"No. You have to remember, all Chinese marriages are conditional. A code exists, one for the men and one for the women. He will keep to the conditions on his side as long as I keep to those on mine."

"I should think that is a most satisfactory arrangement," said Jessica, who loved unwritten social codes. If she were to ask Elaine precisely what those conditions were, she would go down a notch in her estimation. That was how it should be. Good social codes ought to demand a mincing and largely private degree of interpretation. Unlike, say, that piece of furniture on the other side of the room, near the doors open to the garden. Late French Empire, with more scrolls than drawers. And walnut stained, think of it, a dark walnut. One could hardly forgive the Victorians for that.

"I just *have* to see how much it is," said Elaine Kwan, smiling and taking a girlish delight in breaking her own rule.

"You wouldn't dare," said Jessica.

"Just see if I don't," she said, walking over to the dresser, which sat near the door open to the back garden.

"Nice piece," Elaine heard a woman say, coming up to the dresser to look it over. She was a blonde, middle-aged woman with a uniformly yellow tint to her hair.

Then she turned her head toward a young woman, quite obviously her daughter, who was coming out of the garden with a bunch of flowers in her hand. Their petals were dusted with white.

"Aspidistra!" she screamed. "Didn't you see the white powder?"

"They're bluebells," the girl said, sniffing them. "I didn't know they had them here. That lady over there," she added, pointing to Mrs. Wallace, "said I could take as many as I wanted."

Her mother scuttled over to her, snatching the thin blue flowers from her hands and tossing them onto the pavement of the garden.

"Can't you see it's pesticide?" Then, with concern, "You have some on your shirt."

The girl pulled up her blouse, showing her mother a rash underneath.

"You think it did this?" she asked her mother.

Her mother stared doubtfully at the rash.

"I don't know, honey. How long have you had it?"

"I can't remember. Tristan said it was nothing though. But he had to run off to the bank to deposit some money I gave him."

"You mean you lent *him* money?"

"I think he was afraid of asking his mother," said the girl, who went back to scratching her rash. "But I'll go wash it off it you want me to."

The girl went off in search of a bathroom.

"Jessica—oh *Jessica*," the mother warbled across the room. "Jessica—may I call you that? It's Jill. Aspidistra's mum."

Jessica turned around. She did not feel like objecting to almost everything she said, as well as to how she said it.

"I see you and your friend are also looking at this beautiful piece. It's so majestic. I've had my eye on it, too," she said, lowering her voice. "For my *bedroom*."

She moved in closer to Jessica.

"Speaking of bedrooms, I hear the two of you have become—quite the little item."

Jessica bristled. She now felt she had to say something. "You speak of it rather as though one were being placed on offer."

Jill Benning did not hear the correction. "You know what I mean," she said, becoming even more insinuating. "An item. And a nice daily one, I gather."

"We walk our dogs," said Jessica, inflecting each word separately. "Twice daily," she added, putting a chaste emphasis on twice.

"Aspidistra used to walk Wylie for the Nyes," said Jill. "You know, she's very good with dogs. I'm sure she could relieve you of some of your dog-walking chores if you needed a bit more free time, you know, for other things."

Jill touched her arm in an alarmingly mutual way. For a moment Jessica was afraid she might actually wink at her. Jill had blonde hair a uniform color (clearly she could not afford balayage at a salon such as S/Z), and a wind-burned face from doing, well, whatever it was she had done back in Canada. Jessica had to remind herself it would not be polite simply to turn away from this person. But she found herself wondering why, if Canada was so large and empty, it had to send so many of its citizens to Hong Kong, which was, after all, small and already overcrowded.

"I was thinking I might have the two of you over for dinner. Tristan and Aspidistra could come. Just the two of them, the two of us, and Philip, of course."

Jessica heard how Jill paired them together. She wanted desperately to put their relationship on some kind of equal footing.

"Why don't you speak to him about it?" Jill continued. "Maybe Poppy could come, too."

"Poppy?" said Jessica.

"I'd dearly love it if she and Aspidistra became friends. They could have sleepovers, you know. You and I could join them. Watch old movies together. Sort of a girls' night out, but in."

Jessica's face contracted almost involuntarily. Her daughter friends with Aspidistra? Poppy was already very immature, her bed piled with dolls, her walls pinned with little drawings of this and that, mostly flowers. She rarely read a book. She was sure because she kept a little stool next to the door, which had a transept over it, and stood on it from time to time. She rarely saw anything worth seeing, except that her room was a mess. She would not even let Mina in to clean.

Elaine, who had moved away to talk to Mrs. Wallace, a distraught-looking woman in a Chanel suit, came back.

"What did she say?" asked Jessica, turning to her friend with a sigh of relief.

"I'll tell you later," said Elaine Kwan.

"Say what?" intruded Jill.

"Just—an inquiry."

"Oh, I thought you were negotiating with the Wallaces for this lovely dresser. Well, at least with her. Heaven knows where he is. Probably in Phuket with that Chinese mistress of his. But you're right. You can always save a few bucks, you know, with some hard bargaining. God knows these are good prices, but some of these people are in such bad straits, I almost think they'd pay you to cart off all this stuff. Even I can afford most of it."

Confessions of poverty did not resonate well with either Jessica Sinden or Elaine Kwan. Elaine was not happy. She gave Jessica her *where-did-you-get-this-person-from* look.

Jessica registered it right away. A hard woman herself, she knew how crushing her disapproval could be.

The two women were standing there, both thinking of how they could get away from Jill, when Aspidistra came back from the bathroom.

"Oh, Mrs. Sinden!" she said. "I just knew you'd be here. When I told Mama how you went out Saturdays she told me she had been meaning for ages to go out to some rummage sales."

"For ages," chimed in Jill.

"I tried to get Tristan to come with me but he just rolled over in bed and put the pillow over his head. I think he could hear me though. I told him he could get to know Mama a little better. Maybe I can get him to come next week. Because of his business he knows all these buildings and could show off their features, you know, in case we want to move. We could all go together."

"Heaven forfend," said Elaine Kwan, almost involuntarily.

The word whizzed by the Bennings, mother and daughter. Not even a near miss, thought Jessica.

'Why, thanks," said Jill, thinking she had Elaine's heavenly blessing. "I hope you don't mind if I join you. Maybe the three of us could start going. Why don't both of you come over for dinner next week?"

This was just too much for Elaine Kwan. She simply walked away.

Jill paused for a moment, then said, "Is she not feeling well?"

"You could say that," said Jessica.

A week or so passed. Elaine Kwan schemed. To meet Philip Nye she would have to take things into her own hands. Luckily nothing in life gave her more pleasure. Other hands were so unreliable, and they sullied things so! Jessica Sinden might well keep her off from her American for months, and then meeting him would become a matter of mere chance— shopping on Des Voeux Road, lunch at Grappa's in Pacific Place, a stop at Staunton's on Old Bailey. Elaine disliked chance. The outcome would not be precisely adjusted to her social micrometer. To meet him, by which she meant a sort of measured mutual viewing, as at her Inquest, everything would have to be just-so.

The occasion she chose was Simpson's birthday. Goodness knew she did not want to have a large party, but neither could it be an intimate private dinner of the kind she favored. She convinced the head chef of Riposte on Arbuthnot Road to close his restaurant the night of the party so that he and his staff could cook for her. As for the guest list, she went over the possibilities in her head. The Sloane Shaws were probably the best of the lot. Regina Yip she should probably keep to herself. Justine Ho could bring her daughter, Phoebe, who was attending one of the lesser Oxford colleges she supposed to be comparable to Harvard. And there were of course Simpson's clients, one or two of whom might be presentable enough.

A setting for twelve on silver; that would do nicely.

~

The night came soon enough. But there was one surprise. Jessica Sinden came, but not with Philip Nye. She came with his ex-wife.

"Pretty small for a surprise party," said Roma Nye, coming in and looking around. "And Simpson's here, too, I see. So I'm guessing you've already sprung it on him?"

"There are no surprises in Chinese culture," Elaine told her. "Simpson worked out the guest list with me."

"Hm," she said, nodding with approval. "Probably better that way."

"There are certain business contacts I would not know to invite."

"How old is he, then?" Roma asked.

"Why, I think you'd have to ask him that."

"Good," she said flatly, as though receiving instructions. "I will."

Roma Nye pulled her head back tautly as she spoke. She was pale and blonde with long, blue-veined legs that had the elegance of marble. She was not particularly pretty but her straight hair set off her long bony face in a way that made you pay attention to her. She had something. An intelligence possibly, or perhaps it was only a hardness.

"Jessica talked me into coming," she said to Elaine, reaching out and pressing her arm. "She can be very persuasive."

For her friend's sake, Elaine let her arm be touched without withdrawing it. The two women seemed to like each other. Elaine wondered to what extent.

"I don't know many of Philip's women friends," Roma continued. "I just know he likes to have them." She took a sip of a Scotch that a waiter handed her. "And anyway, I'm not his keeper."

Elaine already knew this. Simpson said they divorced a year ago but still shared a flat on the Peak. But they still went everywhere together.

They were to be seen at T'ang Court at The Langham, sampling the steamed sliced goose with taro and soya bean, where Roma took his arm but never his hand. Philip was Roma's date at *The World in 2002 Gala* sponsored by *The Economist* at the Marriott at Pacific Place, where her colleagues liked him, not so much because he talked, but because he was just about the only one at the table who listened.

"So," said Roma, who took in the Kwan living room, with its heavy varnished furniture and old tintypes of women in cheongsams sipping tea. "This your house?"

"Yes," said Elaine.

"Nice place. I live down the street and around the corner. Just past the stop sign. Funny how you never run into your neighbors here. Even though the place is really pretty small."

"You don't walk Wylie at all?"

"To me he's Philip's dog, really. I won't let him up in my bed. Usually he sleeps in the second bedroom with Philip. Wylie kind of knows to avoid me. You should see it. The dog almost leads him there at night."

Biting her lip, Jessica dropped her eyes. Elaine Kwan was more used to the blunt self-disclosures of Americans, even those said to be reasonably well-educated.

"And how is—Philip?" Elaine ventured.

"He's at the theater."

"He is?"

"What did he go to see?"

Roma shrugged. "I don't know. Whatever's playing down there. I don't think he'll like it though."

"He won't?"

"He never does. Goes to all the trouble to get the best seat in the house, then he's always so let down. I told him to readjust his sights. I mean, all the shows he sees can't be that bad."

Then Simpson came up.

"Thank you for coming, Roma."

So Simpson knew her. Odd, he never mentioned it. But then again, why would he? He would not have known her to have any possible connection to this woman.

"How are the negotiations going with the Hang Lung Group?" Simpson asked.

Ah, business, thought Elaine, partly closing down her mind.

Roma's eyes narrowed to a visor slit.

"I put on my naive American act. You know, nice and trusting. And *blonde*," she said, sweeping back her long straight hair sharply with one hand. "Once they see me they usually forget what I know or where I've been to school. They even start talking to one another in bits of coded Mandarin, taken from *The Story of the Stone*."

"You've read it?" asked Elaine, muting her astonishment.

"Memorized is more like it," she said. "They think I don't know Chinese, but just to make sure, they talk in metaphors. Ha! As if I don't know what the Dream of the Land of Illusions is."

This time it was Jessica's turn to look at her blankly.

"Sorry, I see you don't know. It's just a story about some lovers."

"What happens in the end?" asked Jessica.

"Oh, I can't remember. They pair off. They always do. I never see what Philip sees in all those novels he reads. Same story over and over, as far as I can tell."

"*Mo lun yung*," Roma added, this time in perfectly-pitched Cantonese, almost growling it to Simpson, who laughed heartily.

"What did she say?" asked Jessica.

"I'm afraid it's untranslatable." He folded his arms, still amused.

Elaine Kwan knew perfectly well what it meant. Useless, with expletives attached. She was surprised Roma knew them. So she had something, a sharpness, that in one limited context, became an acuity. It was also quite possible that she was simply very good at this one small thing.

"Honestly, I've never read the *The Story of the Stone*," said Simpson. "It isn't in the Hong Kong Curriculum."

"I don't think it's in anybody's," Roma added. "For me it was strictly on a need-to-know basis."

"I hope you don't mind my asking," said Jessica, "but how did you know it would be useful?"

Always so sharp, thought Elaine, pleased with her friend's question.

"Well, one day after work I was telling Philip about it, about how they talked, using names and telling little stories. I remember we were at that little tapas place on Staunton Street. And he said it reminded him of a dream vision by John Bunyan."

"Of course!" exclaimed Jessica. "A Chinese *Pilgrim's Progress*!"

"That's when I realized there was a kind of key to what they were saying. That it was an allegory. After that all I had to do was the leg work."

"It couldn't have been easy," offered Jessica.

"It wasn't," said Roma. "I already knew Mandarin but I had to learn a whole new set of words. Philip said ancient Greek is like that. Every author is like a different dialect. But once you do your homework, it's pretty easy."

Easy? Well, perhaps. Roma Nye was utterly utilitarian. She learned everything she needed to learn, no matter what it was, to do what she needed to do. Thought was action for her. She would never go beyond a certain point, but then again, she would never want to.

Elaine's mind curved back into the line of the conversation. But Roma had already gone on to something else. Some little tidbit about Philip: how, when they were in Central, they always fought about taking the Escalators up the hill. He liked walking. She liked taking them up, lolling, posing, observing and being observed. They rolled past some of the finest stores in Hong Kong, which was nothing if not a place to shop. She liked to keep up a light running commentary on them. Silk was out, chenille was in. A line of ruffles did indeed improve on the tightly-fitted dresses most Chinese women favored. She had been in Hong Kong long enough to know that the Escalators through the Mid-Levels were as close to Madison Avenue as it got. Philip could be *such* a New Yorker sometimes, lecturing her at the Met as if she did not know the difference between a baroque scroll and a rococo shell. Or was it a baroque shell and a rococo scroll? That was Philip for you. The world for him was written in fine print. When she first met him she used to tell him he would have made a great lawyer, but now she knew better. He would not have made a great *anything*.

Rather more revealing than Elaine liked, but then again, it was a crisp account, thin and brief like an American newscast.

"He's good on the phone, though," Roma was saying now.

"Is he?" asked Jessica, who had not known it, and would certainly not have predicted it.

"He's amazing," she chortled. "You know, he can get people off the line in a minute flat."

"He can?"

"Yes. And the whole time he's so polite they think he's concerned about taking up *their* time."

"Perhaps he is," said Jessica.

"I tell him just to let the machine take it. But then he hears the message come on, you know the kind, *This is 852* and so on, and he can't stand hearing it yet again, so he just picks the thing up."

"Poor Philip," said Jessica.

Possibly, concluded Elaine Kwan, construing it in the broad sense her friend certainly meant it in—poor in having been married to her for a time. Certainly she was a very poor representative of who Philip was. But then again, that was not why Jessica had chosen to bring her. She brought her to show Elaine everything Philip was not. It was not that she thought her less good than she should have been. She was refined in the way oil was refined, to a kind of valuable concentrate. But her ex-husband had real refinement. Americans so often confused the two, which is why, Elaine supposed, the two had come to be married. And yet really, when she came to think of it, Elaine could not imagine him saying more than five words to her in the many years they were married—so unlike did they seem to her.

Elaine ushered her guests to the table, taking care to seat Roma next to her. She was glad they had at least one thing in common. Neither of them could abide dogs.

9

mid-january 2003

ROMA NYE knew where the Helena May was, but she had never been there before. It was an old colonial building with high windows where Philip spent his nights with Jessica Sinden. Roma parked in the back lot under Cotton Tree Drive. Circling round front, bending into a high wind, she stopped to look through the high windows of the old dining room. A brittle light from the old chandeliers, strung with drooping glass beads, filled the room. The women sat stiffly, looking at their padded menus. A waiter in black stood nearby, waiting to refill their glasses with luke-warm water. A woman in a long gown, perhaps Mrs. Braveley, the social director of the club, moved from table to table, welcoming her guests.

Mrs. Braveley was waiting for her at the front desk.

"Ah, Mrs. Nye," she said. "Next time you may use the member's lot." She handed her a key to the garage. "We're expecting a storm, you know."

She took two menus and turned into the dining room. A few women looked up from their menus, then down again. A few others pretended not to see her, but stiffened as she passed. Roma followed their eyes to a table by one of the high back windows. The settings were silver and the glasses were crystal. The white linens reached nearly to the floor. Mrs. Braveley pulled back a chair and handed her a menu.

"We can speak later," she said.

Roma suddenly had the feeling of coming into a very large ballroom she could never leave. These women, perhaps six or eight of them, had the place to themselves. Each table had a wreath and an unlighted candle.

Half a dozen tarnished mirrors lined the wall, along with some upholstered white chairs.

Roma's table was next to some French doors that opened onto a terrace. Some trees on the terrace were bending with a high wind. Dark clouds were moving in quickly.

The lights flickered. She watched as rain started hitting the windows in sheets, snapping at the side of the building.

Roma overhead one of the members asking Mrs. Braveley if a typhoon would hit Hong Kong.

Just then Jessica came up.

"A bit early in the season for this," she said, seeing the rain.

"I wouldn't know," said Roma.

Another wind came up. A metal chair skidded off the balcony and tumbled over a low wall.

A few of the women began to leave the room.

Jessica settled into her chair and unfolded her napkin.

"It's just a tropical storm," she said.

Just a tropical storm? Roma's eyes followed the dropping waves of wind. The panes in the French doors rattled in their muntins. A low whitewashed building stood on the other end of the patio in back, its flat roof pooled with water. Close by, a few trees were down over the tram line, stalling a pair of red cars just before the service platform on Garden Road.

But Jessica was busy looking over the menu. She beckoned a waiter in black.

"Benson. Are there no Black Bullace Plums?"

"I'm sorry, Mrs. Sinden. Not tonight."

"Then you would recommend—"

"The mutton is said to be very good."

"What about my veg?"

"Oh, we always have your veg, Mrs. Sinden."

"Good," she said. "Roma?"

"Oh," she said, her eyes still on the sky dark with rain, "I'll have whatever you are having."

"That will do, Benson," said Jessica.

She turned to Roma. "So. I'm here. And you have my full attention."

She was here because that morning Philip told Roma he was getting very serious about Jessica Sinden. Roma liked Jessica Sinden, but it was getting to her that Philip was not home much any more. Never mind that she was rarely at home. He was never at home with her.

He also told her he would be spending most of his nights at the Helena May. Roma opened her clutch and took out the card he gave her. It was the engraved business card of the Helena May, with *x208* written on it using a fountain pen.

Jessica started to smile. "I gave him that to give to you. The writing is mine. He knows I don't approve of sneaking around."

"So people here—*know* about you?"

"Yes."

"Which ones?"

"Why, they *all* do," said Jessica, with an odd trace of gaiety in her voice. "Philip has made quite an impression on the membership. In fact, were it not for his gender, I think he would be offered a place at the club. A club is such a special space. Things can happen here that can't happen elsewhere. Philip seems remarkably at his ease among the members. He's a particular favorite of Mrs. Braveley, the Social Director. I rather thinks she wants *you* to join."

Roma half jumped out of her seat. She wanted to laugh out loud. What was she doing having lunch with Philip's lover? And why had all these people sided with him? A feeling washed over her that all the people in the room were somehow against her.

Jessica remained quite still, regarding her benignly. A few women in the room turned their heads ever-so-slightly.

Another high wind came up. The walls creaked heavily.

Roma overheard Mrs. Braveley telling several women it might be a good idea to go to the basement.

"If you'd like to go with them, you know," said Jessica, several tones above her speaking voice, "we can speak to Mrs. Braveley."

Roma heard how Jessica was covering for her. The rain was raking the windows but there was little thunder and no lightning.

"Mrs. Nye?" inquired Mrs. Braveley, from across the room.

Roma took several measured breaths and sat back down.

"No, it's nothing," said Roma.

"A attack of nerves, perhaps," said Jessica, loudly enough so that it could be heard around the room.

Roma was not afraid of tropical storms. But for the first time she was afraid of what Philip was doing. When she divorced him he did not move out He liked Roma as much as he always had, even though, as a spouse, she had been rather more imperious than he wished. But Jessica Sinden also had a sharpness about her. Caustic, but like cleaning the old varnish off tabletops so you could see the bare wood underneath.

"You're thinking about me, aren't you?" Jessica asked her, pouring tea into two cups from a Brown Betty. "I suppose I don't look the part, do I? Of a mistress."

"That's, uh, well—true."

"I appreciate your hesitancy. I have been trying to help Philip adjust to how I look, as well. You're certainly more presentable than I am. That light dress you're wearing with the open back, for one." Jessica straightened her top of her blouse, drawing its collar firmly around her neck. "Though I might add that it is a bit too skimpy for dinner here."

Mrs. Braveley came to the table. "Mrs. Sinden. The T3 has been hoisted."

"Is the kitchen closing?"

"Why—no."

"Well! Thank you, then."

The lights went off and on again. Mrs. Braveley blinked and withdrew. A few more women moved toward the side door leading to the basement. Several others remained, picking at their salads.

Her fingers trembling, Roma opened her clutch and took out a little brown envelope. She took out a folded document on vellum and opened it. It was official and had a blue stamp on it.

"Look," she said, thrusting it toward Jessica. "This is what's left of us."

It said, DECREE OF DIVORCE, HONG KONG SPECIAL ADMINISTRATIVE REGION.

"Do you ever read it?" asked Jessica.

What an odd question, Roma thought, but then, considering it, she said:

"No. Never. I've just been carrying it around. You know, like a favor at a wedding. You put it somewhere and then you lose it after a while. But," she admitted, more hesitantly, "I take it out and look at it from time to time."

She crammed it back in the brown envelope.

"To remind me of what I did."

"Philip said he agreed to it," said Jessica.

"He did. But I think I wore him out."

"That's not true," said Jessica. "Everyone is exhausting. And a marriage doesn't stop because of a divorce."

"I know," Roma said quietly. "I kept his name."

The green in Jessica's eyes seemed to sharpen.

"I thought I did it for professional reasons. But I didn't want to go back to being Roma Morrow. I really thought of myself as Roma Nye."

"I was once Jessica Bright," said Jessica. "I took Edward's name because I wanted it, too. I've never been good with names, you know."

Naming was so intrusive, she went on to say, so misconstrued, and in this giving of names she was just as bad at it as everyone else. Poppy was a horse's name, Tristan was never as sad as he rightly ought to be, and her other daughter, Felicity, who died some years back, was terribly misnamed, for she was never happy. Only *Sinden* told the world what she really was, and she often felt she married Edward only for his name, which was like a deep still pool of water, a kind of lake where they buried kings with their swords.

"So I could never be Jessica Nye."

"You couldn't?"

'It would just be another bad name. Jessica Sinden is close enough, I think."

'So you will never marry him?"

'I can't say that. I can only say with certainty that I will never be Jessica Nye."

Dinner came, and along with it, tropical storm Yanyan. The lights flickered a few more times and finally went out. The two women ate quietly in the dark. Afterwards, Baker Nicholson sent a car for Roma to take her back to her empty flat on the Peak. The lot where she was parked was blocked by fallen trees and live wires.

10

february 2003

THE TWO OF THEM had a way of communicating through the dogs. Poppy remarked on it. Even Tristan readily saw at a distance how Philip would come at his mother, sweeping up Bovary as they walked along, holding the little greyhound with one hand at a balance point just under her ribcage. They joked about it, calling it *him making a pass at her,* her being both their dog and their mother, who seemed to them, even then, to be an almost incomprehensible object of desire. For their mother never smiled, not even with her American, not even after she began to pin a sprig of iris in her hair when she was out with him. The closest she got to laughter was pretending to be annoyed with him when he snatched up Bovary.

Saturdays were their days for long dog expeditions. It had come to be understood around the Peak that theirs was not a dog walk, but a dog hike, a great running of greyhounds, who, they let it be known, were all lung and leg and needed this sort of thing. They went far and wide around the Peak, not avoiding its steepness but seeming to revel in it. They went along Lady Clement's Ride and over Peel Rise and down the Aberdeen Reservoir Road, skirting the mountain tops and the terraced sides of paths so steep they suddenly became staircases, passing too through the long wastes of gun emplacements built long ago to keep off the Japanese. They climbed high enough to see the uneven lines of skyscrapers on the Kowloon side of the Bay, and the scars of the old Anderson Road Quarry gouged in the hillside of East Kowloon, and beyond them, the far ridge of the connected hills at Pat Sin Leng.

Going over the roll of a hill that Saturday early in February, stamping her feet first, not so much to get the dirt off them as to remind the ground who was who, she said to Philip:

"Well! What would you say if I just kidnapped you sometime, and took you somewhere, say, to Thailand?"

"You have a house there, Jessica."

"You think I'm putting you on? I'd tie you up."

"Since when have you needed to do that?"

"I'd fill you full of marmite and crackers."

Philip knew just how to take this. She was such a frugal eater.

"You're not telling me something," she said.

"I thought you liked privacy," he said.

"I do," she said, becoming rigid. "But only to a degree," though, pausing to think it over, she was not exactly sure what that degree was between her and Philip. It always seemed to be changing. So she said: "I think I shall just stand here until you tell me."

So he told her that she actually hated marmite and the only reason she served it was other people did, too.

"You're still not telling me everything, Philip."

She put her hand on his arm, which felt warm even in the chill of a January day.

"As long as you don't tell anyone else," she said, giving him her best half-smile. "I don't mind." Then, seeing something out the corner of her eye, she jerked her head up. "Bovary? *Bovary!*"

Bovary had picked up a stick. Jessica called out her name, and she snapped her head around, dropping the stick. She did not like it when she picked up things on their walks.

Wylie snatched it up and stared at Philip.

"Well?" asked Jessica.

"Well what?"

"Aren't you going to chastise her?"

"What would you have me *say*?"

"What you say doesn't matter with her. It's your tone that does."

Tone was everything to Jessica. It was how she herself heard things. Philip once called her a creature of inference. She was well aware that she did not know him well, not yet. She had to listen to him carefully to tease out his history, inferring it as she went along. Jessica mostly had lived her life in a British and European world, as well as whatever part of the Chinese world that had managed to accommodate itself to it. But Philip Nye was in the American grain.

It took her some time to see that he was not American in Poppy's sense of that thin layer of American culture that seemed to cover everything nowadays like dust blown from a distantly erupting volcano. Philip was as ignorant of American television as she was. He never watched movies. Large visual images, unless they were as rigid as tapestries, made him uncomfortable. Jessica was surprised to learn that he had never been to California. He was from a more deeply impacted layer of America, northeastern in nature, and it took some piecing together on her part (for despite what he said, he could be as undisclosing as she was), to see what that was.

Philip Nye had been his name, she found out, and his father's, and his father's before him. It was not an old name, not in the British sense that any of them had been someone or done something, but they had always, as she understood it, *almost* been someone or done something. There had been Nyes on the edges of everything American for generations. A Nye declined to sign the Declaration of Independence. A pair of Nye brothers paid substitutes to fight for them in the Civil War. Nye was nigh, but, to hear him say it, not quite there at all, except, perhaps, for Philip's grandfather, who had been an Under-Secretary of Commerce, though one of no note, under Averell Harriman. Other than him it seemed to her the Nyes were wealthy nonentities. They did nothing other than go to Harvard, after which they became lawyers who never practiced law, doctors who never saw patients, writers who never published a word. It was life lived just short of living, just below the threshold of crossing over from *not-quite*, to *barely*. And yet, he once admitted to her, they were perfectly upright about it. Nye was considered a good old name in the Hudson River Valley, where Philip had been raised in a fine old house overlooking a bend in the river. His father pottered around in the garden and collected old books. His mother drank rye whiskey and did not like leaving her bedroom, saying the light hurt her eyes.

One thing he did have, though. Philip Nye had a way of knowing people. Not over the long term, but knowing where they were, how they felt, in the pulse of a moment. From very early—who knew when, but it had been before Harvard and even before Horace Mann—Philip could see through situations and into people, who were diaphanous to him. And yet the seeing was so casual with him, the way he lingered in front of them as though he was looking into a shop window. He tried hard to hide it under a studied American casualness, looking down, dressing dumpy, pretending to be shyer than he was. But there he was and out it came: a sharp focused seeing of people. It was never intrusive. He never gave one the sense that he needed people. He always held himself back a little from life, in that ancestral way of all the Nyes. But he was never at a cold remove, not the way she was. The world, instead, was a great sad comedy lurching warmly across his field of vision. He had laughter without rancor, and a smile without a sting. He seemed to take hold of people, lightly, turning them round, watching the light fall on them from various angles. Jessica wondered how much he had been able to infer about her, and about Felicity. Very little, she concluded, always meaning to tell him more than she actually did.

Not that he felt a sense of other people continuously. He did not. When they were absent they were not there for him. Not even she was. Jessica wondered how, if he had such a sharp sense of the existence of others, he could ever manage to be alone. What did he think about if, only thinking about others, there was no one else in the room? She was not sure. She was only certain he was not preoccupied with himself. Perhaps it was then that his life was taken up with Wylie. His little dog hated discomfort. Philip was forever arranging pillows for him, tugging at a comforter, or pushing Wylie's thin body back onto the sofa when, asleep, he was in danger of falling off it. Jessica almost thought it was a pity that such a fine intelligence spent itself on such small things, but it was an *almost* because it did not bother Philip. She had never met a more contained man. He was neither this nor that, but he was very much unto himself. He always seemed to be resting.

She was surprised how few women noticed him. He was tall and handsome but there was something in his manner, absorbed from generations of Nyes, who had been, it seemed to her, invisible to life and time, that set him apart and made him not a possibility for them. Perhaps, after all, that was the real reason for those red bootlaces of his: it was as though, in them, Philip had contrived a slightly ostentatious form of anonymity, insuring that, when he left the room, everyone would remember his laces, but not *him*.

But there was more. When he was twelve Philip passed out when he was walking down a hallway in middle school. He told the nurse it was the din, the press of bodies, the confusion of voices. He asked to be sent home. But the nurse concluded his blackout was caused by his backpack lying across his main artery—and made him stay in school. So Philip started walking through the halls with his hand on his heart to keep it from jumping so hard. Like the pledge of allegiance, only all the time. Passing periods were the worst. He went into the bathroom and dipped his head in a toilet. Nothing came up. He tried to get back to the classroom. Every footstep felt like walking though tar. He tried thinking out every step in advance but it didn't work. The only place he liked being was in his room at home, or locked up in the back seat of his parents' station wagon.

It got better after a while, but only a little. He got therapy; took drugs. He learned a name for what he had, *agoraphobia*. Learned his mother probably had it, too. They transferred him to a small private school. He managed to get through Horace Mann because the classes were so small. But he almost flunked out of Harvard because he didn't like going to big lectures. He went for a classics major because there were only a few people taking classes about dead languages, and even then, there was more safety in obscurity. His senior thesis was about Eusebius. He made sure his interests always kept him apart. *Apart* felt safe.

There was a period after Harvard, when it was clear he couldn't go on in school, when his teachers and therapists tried to push him into vocational training. He took up house painting for a while. One summer he painted a family's house on Martha's Vineyard because it was empty and he could live there while he was doing the job. Then Roma Morrow showed up, back early from some trip. She always said that was why he got involved with her. To make the best of it that one summer, when, after all, he counted on being alone. She seemed to have broken him in a bit over the years. She took him to small theaters, churches and museums where it was quiet, and even to big cities, though they always wound up living in small places near them like the Peak.

⁓

Philip had one other quality Jessica came to love. It was his saving grace, because it made his phobia livable. He was a great appreciator. It was his nature to enjoy the things around him without any bitterness in his enjoyment of them. He saw practically everything around him with finely shaded taste. He was the only person she had ever met whose outlook was so aesthetic. The world for him had no gods in it except for beauty and proportion. Just last week she had to go to a funeral down at St. John's Cathedral on Garden Road. She took him with her. Someone had died of some new kind of flu after visiting the Mainland. Someone Felicity knew from school, one of her teachers who helped her get into Oxford. Edward hardly took any interest in their children's education, and he was the one who suggested that she bring Philip along.

So she took him down to St. John's for the service.

"Such a poor excuse for a Cathedral," she said, entering the nave. She picked up right away on a certain monotony in the ornament, most of it wood pasted over plaster. "Such second rate Gothic."

"Oh, but I like it," he told her. "At least there's wood in it. The old Gothic churches, you know, the *really* old ones, are such cold damp places made of stone. And look, it's right across the street from the Helena May."

Her eyes followed the limbs of the pitched wooden ceiling. A row of narrow and tall windows reached up to it. Little vines carved in stucco around the arches added a delicate touch to the high, severe windows. Philip was right. It had all the beauty of Gothic ornament without any of its rudeness.

"It's not so bad to copy something, is it," he asked her, "particularly if what you're copying is pretty great?"

True. When Felicity was in Middle School pretending she was a girl monk, she made detailed drawings of the Limoges reliquary. She simplified it a lot, making it more copper than gold, softening the enameled angels too, rounding their triangular eyes and making their stiff hair a little curly. But there it was still—the very thing itself—the long fall of the robes, their sleeves flaring at the ends, the straight noses and small mouths with pinched lips. She had caught the spirit of it by copying it! She wondered if Philip had seen them in the hallway leading to her bedroom on the Peak, and then she realized, with a start, that he had never been that far into her flat. The bed where she slept nearly every night, he had never seen. And her bathtub, with its little row of seven devotional candles mounted on a shelf over the spout. They too were Gothic of a sort, weren't they? Copies of copies, and yet she loved them so.

"Your name, too?" he said after a moment. "It's like this cathedral. It's a copy, isn't it?"

"Yes. Sinden is a corruption of St. John."

His eyes widened. "Yes, and you rather like it now, don't you? Your family's past being—concealed by its own name."

Yes, but more. Philip couldn't have known how badly, when at twenty she married Edward Sinden, she, in her maiden's heart, wanted to be the consort of a St. John of the Cross, a crusader with his lance set against the infidel, his shield a red cross gules with a white hound rampant, a real coat of arms she would never show to anyone unless it were on a lintel of one of her houses back in the Home Counties. And how, really, could he have known how grateful she was that, now, as a matron of the Peak in Hong Kong, nobody knew there what an old family she was from, save for the few who were themselves from old families. It was such a pleasurable mirroring effect. It let her walk among the historyless full of her own undisclosed history. It made her family's past secret, private almost by definition.

And yet he intuited it at just the barest hint. It made implication so fun. Inferences just spiraled into infinity when she was around him. It was as though he had nothing better to do than listen to her, listening, as it were, between every line as though, really, he was listening to poetry.

An usher showed them their seats. Near the altar, covered by a quilted strip of fabric like a table runner, was the coffin. It was not metal and square, but wooden and angled, the shape of the body inside it. Widest at the shoulders, it made Jessica think of Felicity's sharp shoulders, sharp even in death. Death was so angular.

Philip put his arm around her. She liked that he did it, that he claimed her, and here, where his claiming would look like a consolation. It was such a quiet gesture, so like him to make, and yet he seemed to know that was what she was feeling was grief for Felicity, grief by association.

"What was his name?"

"I–I can't remember."

"It's just that the coffin is made of oak. So odd; all the way out here in China."

True; After twenty-seven years Jessica was still very aware that she did not know the names of the trees in Hong Kong. Oak, maple, birch, chestnut: these were names she knew, and they were full of feeling.

"Douglas. Douglas Tracey," she said, almost blurting it out. then she found she could say no more. Why did people have to buried in boxes? Felicity was still inside hers, half a world away. Was her face still her own, or had death taken that, too? A phrase trembled through her mind. *Half in love with easeful death.* Keats, but really, it had to have been Felicity, since the few lines she knew from poetry always came to her through her oldest daughter.

The funeral service started. The celebrant came down the aisle to meet the body at the door of the church. The organ was old and rasped out an *Introit*.

"So like lungs," whispered Philip, hearing the organ. "I like these old ones. It's good just to hear the air leaking out of them."

Again, that rightness. Jessica let the words of the service wash over her.

> *For none of us liveth to himself,*
> *and no man dieth to himself.*

They came and went through her mind.

> *Neither death, nor life, nor angels, nor principalities,*
> *nor things present, nor things to come, nor powers,*
> *nor height, nor depth, nor anything else in all creation,*
> *will be able to separate us....*

She did not hear the rest, but what she heard sufficed. It was beautiful, even though it was such bad magic, the priest like a magician telling you his pretty assistant was still alive inside the box, ready to come out in her spangled dress and take a bow after he made a show of sticking six knives in the box and pulling them out again. Lies, and yet they did not seem to bother Philip. She liked that about him, his sad heart and quiet breath that was something of Felicity, reborn.

She pressed Philip's hand and felt him returning the pressure. He was there. She was glad. Death was only a few feet away, but the feet between life and death went on for miles and miles.

"Did you know him?" Philip asked her during an interval of silence.

"Who?" she had to say, still following her own thoughts.

Philip's eyes drifted to the coffin.

"Oh, him. Barely. He was one of Felicity's teachers."

"The one who sent her to Oxford?"

"Yes. A drama teacher. He took her aside early and prepared her for it. He loved the old mystery plays. Felicity knew parts of them by heart. Oh, what was it—"

She paused to remember, then said:

Lorde, oure beestis lyes dede and dry
Both oxe, horse, and asse
Fallis dede doune sodanly.

"She was like you, Philip. She read about the ten plagues of Egypt, and felt bad for the animals."

Philip breathed heavily. "Do you wish—"

He paused.

"What, Philip?"

"That you could have gone. I so wish you had been given something just as good."

Jessica took a moment to collect herself. It was something she could hardly admit to herself. Edward had gone to Edinburgh. She had a year at Sussex, that was all.

"Felicity used to write me from Oxford," she said in a low, halting voice. "Long letters—as though she wanted me to see it. Every detail of it."

"I wish I'd met her."

"Yes," she said quietly. "I do, too."

Philip squeezed her hand, and then the service started up again.

When it was over they paused outside the cathedral, lingering in a little plaza around a big Celtic cross.

A number of people milled around, expecting a hearse to pull up at any moment and begin the short drive to the Protestant Cemetery, a series of terraces rising above Shan Kwong Road in Happy Valley.

"Strange," she said after a bit. "Is there no graveside service?"

"Maybe that's just for the family," said Philip.

"No, no," said a clergyman, overhearing them. "He will be going back to England."

"Ah," said Jessica, thinking of the downs where Felicity was buried. "I perfectly understand."

"But only after—cremation. They have protocols for infectious diseases, you know."

Jessica and the clergyman eyed one another uneasily.

"They won't send him *there*, will they?" she asked after a time.

The clergyman gathered his robes and pursed his lips. "Yes, I'm afraid so."

"But I thought that was only for the Chinese."

"So did I," said the clergyman. "But apparently not."

Philip had no idea what they were talking about. Leaving the plaza, and passing under a tall arching row of trees on Garden Road, Jessica told him.

There was the crematorium at Cape Collinson. It overlooked the road to Shek O. From the outside, Jessica said, the building resembled an abandoned concrete fortress. Inside was a vast windowless gray hall. At one end of the hall was a line of rollers leading to a small curtain in the wall. It was meant to be unobtrusive, but really it reminded Jessica of an airport security check where you put shoes in trays which rolled along, disappearing behind a curtain of dangling rubber flaps. Funerals there took all of five minutes. A clergyman pressed a button and the coffin glided on ball bearings into the wall. There were no flames. It was a way of cheating death, but death could never be cheated. Of that she was certain.

11

late february 2003

DR. SINDEN LEFT WORK early in the afternoon and took a taxi to Hung Hom Station in West Kowloon. He sat alone at a table in a small café there, sipping an espresso and looking over a small card that came in the mail two days ago. *Conference moved to Foshan Municipality.* Then an address and a hotel to report to. He read the message several times, wondering who decided to call this a conference. Sixteen doctors, all epidemiologists, were heading to a small hospital on the north side of Foshan, where there was an outbreak of the yearly flu. It was where an old teacher of Felicity's died while he was staging one of the old York Mystery Plays, which Felicity so loved.

Dr. Sinden knew that hospital. It was a large gray building with a large courtyard, built in the forties or fifties. The fittings were made of porcelain, and in the corridors there were rows of old photographs of doctors with little round glasses and nurses in long skirts. Like a lot of hospitals in China, it was both old and new. He'd asked his wife the other night if she was comfortable with him going because the resources there were often so limited. He tried to tell Jessica that this outbreak might be more serious than they were letting on, but she barely paid attention, instead toying with a new harness she'd bought to replace Bovary's old collar, following the recommendation of her new American dog-walking friend. Finally, she said she supposed the flu was nearly everywhere this time of year, and that it did not matter whether he volunteered and went there, or waited for it to come here. Really it was all the same to her.

The rise was tremorless, one of those fast new electric trains China was so proud of. It did not take long to get out of the city. The train flew over the land like a water-skater over the calm surface of a lake. Out the window, he saw a wash of green with yellow paddies of rice ruled lightly across it. There were brown roads and blue canals, fields with flowers grown for rapeseed oil, and ditches filled with muddy water. The train would hiss along for another half an hour before they came to the border at Futian.

So Dr. Sinden began a mental game that he sometimes played with himself in medical school. He called it viral roulette. He had a little red-and-black roulette wheel he'd fitted up with special labels based on the Baltimore classification. The first spin gave him the host, and was divided into five sections: vertebrates, invertebrates, plants, fungi, and bacteria. The second spin gave him the genome: dsDNA-TR, dsDNA, ssDNA, ssRNA-RT ssRNA+, ssRNA-, dsRNA. And the third spin gave him an analogue virus that had already been named, all the usual ones plus many others, to give him a clue to go on, and these were numbered 0 to 36, just like on a roulette wheel in a casino: from the coronaviridae among vertebrates to the cytoviridae among the bacteria. He'd spin the wheel and watch the ball go round and round: nature was like that too, a spinning wheel dropping its balls where it might. No one ever seemed able to predict which ones were going to show up where. So Edward let chance do its work, then took what came and tried to work with it.

The first ball landed on VERTEBRATES.

The second ball on DSDNA.

The third ball on POXVIRIDAE.

Good, he thought, it's a start. He took a sheet of graph paper out of his briefcase and set to work. Poxviridae belonged to a group that included, most familiarly, Herpesviridae, Adenoviridae, Polyomaviridae, Papillon-viridae, and Iridoviridae.

So, for this scenario, the virus was going to be one of the pox viruses. All these viruses were enteroviruses, herpes simplex, HIV, mumps, West Nile, and they could cause—

Viral meningitis.

Ah, meningitis *again*, said Dr. Sinden out loud, thinking of this odd convergence of change. Viral meningitis was just the chance blow that struck his wife when she was a girl. He knew only odd facts about the first occurrence. Jessica was very young. She said she felt a slight trembling in her lower back. The trembling did not go away. It spread down the left side of her spine and into her pelvic bone. She felt pulled downwards, down to the ground, down to where Judy was, as she put it.

The conductor came by, scanning his ticket. Dr. Sinden was spinning his little wheel and making notes. Then he went off and came back a few minutes later, this time with another conductor, a taller man with a red stripe on his hat.

Together they approached him slowly. Dr. Sinden made no effort to hide the wheel. They seemed to be commenting on his open use of it, though Edward was not sure. He had only some Chinese, and they spoke very quickly.

"No gambling on train," said the tall conductor at last.

I'm not the gambler, thought Dr. Sinden, smiling to himself. God is. Not the proud controlling God of Jessica's father, but the blind gambling addict that was nature. But what he said was,

"Yes yes of course."

"And *that*," said the smaller man, pointing at the wheel. "That not good in China. Police not happy."

Edward feared little from the police in China. They tended to keep well off from British subjects, especially medical people. Though there were Chinese police in Hong Kong, you rarely saw them. They tried to keep a low profile, biding their time, even if that time, he imagined, was the span of nearly fifty years until Hong Kong was to be folded back into the Mainland.

"I understand," he said.

The shorter man moved close. "Put in bag, and not open."

It came to him that perhaps they suspected he was a spy, and that the chemical equations rounding his wheel were part of some elaborate cipher. He could explain it if to them he had to, but knew to avoid having to. So he put his wheel in his briefcase and the men went away.

The passage across the border at Futian was something he never got used to. It meant going from the free-for-all that was Hong Kong to the unfree-for-all that was China. You crossed from a carnival into a cynosure, where, unfortunately, all the attention focused on you was bad, a bit like what he used to feel crossing through Checkpoint Charlie from West Berlin into East Berlin. And it was poor there, too. There were concrete housing blocks separated by branches and straw shacks and wide plots of waste land. Under the mild yellow light, Dr. Sinden saw stagnant creeks bordered by roofless red brick buildings and rows of small houses with one wall open to the street. Everything seemed so exposed. These were places Westerners were rarely allowed to visit, but still, they could not really prevent them from passing through them rapidly on the train line.

The station platform at Guangzhou South was light and modern. Following the parallel red and yellow lines on the long platform, he passed small stalls selling edible birds' nests and sharks fins, strange tastes probably developed long ago to keep off starvation. But now they were being sold as luxuries in bright red lacquered carts stamped with heavy yellow Chinese characters. The Year of the Sheep was coming too, and that motif seemed to be everywhere on offer, on bowls, chopsticks, soup spoons, and high haughty pottery that made him think of funeral urns. The main hall had a large panopticon that reminded him of a Victorian prison.

A man at the curb held a small sign, DR. SIN TIN.

Dr. Sinden walked up to him.

"You Tin Sin, Doctor?"

"Yes," he said, accustomed to his name being rearranged in various ways around Asia.

"Ride not long, but many traffic," said the driver, leading him to a waiting car, a silver Mercedes with Foshan Municipality license plate in green rather than black, which meant that it was government car allowed to leave the province.

Dr. Sinden was glad to settle into the back seat and rest. No lines of interrogation here. He let himself doze off for a little, opening his eyes for long enough to see several police cars around them, one in front and one behind.

He woke out of a hazy sleep with a slight jerk. They were there, the driver said.

"Already? "asked Dr. Sinden.

He expected he was going to be taken to the hotel but the car pulled up to the hospital, the First Peoples Hospital of Foshan. The two police cars idled nearby.

Then his door popped open.

A man poked his head in. He had a thin face, kind eyes, and a mask pulled under his chin.

"Dr. Sinden. I am Dr. Ma. Come, come."

"My—bags?"

"You will not need them. We are all sleeping here now. You'll see."

Dr. Sinden had been there once in the nineties, part of some delegation there to look into—he forgot what. But the old postwar building had been swallowed up by planes of glass and aluminum, punctuated by columns of concrete and cross-girders of steel.

He followed Dr. Ma. The doors swished open. A volume of chilled air hit him.

Too cold. More like an operating room than a lobby.

"We have to assume," said Dr. Ma, tapping a file he held under one arm, "that transmission must be minimized in all spaces leading to the amphitheater, as well as in the amphitheater. Thus the chill."

The doctors and nurses were all in scrubs and masks. The chairs had been taken out of the waiting rooms. He saw no patients. Aside from the medical personnel, the hospital appeared to be empty.

"This is now," Dr. Ma continued, "a *dedicated* hospital."

"Dedicated to what?" Dr. Sinden had to ask.

"They only just named it. It's a kind of—coronavirus."

They came to a set of double doors that opened into a long corridor.

"There are three levels of sterilization before you can enter—well, what we call the amphitheater. It is of course the hot zone. You are undoubtedly familiar with these protocols."

"I didn't know it was that bad."

"Nobody did. And I'm afraid we don't even know what we should expect from it yet. The whole thing is so—unpresidented."

Here he paused. Dr. Sinden clearly heard this small slip in this educated man's English. He of course meant "unprecedented." But being who he was, it pleased him. *Unpresidented*, were it a word, would have to mean something so strong and unexpected that it was capable of evading the central control of a political power like a presidency.

Dr. Ma continued: "We don't know where it made the jump. In some wet market, probably."

Dr. Sinden knew these places. The Yau Ma Tei Street Market in Hong Kong, the Shekou Market in Shenzhen, the Yu Lin Market in Chengdu. They were slaughterhouses, swishing in blood and guts and melted ice. But besides the cages with live animals, chickens and geese and ducks and rodents, there were places to eat and drink, noodle shops, stalls full of yellow poached eggs and red carrots, and tea counters serving the local drink, Yuan Yang, tea mixed with coffee.

They came to an alphanumeric panel. Dr. Ma raised the clear plastic lid and tapped in a series of numbers, or perhaps they were letters. Dr. Sinden heard a series of clicks, then a low hum, then some dotted green letters glowing on a screen, MA ZHANG YONG.

The doors slid open. They were at the first station.

Nothing seemed amiss here. It was the usual scrubbing up, holding his arms out to be wiped down, a nurse handing him a towel. He unbuttoned his shirt, loosened his pants, then slipped into green scrubs. When he turned around, Dr. Ma was doing the same thing, even though he was already in scrubs.

"New protocols," said Dr. Ma, smiling. "Very strict."

They moved through the long hallway to the second station. The corridor was a bright blighted white, as though the light itself was sterilizing.

Doors opened into a lab lined with a row of stainless steel tubs.

"Hexacholophene and methitol bath," said Dr. Ma. "Sixty minutes. Then fifteen minute wipedown with monochlorophin."

The baths were not soothing. The solution had a high specific gravity that seemed to press on on his pores. Afterwards they were rubbed down with disposable wipes and given new masks with double-layer carbon filters. They had to wear them from now on.

Then they changed into white Ethylene Oxide 10-6 gowns and moved to the third station. A row of UV and IR irradiation booths stood behind glass doors. They took off their clothes and went for three cycles in each, with five minutes of rest in between. Then they discarded their old whites in bins that were quickly wheeled out of the room by attendants in cleanroom coveralls. Dr. Sinden and Dr. Ma suited up in new whites, spunbounds with A7 liquid barriers, one sleeve of each slashed with red.

Red, for the hot zone.

A last row of double doors opened with a pop. Dr. Sinden could suddenly hear the hum of respirators—a long circular plunging sound like the piston of a car, only filled with air rather than gas.

The room was large. It must have been an operating amphitheater of some kind at one time, but the chairs had been cleared out and beds and partitions installed.

There were maybe sixty patients there. They were all turned face down. Turn them back over, explained Dr. Ma, and they wouldn't be able to breathe even with help. We don't know why that is, but it is. Dr. Sinden saw they had been intubated, but even more. Oxygen rich solution dripped into their arms. Small amounts of plasma drawn from the handful of patients who had recovered were being used experimentally on two or three of the sickest ones.

"None of these people in here have breathed on their own in over a week," said Dr. Ma. "The virus goes straight for their lungs."

The days turned into nights, and into days again. Dr. Sinden lost all sense of time. Some of the patients died, and some didn't. They didn't know why. Some lungs darkened with fluid and others lightened with air, that was all.

He got one chance to call home. A hospital monitor sat in the room and dialed the number he gave her. She was a dry woman with straight bangs and inflexible eyes. She was there to cut off the call if necessary.

"Hello—Jessica?" began Dr Sinden.

"Daddy, this is Poppy."

It wasn't the first time he'd made that mistake. Felicity used to sound a lot like Jessica, too. It was as if the one thing his wife was able to reproduce successfully about herself was her voice.

'Mama's taking a bath.'

'Get her out, Poppy.'

'But she's lit all her candles.'

'I said, *get her out.*'

Poppy put down the receiver and he heard some shuffling and footfalls. The opening of doors and the snapping of towels. Then his wife's voice:

"Edward, I—"

"Jessica, I am in Foshan. I have to stay here longer than I thought."

"Well!" she exhaled. "Is there some kind of emergency?"

The monitor shook her head, her finger hovering over the off button.

"Not exactly," he said, hoping his tone alone would covey worry, or at least some sense of urgency.

"Well, then," said his wife, who seemed preoccupied.

"It's just that I don't when I'll be coming back," he continued. "Maybe in a week—"

Shaking her head, the monitor caught his eye.

"Maybe in—three or four."

The monitor nodded slightly.

"Yes, very well, Edward." He heard her sighing. "How is your hotel this time? The last one you stayed at, you said the elevators didn't work."

There was no hotel there, just a cot in the room off the amphitheater with a thin blanket and a flat pillow.

"Quite good," he said.

"Really?" she asked. "You always seem to find them so sub-standard."

"This one is—*special*," he said, hoping she would catch the inflection. But she didn't.

"Well, good then."

"Are some of your friends there with you?"

Not yet, but Edward decided to lie. "Yes, Ma Zhang Yong," he said, carefully enunciating the name. There was a chance if she searched for this name that she might begin to find out what was going on, but she seemed so incurious.

"You know, Ma Zhang Yong."

"Who?"

"Surely you remember his name. Ma Zhang Yong."

"Ma Zhang Yong," she repeated.

"That's correct," he said.

"Oh, good," said his wife. "At least you're not alone. You and—Ma Zhang Yong."

She said it ironically, because she must have known very well that he knew no such person. But Dr. Sinden felt certain the monitor could not detect the irony.

But he hoped Jessica might remember it—if only for later.

Even so, his wife sounded a little strange to Edward. She liked being alone, and so did he. He wondered why she would say that. Perhaps she picked up on what he said. Perhaps not. He simply did not know.

The work was endless. More patients came in. More died after some time. Many just came in and died right away. But one woman fought for life with all she had in her. She was an elegant woman who reminded him of his wife's best friend, Elaine Kwan.

He got to know her a little because he admitted her. He saw so many patients who were very sick. But when she came in she was complaining only of a slight cough. Triage sent her to him because the cough had that telltale sign—the ring of a bell. And because she asked to speak to someone in English.

She wore a Chanel suit and a string of cultured pearls. Her face had just the slightest trace of makeup. Her hair was soft and not stiff—a sign of hair care at the level of *S/Z*, the salon near Arbuthnot Road where his wife went.

"I'm expecting to be evacuated, and quite soon you know," she began in clipped and precise English.

"I see," said Dr. Sinden.

"Do you then?" she said sharply. "I understand our medicine is *the finest in the world*," repeating a stock Party phrase, "but I have—my own preferences."

Meaning she was expecting to be transferred to one of the small private clinics available to those who could pay for them.

Dr. Sinden confined himself to the strict truth. "Our care is unmatched." He said it in his finest London accent, knowing, in fact, that there was no care to be had for this disease anywhere in the world but there. That this was it.

"Ah, good, then. May I venture to reserve a room?"

Dr. Sinden found himself wondering how her English got so good. Perhaps she was related to someone high in the Party.

"We have our protocols," said Dr. Sinden.

"I wish to be treated by you, personally," was all she said.

Later that day, he met her at the amphitheater end of that long white corridor. She tried to hold back the fear rising in her eyes.

"I want to go back, Dr. Sinden," she said. "These people here are all very sick."

"You're here now," he told her, "just as I am."

She clearly heard how he was saying, *They won't let either of us out.*

She was given bed 12A. At first, Dr. Sinden hoped she might be one of the few who reached the amphitheater who got well enough to be discharged—but it did not fall out that way.

That night—his tenth at the First Peoples Hospital—he intubated her.

"Will I still be able to talk?" she asked before he began the procedure.

"A little," he said, but he could tell right away that she was the kind of person who was used to talking. Intubated, a tube down her throat, he would only be able to ask her yes-or-no questions she could answer by shaking her head or blinking her eyes. As he explained: blink once for yes and twice for no.

Still, in off hours, she tried to tell him little stories. In slurred words and short blinks.

"Mh Mhn."

"What?"

"My *Mhn.*"

"Your—son?"

One blink.

"Do you want me to contact him?"

Two blinks.

"Dhc Thr."

"Doctor? "ventured Dr. Sinden.

One blink.

"So your son needs a doctor?"

Two blinks.

Dr. Sinden paused. Her eyes pleaded with him to understand.

"Oh, yes," he said at last. "I think I get it now. You son is a doctor."

One blink, and Dr. Sinden swore he saw a smile lighting her eyes.

"Vhy Phhd."

"Very—something."

"Phhroud."

Dr. Sinden smiled, for the first time in days.

"You're very proud of him, aren't you?"

One blink, then she closed her eyes, drifting into a heavy sleep of sedatives, which ones, he didn't know, because the charts were in Chinese. But he could distinctly hear the telltale sawing in her lungs. It must have taken everything she had left in her to tell him that she was proud of her son.

She died a few hours later. He tried to check in on her from time to time, but he was not able to be there when she died. When he came back, they were already packing up her body in plastic. He opened the sheet folded lightly over her face, and touched her cheek.

It is meet and proper for a mother to be proud of her children, he considered, in that ancestral way of all the Sindens. He tried to remember her name, but Dr. Sinden could never remember the names of any of his patients.

~

Then for a time, it was slow. The dead woman was covered in a plastic tarp and taken out. Quicklime in a mass grave near Nanhai waited for her.

Edward stepped outside into a small courtyard off the amphitheater. He would have to go back in through the long corridor, a time-consuming process in itself, but he needed a break. A few nurses who were smoking quickly shuffled to the other side of the courtyard; he would never be alone here in China. So he turned his eyes to the sky. At last it became an ordinary day. A thin mesh of clouds covered the sky like a sheet dropped over the disease. His ears hummed. In the far corner of the courtyard, two nurses' aides, a man and a woman, had put a wood box between two folding chairs and were brewing tea over a small propane stove. One of them poured boiling water mixed with tea leaves into two small cups. Dr. Sinden meant to stay well off from them, but the man caught his eye and motioned for him to draw near.

"You—English man?" he asked.

"Yes," said Dr. Sinden.

"You—very good man—be here now."

Dr. Sinden did not think of himself that way, as either good or bad, but he nodded and let the remark pass.

"Many very sick. But look—"

The man then opened a small satchel and took out a can of condensed milk.

"Have—this."

It was a can of Carnation condensed milk.

"Very hard," he added.

So it was very hard to find. The man cradled his small treasure.

"So—for you."

Before Edward could stop him, thinking that this can of milk from America must have cost him half a week's salary, the man took out a knife and cut a small slit in the lid of the can.

The woman then stood up took a third cup from her satchel. She motioned for Dr. Sinden to take a seat.

"You—Doctor—Hero of the People," continued the man.

Dr. Sinden knew approximately what that meant in Mainland China, but still he felt uncomfortable with the phrase.

"You—*Doctor*—sit."

He said it in that Chinese way Dr. Sinden recognized, as a cross between an invitation and a command. So he sat.

The woman spoke for the first time.

"Tea, with milk," she said, in a nearly perfect English intonation.

The first man frowned, then smiled, then said: "My wife no English. Just 'Tea, with milk.'"

"Tea, with milk," repeated his wife, smiling to show a gray row of teeth, and handing him a cup of milky tea.

"Yes, yes," said Dr. Sinden, trying to smile back. "Tea with milk."

Dr. Sinden surmised the two had been married for a long time, and this was how they managed to see one another. Once a day, in long days that only seemed to lengthen out into other long days, they came together in this little drab courtyard, treeless and gray-walled, and brewed tea. Sipping, Dr. Sinden let himself look them over. The woman was dressed in a faded white cotton gown, clean but very old. From time to time she leaned over and lowered the flame on the tiny propane stove; gas was surely another expense to be reckoned with here in China. The flame dropped from white into blue, giving off a wavering stream of heat. Her husband came near to the stove and stretched his hands out to it, trying to catch a bit of warmth.

Leaving China, it was the one thing he came back to, long afterwards. That quiet cup of tea with those two poor people, doing the best they could in a bad time. He wished his Chinese had been good enough to tell them how much he admired them. But telling them this would be too much for them to hear. Warmth was withheld in Chinese culture from most public contexts; you had to infer it from a frozen formality. The couple were sharp-faced people who averted their eyes from him when they spoke, and looked at the ground while they drank. He remembered how the hot tea scalded his throat, and how he shivered from its bitterness.

How the man sipped his portion with deliberate small sips, swishing the tea around his mouth before he swallowed it. How the two of them then threw the tea leaves on the ground when they were finished drinking. And how, before leaving to go back into the hospital, the woman pressed a small cloth pouch of tea in his hand, saying,

Nidou. Bei lou po.

Here, it meant. For your wife.

12

early march 2003

THAT SATURDAY they decided to stay closer to home. There had been a rash of dog poisonings on Kennedy Road—more needless deaths. It would not be good to go too far afield. A walk around Victoria Peak would still leave enough room for them, Jessica hoped, seeing how Philip was bringing a blanket and a small pillow.

"I like leaving room," she told Philip, adjusting Bovary's collar as they were about to leave from her back door.

"I like the room you leave me," said Philip.

Jessica smiled. For Philip had found out that she actually enjoyed a light sort of sexual banter between them. She liked that it was a completely private mutual sphere of reference. Sex was just enough of an extension of her personal privacy into a single, other, person, to appeal to her. She herself felt her body to be unprepossessing but knew how it appealed particularly to him. And Jessica loved nearly every form of exclusivity, whether social, aesthetic, physical, or sexual. With a very discreet man she became a very discreet woman, that is to say, very willing to do almost anything with him and very unwilling to let on that she did it, except with him of course. One was absolute, but she was finding out that two could be absolute, too.

They liked starting with a loop around Harlech Road and seeing where it led them, even on days early in spring when they planned to take a longer walk. It was one of the most gracious walks in Hong Kong. People composed themselves to walk here, as though they were visitors to the Peak on a day pass. Men offered women their arms; women took them. Even children restrained themselves. The slopes were well tended, more manicured than most in Hong Kong, where they sprayed concrete over almost any hill. It made for a feeling of battlements rather than public works, a kind of uncivil engineering, Edward had called it. But Harlech, like the Peak itself, was a world apart.

They came to the little junction near the playground at Hatton Road. One road led to the cliffs at La Fu Shan, another to Pinewood Battery, while Harlech connected with Lugard Road and continued around Victoria Peak. Philip paused, looked around, he slipped his hand under her blouse, pressing the small of her back.

"Philip," she said. "Someone might see."

"Let's go somewhere where they don't."

He turned up the path toward High West, and she followed. The dogs raced ahead of them. So lithe and fast these greyhounds! She never ceased to admire their tautness. They had a readiness-is-all quality no other creature had. Philip admired them too, but he said it in his own American way. Zero-to-sixtying, he called it, and perhaps that was what he was doing now, a jump in his step as he led her into the woods.

He was off the path and she followed him into a very small clearing, the size of a closet, enclosed by a small stand of cotton trees.

Kissing her, he started unbuttoning her blouse.

"Philip," she said. "Not here."

"It's all right," he said.

"No, it's not all right. Someone might see."

She said it excitedly, her pulse lunging, so he went back to kissing her. She leaned her head against him.

"I really want to," he said.

"I do, too," she admitted.

She almost pushed his hand off her shoulder but she did not want to. The side of his cheek rested a little above her breast. She rotated her hips a little and hooked one leg around his, pressing her pubic bone against him.

"But there are other people around," she added again.

"I don't see anyone."

"Can't we go somewhere a little more private?"

"No," said Philip, pulling off her blouse.

And then—she giggled. Mrs. Jessica Sinden giggled. She didn't understand why. She never giggled. She was such a low alto, and it made her voice into a high soprano. She covered her mouth, almost afraid of the sound she was making.

Afterwards, Philip thought her eyes, which were always beautiful, were startlingly green against her flushed face. One arm was behind her, her wrist curled over the scars on her spine. Up close she seemed to have no lines in her face. She was always a little stiff after they made love, as though her frame had been placed in a cast. He sometimes wondered if she was all right. Jessica Sinden was so unused to making love. She must have had sex to have had her children, but the only thing she said about it was, *It went so quickly, Edward still had his socks on.* She had Tristan when she was thirty-eight years old. He supposed she was actually fifty-eight or fifty-nine.

"What are you thinking?" she asked him, withdrawing her hand.

"About your age," he said.

"Do you want to know?"

"Yes," he said, "but I have a greater tolerance for approximations than you do," he said, knowing, too, that when he first met Jessica she usually gave the shortest possible answer to questions put to her, though that was changing as she was opening up to him.

"Nearly everyone does," she said, a little more sharply than he expected. Not that that in itself it was anything new. It just took him a while to accept the suddenness of her sharpness, and to realize that she did not mean to shut him out by means of it. No, she was simply sharp, sharp the way her face was angular, sharp the way a key was jagged so that it could fit into its one hole, and turn the lock.

Jessica was starting to look around her, seeing again a few large evergreens, camphors with the pale bark and black fruit, bamboo palms, the ever-present cotton trees with their soft, thick trunks. She imagined that later in spring she would pick Philip some red flowers with their five pretty petals. Not quite the Helena May, but not quite a picnic either, with not even a blanket to put under them. Next time she would be better prepared. She had a good map of the country parks and would mark out some places they might be able to go to later in the spring. This place was off the path, but still a little too near one. She would like to lie naked with him in a little spot of their own, and she would bring a sheet, too, as well as a light blanket, for a chill might come upon her at any time, even in this heat.

"The dogs," she said, her voice changing, coming back down to its usual alto. "Where are they?"

"What?" said Philip vaguely, rolling onto his back.

"The dogs, Philip."

"Somewhere around here. Certainly not far," he said, pulling his pants on. "Maybe down that way."

She pulled down her skirt.

"I suppose these things were designed just for this," said Jessica, smoothing down the sides of her skirt. "Ease of access."

He slipped his hand under her skirt, feeling the plush of the hair underneath.

"Philip," she said. "I'm dressed now."

"Alright," he said, pulling back his hand. "Come, let's find them."

They did not have to go far. Just beyond the clearing was a little path that led to the main steps up High West. It was an out-of-the-way place. The only people who went there were people, like them, with dogs. She saw it first.

"Oh, shit," yelled Jessica.

She picked up the piece of chicken covered with purple crystals. "Shit. Shit! *Shit!*"

Wylie was a few feet off. He was already vomiting, or trying to.

"Bovary's not here," Philip said anxiously. "Maybe she didn't have it."

"No, I know her," she said. "She'd take it away somewhere so Wylie couldn't get it."

"We've got to find her, then."

Philip picked up Wylie, whose vomit, mixed with blood, spilled down the front of his shirt.

"You go—"

"No, we should stay together. I didn't bring my phone."

"You didn't?"

"I never do. Not when I'm with you." He paused. "Where would she go?"

"Not far," said Jessica, trying to keep up hope. "A lot of the brush is too dense for her. And she wouldn't go uphill."

"Then down here." Philip pointed to the toilets on the other side of the playground.

"God, she doesn't even like being outdoors."

"Try the bathrooms," said Philip.

She went in one. He went in the other, not even noticing it was the women's. Bovary was there, collapsed on the concrete floor, unconscious.

He came out carrying her.

"The closest Vet—"

"Mid-Levels."

"Call them first and tell them we're coming."

She got on the phone. He tried to listen in but she waved him away. Reception was often bad on the Peak, especially near the TV transmission towers on top of Victoria. She spoke loudly into the phone, then strained to listen. Then she flipped the phone shut.

"It was Dr. Briden. He told me they've already got six dying dogs. He said to wash out their mouths and try to induce vomiting."

"Will he take them?"

"Of course he will. But it sounded like chaos behind him. It's bad, Philip, really bad. Another call came in while I was talking to him and he said that the ones who swallowed a whole piece weren't going to make it."

They had a slight bit of hope. Italian greyhounds were notoriously fastidious eaters. They sampled things, and rarely ate anything quickly.

They ran as far as the Peak Café. A Chinese couple getting in a taxi waved them in as soon as they saw the dogs. The man said two men had already come by carrying a black lab. The dog was barely alive.

The veterinary was twenty minutes away. The cab jumped into high gear, taking them past places they thought of as *theirs*, the sharp crossing to Plantation Road, Gough Hill Road, where the police station was with its spigot of potable water for the dogs, the turnoff at Guildford down to the German-Swiss School, where there were often dog groups at twilight. Such things now seemed impossibly distant. The dogs were quiet in that way animals had when they were in a lot of pain. They seemed to recede into themselves like a tide falling back too far, preparing for death. Wylie's paw trembled. Philip tried to steady it but Jessica took his hand off. He needed to tremble. Let him. She felt the heaviness of Bovary limp in her lap. Her jaw was ajar. Her tongue fluttered. Her nose was dry. Her eyes were milky and remote. Death was there. She felt it. Not walking but running. The taxi was going fast but death was going faster. They didn't have much time.

The veterinary was on Mosque Street. Dr. Briden was there. He knew both of them. He said three dogs were already dead. A fourth was near. She noticed the other people in the waiting room. The looks on their faces. Oh no, not more. One woman sat slumped on a pile of dog beds. Another sat on a scale, its weights swinging every time she shifted herself. A man stared helplessly at a large chart of different breeds of dogs. *The boxer is a fierce dog who makes a loyal companion animal. He is a friend for life.* It clearly made no sense to him. The dog poisoner saw them as just dogs.

Dr. Briden took Wylie first. He was a slight, tidy man with close-cropped white-blonde hair who wore a narrow knitted tie, beige striped with blue and yellow, tucked, military-style, between the second and third buttons of his shirt. They were the colors of the Royal Regiment of Fusiliers. Good. He had been well-trained and would remain calm.

Philip was torn about Dr. Briden taking his dog rather than hers. But Bovary was unconscious. The doctor was right. Wylie had a better chance.

Just then Philip edged toward Jessica across the room. The muscles in her throat stiffened. She found herself moving toward him involuntarily, her eyes tearing. She thought of wiping her eyes. She never thought of wiping her eyes. She did not care about being seen. She never cared about not being seen. So this is love: she felt herself softening as he came near her, coming as something warm and full of light. Other people had always been such cold, dark presences for Jessica. One acknowledged them, of course. Gave them gifts; wrote them cards; served them marmite on crackers. But now she did not want to do something for him. She wanted to *be* something for him. Her first inklings were silly and soft. Perhaps she would do her hair differently. Grow it out (for some reason she had always been saving her hairpins). Or stop coloring it. Philip liked it that she was a tad older than he was. She would tell him she was fifty-nine.

Tristan had come in with Aspidistra. Philip must have called them. They knew to go to him first. He would tell them what they wanted to know. What he was feeling; what the other people in the room were feeling; even what they felt. They would not ask her. Tristan knew not to and Aspidistra was afraid of her. They grouped tightly around him, asking all sorts of questions she considered irrelevant. Were there dog ambulances? Could they donate blood to them? Had any dogs they knew from the Peak died?

Nothing stirred in the clinic. The vet was in the back room, working at his large stainless steel table. She respected his intensity but knew he did not care a jot about any of the dogs. He had a greyhound there, not as a pet, but as a blood donor. He said the dog gave him no trouble. She heard how he said *the dog*. If the frail, brindled creature had a name she never heard him use it. And yet the creature had a whole little ceremony for making his own bed, starting, circling, then seeming to change his mind, then starting again, pawing at his thin blanket, digging out a little alcove in it then dropping his weight, rump-first, not so much satisfied as giving up. He was sleeping now in his defeat. Jessica had a lingering awareness that the reason she liked animals so much was because it was a kind of British Empire she had over them. Kipling's world, but not the white man's burden. The burden of humanity for those creatures they have subjugated. Jessica acutely enjoyed feeling responsibility, but she could only feel it when she imagined herself in an implicitly superior position, watching over the inferior realms, as with her children. Philip was rather more democratic in his feeling for animals. He saw Wylie as his son. She would not have said son, but captive.

Poppy came in with Mina. Mina wandered off to talk to the other maids.

She tried calling Edward at the hospital in Foshan. She had a hard time getting a direct connection, but finally, she got through.

"Edward!"

"What, Jessica? What?"

"It's the—"

She choked with a sob.

"The dog. Edward, the dog! I'm at the Vet."

"You mean you called me about *the dog*?"

He paused and took a deep breath. "I've got other things on my mind right now, Jessica."

"Bovary has been poisoned, Edward."

"What? Are they sure it's poison? Have they intubated her?"

Jessica paused, not knowing why he would ask that.

"Why, no. She's getting a blood transfusion."

"Good," said Edward. "Is there anything else?"

Jessica heard a series of sharp piercing beeps. "Dr. Sinden," she heard a woman's voice say somewhere behind him, "Dr. Sinden! *Dr. Sinden!*"

"I've got to go, Jessica."

Then the line went dead.

She thought, *How dare he?* But then she also thought: *How dare I?*

Jessica felt the hardness in her returning. Again she started to hear the familiar litany of Mrs. Jessica Sinden. *She* was responsible for this. *She* let herself go with Philip. *She* let her attention lapse. *She* eased her vigilance, never mind that before, she had never known for what, or even why, but here was the proof. Any slackening of resolve courted disaster. She had always felt it, always known to impose it on her children. But before this it had only been an article of faith. A mighty fortress is our God: the God her father instilled inside her was a watchful God in a high tower, and she had fallen asleep in it. Jessica looked over at Philip. He was a good man, a responsible man, but like her he had lapsed. She felt the slippage in him too. She made him slip. His love for her blurred the hard clear edges of things. It made him vague. Vagueness, even for a moment, was death. She looked over at Poppy. She had a potential clarity in her. Unlike in Tristan, it was there to be had. Jessica would not let her go to acupuncture school. Needles buzzing and popping, what kind of a parody of medicine was that? Needles would not save Wylie and Bovary. Only a hard intervention would, a tearing open of bodies with knives, a pumping in of chemicals synthesized in a laboratory, a relentless attention of trained intelligence. Focus. Cold focus. Unrelenting cold focus.

She looked up. Poppy had her hand on Philip's shoulder. She instinctively liked him. Some of her long hair fell on his jacket but she did not brush it away.

The bright light in the hallway was caustic. Philip had called Roma but she said she could not come. Work called. Jessica understood that, but she also knew what that would mean to Philip. He would finally leave his ex-wife. He would not continue to share a flat with a woman who preferred paper to flesh and bone. She knew how much he loved holding her bony frame, saying once that he was insinuating himself into her very joints. Such a Philip phrase!

She tried to sort out what she felt about him, but the more she thought about him, the more she thought about Edward. Over the phone Edward was as cold as a morgue. Trying to listen to her, but only just. There was always something halfhearted about Edward's propriety. He was responsible and willing to observe the forms, but he always kept himself at a slight distance from them. *Keeping off appearances*, he said sometimes, in his punning way. He had always kept off from her, too, leaving her to her own devices. He took on long hours at the hospital, often volunteering to help out at hospitals in Guangdong Provence when they were shorthanded, not because he liked the work or was especially generous with his time, but because he did not like facing their essential separateness, which he nevertheless had no inclination to undo. The truth was there were a thousand places Edward could be and not be at home, and Foshan was one of them. That left her here with Philip, which was all that mattered.

13

march 2003

THE DOGS RECOVERED. But Jessica had no idea when her own life would return to normal, if there even was a normal with Philip in it. She felt unable to make plans. If the dogs could be taken from her by some lunge of chance like that snake she killed with Tristan's bat on Homestead Road, her whole world could fall apart at any time. She remembered Bovary's mouth full of blood, so much she couldn't even whimper, and Wylie's blood running through tubes to a pump which turned in slow agonizing circles. And Edward still in Foshan, calling from time to time to say, in his monotone way, how some people there had some kind of catarrh. She wondered why he chose such an old, obscure word for a coughing sickness. And then he became so technical, as though he was talking in code, saying this catarrh was caused by something called a coronavirus: a blight shaped like the crown of the sun. She heard him trying to pass lightly over it, as he often seemed to do in these calls from China, saying, it looks we're going to have to deal with this *Pretender to the Crown*, as though the virus had an ambition to rule, but he also said, more menacingly, that it was aptly named, because you can only see the corona of the sun during an eclipse—while the sun is being snuffed out by the moon. What a thing to be coming over poor China, all of it in the spring, which this year seemed full of an extraordinary sweetness in the trees crowding her little side garden, the yellow acacia, the white magnolia, and her favorite, the red cotton tree.

After the poisoning, Jessica and Philip did not see one another for some time. The dogs were too weak to walk, but that was not it. They had exhausted something between them. She did not know how Philip spent his time. Sleeping, probably, which was how she seemed to spend hers. Poppy, who always managed to divine the direction of her thinking, used her inert interval to race to enroll in her acupuncture program, making sure to have her father pay so much for tuition, texts, and supplies that her mother would consider it wasteful to withdraw. Tristan was rather more gentle with her. He tried to get her out of the flat and into her little side garden. Listless for the first time in her life, she allowed him to lead her by the elbow to the garden. He even bought her a nice hardcover edition of *Keep the Aspidistra Flying* for her to read, a little in-joke between them she was quite pleased with.

Jessica Sinden did not like being secretive but knew how the attack on the dogs had changed the parameters of things between them. They had been outed. Before, everyone knew they were a couple but had been willing to look the other way. But the poisoning changed all that. They were all looking their way now. Both their pictures had been in the *South China Morning Post*. A special police squad was investigating the attack. The dog walks were no longer their little private domain. If they ever walked them again nearly everyone on the Peak would stop and ask them how the dogs were. Bovary and Wylie were now celebrities. They themselves were something like celebrity-consorts. It would take some doing to escape all this attention. It was why they couldn't see one another just now. Even the Helena May might be iffy.

One morning late in March, she was reading *Keep the Aspidistra Flying* in the garden—or trying to, because she never got more than a few pages into anything—when she looked up and saw—Aspidistra Benning.

Aspidistra was in a long peasant skirt. Her yellow hair was pinned up. Her top had slipped a little and Jessica could see the strap marks on her shoulders. She had blond hair on her arms and held her legs close together, one knee bent and turned inward.

"He sent you, didn't he?" said Jessica, putting the book down.

Both of them knew the *he* was not Tristan, but Philip.

"I'm walking Wylie again."

"But you don't really walk him, do you?"

"No," she admitted readily, sitting next to her on the bench. "He just pays me for it. I go over and sit with him. He hates to let Wylie out of his arms."

"Oh, Philip," said Jessica.

A few moments passed in silence.

"And I suppose he did not tell you what to say?"

"No," she said. "Not at all."

"He wouldn't," she said affectionately.

"I was kind of surprised," Aspidistra said, "but he said, 'Just go. Whatever you say will be right.' Why do you think he said that?"

"Because you love Tristan."

Tears came to her eyes. "I do, Jessica. I do so. I want to—"

She paused, not being able to say it.

"I brought you some fruit," she said instead, fumbling with a cloth bag at her side. Her hand trembling a little, she took out a plastic bag with three slightly-misshapen apples in it.

"Want to what?" Jessica asked her softly.

"Want to have a child with him."

"Oh, dear," said Jessica, but without hostility.

"I wouldn't need to marry him, you know. I don't want what he has. I just want a part of him I can love and keep. I'm so afraid he's going to leave me. I feel a coldness in him sometimes I can't understand. When I hold him I feel I'm holding a statue that has to will itself to move."

"How—apposite," said Jessica, not letting on how startled she was by the image. For the first time she looked directly at Aspidistra. She had pretty green eyes and an open freckled face. The girl did not have insight by intelligence, but she had insight by feeling. That must have been why Philip sent her. He liked her and wanted her to know it. He wanted her to allow them to marry. He figured that she would, inadvertently as usual, say some deep disclosing thing that would endear her to Jessica.

Aspidistra put the bag of apples on the table. Jessica smiled.

"It's funny how Philip knew that I could help you. I thought you didn't like me."

"I don't, or rather, I didn't."

"It's Mama, isn't it? She has her eye on everything."

Jessica found herself liking the daughter so much that she chafed at being reminded of the mother.

"She makes me study before I come over here," Aspidistra went on. "She has a big book about Limoges enamels and knows how much every piece is worth. She said if you were to give me that reliquary as a wedding present, she could retire at home."

"You mean she'd go back to Canada?" asked Jessica, considering that the gift might just be worth it.

"She wouldn't stay here one minute longer than she had to."

"Even for you?"

"Especially for me. She likes it here only because we have two incomes and can afford a bigger flat." Her eyes strayed around the garden. "I mean, this is quite a change from the high rise we live in."

Jessica found herself wondering just what Aspidistra did for a living.

"I'm a nurse," she said, and in that moment Jessica saw something of what Philip saw in her. She had foresight as well as insight.

Then she stooped at an empty flower bed near the pergola, once coated with pine needles, filled now with water. "You used to have a row of rocks around them," she said, looking down at the shallow pond. "Didn't you? They made for such a nice border."

Aspidistra took a plastic toy boat from the bucket at the edge of the pond. The boat was long and narrow and slid over the water, its bottom stroking the lotus leaves resting on the surface.

"Such a little Hong Kong scene," she said.

And so it was, though not out of nature but out of some hotel lobby in Central, where iridescent orange koi zigzagged across shallow ornamental ponds, below a mural of ducks lifting up into flight.

"I mean," said Aspidistra, "it's such a small pool of a place."

Jessica looked down at her small tiny fish darting among her carefully-placed reeds.

"Except the fish jump occasionally," Aspidistra added, reaching out to touch the little pearl-colored Buddha Jessica had placed on a pedestal at the pond's edge, moving it a little off-center.

Jessica reached out to adjust the Buddha a little, putting it back just where it was.

"Oh, I can do that for you," said Aspidistra, centering it.

"I'd been intending to make a little fountain under it," explained Jessica, turning the Buddha just a little more to face her, "but I just haven't gotten around to it yet. So I built up the ledge, and put in the fish, trying to make into a reflecting pool of sorts."

"It's very nice. May I?"

"Be my guest."

Aspidistra slipped out of her flip-flops and stepped over the ledge into the water, letting her skirt drift on its surface away from her, then pulling it up suddenly with a tug of her wrist. Squinting in the sun, her toes curling in the water, she leaned over, unpinning her hair. Jessica watched as she skimmed the surface gently with her hand, her long blonde hair falling over her face, the tips of her hair darkening as they touched the water. Then she reached out and touched the little filigreed railing she had put up around the reflecting pool.

"I like it very much here," Aspidistra said.

"So do I," admitted Jessica, her cheeks twitching a little.

"It feels so much like you here."

Jessica widened her eyes. That was just what Philip said.

"It's nice to feel the sun, too," Aspidistra said, laughing lightly in her offhand way. "Really feel it on my skin."

"Yes," said Jessica, blinking, knowing full well she felt the same way.

The wind picked up, a warm breeze, but Jessica shuddered slightly in the heat of mid-day under a sky pale with thin clouds.

"Are you cold?" asked Aspidistra, noticing how when Jessica moved her limbs, she moved them with a sigh.

"Often," said Jessica, answering her as she would answer Philip. She accepted that Aspidistra was his messenger, and that in talking to her, she was in some measure talking to him.

Aspidistra stepped out of the reflecting pool and sat on the grass. She pulled on a blade and chewed on the end.

"Want one?" she asked.

"No, thank you."

"You sure?"

"Well, then again—I mean, why not?"

She took it from her as though she were taking it from Philip.

"If you tug too hard on the blades," said Aspidistra, "the dark green part comes out but the light green part that's a little chewy stays in. You've got to reach to the bottom of the blade and massage it a little, then ease it out. Then it comes out looking like a green onion."

"But not very oniony in taste," said Jessica, chewing on hers.

"No. Rather bitter and slightly sour. I tried chopping up the light part and using it in a salad once."

"And?"

"Tristan ate it without looking at it."

"That sounds like him."

"I'm always trying to get him to pay more attention to what he eats."

She pulled out another blade of grass.

"Mr. Nye likes things like this, too. Does Dr. Sinden?"

Jessica had never been asked. If she supposed anything, she supposed he actually didn't like eating at all but did it because it was physically necessary. Usually he read while he ate, even if she was there.

"You don't have to answer," Aspidistra said. "Tristan is always saying I get too personal with people. That's my mother in me. But I think that he's too impersonal with people. Don't you?"

Jessica genuinely did not know how to answer this. She had arranged her life so as never to have this kind of conversation. And yet here it was. Philip was always personal with her. She was personal with Tristan and Poppy but did not allow them to become personal with her, ever.

Relationships with her were always a matter, not of degree, but of kind. The category, son, daughter, husband, dictated the content and form. But now it was the category *lover* that had broken the form. There was a kind of walllessness between her and Philip. And now the walls were coming down between her and, of all people, Aspidistra Benning.

"Tristan gets it from you, doesn't he?" she heard her saying next. Again that incisiveness, so unexpected coming out of a gangly twenty-year-old in a peasant skirt and flip-flops—but still, being who she was, it made her squirm. The girl would take some getting used to.

"Yes," Jessica heard herself saying. It was like the first time she talked to Philip in the salon. Something about this girl compelled attention. Right then and there she made up her mind to make sure she married her to Tristan. She loved the angels on the reliquary with their red-tipped wings. But she began to sense that she could love this girl more. She marveled at the feeling. Philip was helping her, even now.

"I think he wants me to tell you something," Aspidistra continued, "but he's the kind of person that keeps you guessing about that sort of thing. When I asked him if he had any message for you he just said he didn't want to put any words in my mouth. But I told him that if I were him, I would just take you in my arms and go off to some little romantic spot. I know he's got a little place he likes to have dinner at in east Kowloon. It's way off the beaten track. Why don't you just go and meet him there?"

There it was. The message. She had delivered it without knowing it. He wanted to take her away but did not want to come over and tell her that. He wanted to keep his distance but he wanted to see her. How he managed to instill that in Aspidistra Benning was a mystery to her, but right then and there, watching Aspidistra Benning pull down the straps on her top, so as to tan her shoulders evenly, she made up her mind to meet him that evening in distant Ngau Tau Kok. She knew just where it was, near the old airport.

14

march 2003

THE OLD AIRPORT at Kai Tak was one of Philip's favorite places in Hong Kong. A dirty old runway jutted out of East Kowloon into the bay, seeming as though its purpose had been to deposit the planes in the water rather than the air. A few tin signs mounted on a chain-link fence, warning people to keep out, flapped lightly in the wind. It was pleasingly derelict in a city where dereliction amounted almost to a taboo. Philip liked its emptiness. The runway had closed a few years back. Now it looked like a wide empty avenue in a city shut down by the plague. There was something disembodied about it, even ghostly, the spirit of the city becoming, here, something like a spirit itself.

Every time he came he thought of breaking the lock and walking down the runway to the water's edge where the turf crumbled into the bay. But he never did. Usually he sat on a concrete bench at a bus stop across the street. Today he stood with his fingers hooked into the diamonds of the chain-link fence. He loved the quiet hum of the place. The streetcars and omnibuses and blue panel trucks of the city were somewhere else. It was a time out of time, a moment in late March where the blue morning air had a crispness that made the sky almost neutral, a place out of place, so he could be alone with his thoughts.

"What are you looking at?" asked Jessica, coming up to him, for this had been their place to meet. He had his hair slicked back, though just with water. It made him look so clean. She liked that. Though she wished he would not wear such baggy pants. She would like to be reminded of his body, not caring if, by chance, other people also were.

"Nothing, really," he said. "Just the runway."

Jessica was silent for a moment, then said, very carefully,

"Poppy came out here once. After the airport closed, but before the fence went up. She dug up a rock from the runway and gave it to me for my birthday. She said that thousands of planes had landed on it. And that if I put it to my ear I could hear the screech of their wheels."

"Did you?"

"Well!" she exhaled. "Not in front of her at least."

"So you minded? That she gave it to you, I mean."

"I told her I most certainly did. That such a thing was not appropriate as a present." She paused, turning her toe in the pavement. "But I still have the rock. I keep it in my dresser at the Helena May." Then, more quietly, "And I take it out and listen to it from time to time."

Philip smiled mildly. It was hard for her to tell him things like this. Poppy—a rock—its sounds. It sounded much too sentimental for Jessica Sinden. But only sounded. It was there in the way she looked at Poppy when Poppy did not know she was looking. She had a sly satisfaction that her girl was of a finer grain than her son. Children so often offered diminishing returns, she confided in him more than once.

"And I," he began, more lightly now, "know a nice little place in Amoy Gardens." He turned around. "It's not far."

Hand in hand they walked down Wang Chiu Road, seeing its little stores, so Chinese here in far Kowloon. The stores had little artistic touches Philip liked, one selling flowers made of cloth and paper, another selling rice displayed in large bowls glazed exactly the color of the rice itself, a slightly translucent white for Chinese rice, an off white for Thai, a dull cream for Indian. They passed another still with seven great jars lined up in front of it. The store had no front wall and inside were bamboo containers sealed with mud. In the corner of the room was a small street altar with a bowl lined with rice-straw and piled with apples. Most of the other stores also had these small altars. They gave the street an astringent herbal smell that Jessica should have liked, but didn't. Bitter herbs were someone else's severity. She liked the feeling of a regimen that had a point of origin somewhere deep inside herself. Chinese pills were similarly strange, small and brown and round, the size of BBs. She had seen the way her husband examined the ones Poppy brought home.

"How on earth can you tell them apart?" he'd asked her.

"I think you have to be Chinese," Poppy told him.

Well! Jessica was not. Nearing Amoy Gardens, she tried to fathom what Philip saw in all this, hoping that he was not going to take her into one of these places.

He did not. Thankfully Amoy Gardens was a large and modern housing estate with a small mall in it. A small crowd had gathered at the entrance for some reason—a Chinese reason, Jessica supposed, so it did not really apply to them and she paid no attention to it. It often made life so much easier, so much lighter, not to know what was going on around you. It also made for a certain cloistering of thought. She simply saw what she preferred to see. Today she noticed how many of the Chinese in the crowd had perfect posture. They so often did. It made them look like puppets with strings running through the centers of their heads. Or like those statues she had seen on the Mainland of warriors buried at celestial attention. Admirable. She once tried to tell Poppy if she was not careful about her posture she was going to end up stooped in the grave for all eternity. Perhaps, though, if Poppy went through with her plans, such as they were, to become an acupuncturist, the Chinese would teach her to stand up straight. Perhaps, too, they would teach her how to walk. For all her efforts, Jessica felt Poppy still walked like a small windup toy.

Lunch was perfunctory. They ordered it off a shiny laminated menu. The food was spongy and gelatinous. The Bok Choy was covered with a sauce that congealed around it like varnish. But Philip had been right about one thing. They were really quite alone. In an empty restaurant they sat on the same side of the booth, and she let him kiss her. On the cheek only, for they were in public, but she felt herself, in spite of herself, wanting to be close to him and hoped, despite her qualms, they would go to the Helena May afterwards. Enough time had passed since the poisoning of the dogs. And now the newspapers were full of rumors of some new kind of bird flu on the Mainland. Oh, never mind; Edward would tend to it. That was a yearly event, and in any case the flu season was almost over. The Chinese could often be such nervous nellies. Elaine certainly was.

Outside the commotion had increased. Some of the posturally-correct people were arguing with the police, who were of course maintaining perfect posture, though Jessica supposed that was a matter of compulsion, not volition. Force was so unseemly, though it might sometimes be necessary in situations such as this one. Better to keep well off from it.

"Something's wrong," Philip said.

"Perhaps their rents are in arrears," said Jessica. "They so often are."

"No, it's worse than that," he said. "Those police are wearing riot gear."

Jessica had not noticed. Whatever the Chinese had to do to keep order among themselves was quite all right with her, so long as they left her out of it.

'I'm going to go ask."

'Philip," she said, not pleading, but a little exasperated at the interest he took in matters beyond his ken. "It's not worth it. They won't tell you anything."

"Not directly," he told her.

She watched him go over and talk to the police, who always had at least some English. Jessica looked down at her lap. The left side of her sweater overlapped the right untidily. She started to button it, but the bottom button fell off without seeming to be loose. Mina again. She so often failed at small tasks. Jessica felt it was directed at her and that it was cowardly to get back at her this way. She smiled to herself. Edward, inimitably, would say *coweredly*, because Mina cowered so in her presence. She was afraid of her, to be sure, but she thought of so many ways to get even. She was from the Philippines. They had some taste of democracy under the Americans, and they wanted more. She positively simmered under her submissiveness. She heard it in the way she called her *Mum* instead of Jessica or Mrs. Sinden. Mum's the word: it was a way of silencing her name and reminding her that she was nothing more than her employer. Jessica did not want to be reminded of Mina's humanity. She felt she should keep it to herself, or reserve it for Sundays, when she, along with all the other maids in Hong Kong, went down to Central to picnic under the great open arches of the ferry terminals lining Victoria Bay, winding pipe cleaners into little dolls that not even the tourists bought.

"I suppose," she told Philip once, "your views are rather more democratic."

"Rather," he said.

She waited for him to say more, hoping he would, but he didn't. His views could be so unexpected. Seeing a headline, something about Iraq, the Americans invading here or there, he simply shook his head and quoted Mill. *There is no reason that all human existence should be constructed on some one or some small number of patterns.* It was so right, so seeing. There was no reason for the war in Iraq other than that. Philip, sadly, did not expect democracy here in Hong Kong, but he could not keep a certain sadness from washing over him, a wish that things could be better than they were, even though they weren't.

She slipped the button into her pocket. She would sew it on later, herself, late at night after everyone had gone to bed and she had checked to make sure they had.

Philip came back, sliding into the shiny plastic banquette.

"I should have listened to you," he said. "That one woman was very sick."

"What woman?"

"She's slumped in a chair. There's an ambulance down the street, but they won't take her."

"Really?"

"I think we should go, Jessica."

Jessica slid out of the booth, standing up.

"Something is going on," he said. "Something not good."

Jessica heard the way he said *not good*, knowing him well enough to hear he meant *very, very bad*.

"I said I think we should go, Jessica."

"Yes," she said, putting her hand in his, a little irritated. "I heard you the first time."

Her barrette had slipped. It held only a few strands of hair, which she was growing out because he would like it.

She swung down the street with him, pushing up the barrette, eyes riveted on the woman in the chair. She was so still she seemed hardly to be breathing.

"Don't look at her," said Philip. "They'll think you might know her. That's what they're doing. They're asking who does."

"What should we do?"

"Just hurry up."

"I am hurrying," said Jessica, quickening her pace.

When they had made it back to Kai Tak, near the runway, Philip paused. Both of them were a little out of breath.

"I think they were trying to seal off that building," he said, catching his breath.

"But why?"

"I don't know, but that woman in the chair—I think she was dead."

For a second, his fingers touched hers. They were so thin it didn't seem to him they could hold anything heavier than a toothpick. But they were strong. He knew they were strong. He had seen her lift things he could not, a wheelbarrow, a bag of fertilizer, even a small air conditioner.

"Let's go," he said, putting his hand on her back, directing her toward the ferry pier at Kwun Tong.

—

Landing on the Island, they went directly to the Helena May. Philip had his car in a lot at North Point, but Jessica insisted on driving it because she knew the all one-way streets in the neighborhood. They parked in the lot under the ramp in back, so dark and snug it was almost hidden, and walked around to the front entrance. Benson nodded lightly as they passed through the dining room, but other than that, no one raised a head. Good. The consensus was holding. Then they went back to their room on the other side of the garden.

They felt very close to each other, and, undressing, held each other for a long time before making love.

"I feel so happy," she said afterwards, wound around him, her leg over his hip, dripping on him, thinking about how nothing about their love was prospective. She liked what they were, here, now, wanting, not what they didn't have, but only what they had. "It feels undeserved."

"What do you mean?" asked Philip.

He wondered if she had been as struck by the dead woman in the chair, as he was. But she wasn't. It had been a Chinese death in a Chinese part of town, and she seemed to have already forgotten it. The only thing she said was that Edward was off studying some new disease somewhere in China. Philip was struck by her ability to put things out of mind, especially since he did not have it at all.

"Edward makes an effort to understand me," she began to say, answering him. "And in a cumulative sort of way I think he does. But it's not natural. Not like with you."

"You've never known that before?"

"With Poppy. I could always tell what she was feeling before she knew what had come over her. With Tristan it was different. He was just another male in his technical world. A world of objects he moves around, the way Edward does the implements on his surgical tray."

Philip, listening to her, seemed to recede into some deep place inside himself.

"You're thinking something, aren't you?"

"Yes."

"You don't have to tell me if you don't want to."

He stopped to think. An American woman saying that would be prying, trying to make him feel guilty about not telling her. But with Jessica—he was beginning to feel that for her, the highest degree of intimacy was a kind of sustained mutual reticence, a togetherness while being alone. It's not that she liked not knowing. She didn't. But she was willing to be protective about him not telling her, knowing, that if he had closed the box to her, it would be closed to the world until he chose to share its contents with her. It gave him a feeling of her superintending his privacy, a feeling of quietly enclosed guardianship which, for her, was almost more intimate than intimacy.

But he was who he was, so he told her.

"I was thinking about Roma."

"You almost never talk about her," said Jessica.

"There's no need to," he said. "She's a perfectly congruent person."

"But what were you thinking?"

"How, if she saw us here, she would be happy that you look older than she does."

"Happy?"

"Looks are power for her. She knows if she dresses a certain way, tilts her head, just-so, lets her hair swipe her shoulders, she'll get exactly what she wants. She'd take one look at you and know that you couldn't do it, and feel superior to you."

"And my wealth?"

"Wealth is just one part of the equation for her. Wealth, power, looks. She wants it all."

Jessica sat straight up in bed. She often did when riveted by a thought, or taken with a conundrum, and Philip liked seeing the droop and sway of her breasts when she did. She caught his eye.

"They can't be *that* fascinating."

"Yet you used to be so proud of them."

"Yes," she admitted. "They stood up so well."

"When did they—"

"In my forties, I suppose."

"Did you ever think of—"

"Plastic surgery? Never. No one ever saw them. I don't suppose Edward has seen them these fifteen years."

"Really?" he said, cupping one and kissing it just above the nipple.

Philip found himself thinking about Jessica's looks. She was not beautiful. She had a small pinched face, a sharp little nose, and a tight flat mouth. The veins in her arms were hard as twigs. Yet she had something, something that came and went, a feeling of being bound, constricted, tied up. Her stiffness could be sexy. It showed how much she was holding back, how much she was holding in. He saw the way she would pause in front of the stores on Des Voeux Road selling medical implements, braces, binders, supports, straps. She admired them.

Reminding her of this, he listened, without surprise, as she said, "I wish I could bind my children in one of those braces, and tighten it from time to time."

Then she laughed and said it was time to go back to the Peak. Mina would be making dinner. Philip started shuffling around the room, looking for his underwear and socks.

"Tristan might like it," he said, looking under the bed. "But you'd lose Poppy."

"I know," she said. "She's already almost American."

"And you've done everything you can to prevent it, haven't you?"

"Yes. Everything," she said, stepping into the dance leotard she sometimes wore under her blouse and pants. "But I'm afraid that being American is an inborn tendency. It can't be helped."

"Jessica," said Philip, touching her arm softly, liking how closely the leotard fit her, "I think you're selling Poppy short."

Jessica moved away sharply. "I wish you wouldn't touch me like that, Philip. I prefer a firm grip, you know that."

"Yes," he said, "I know. I keep forgetting."

"I dislike timidity in all things."

"Gentleness isn't timidity."

"It's hesitancy all the same. If you want to touch me, touch me. Directly. Decisively. Do it. Move me around. I will submit to it for as long as you like."

"Where's the intimacy in that?"

"The intimacy is in the fact that I would allow no one else to do what you are doing. If you're to cross over to me, you're not crossing over to some small spongy thing. Take me as I am, Philip. I am a hard thing at heart."

"I know that, Jessica."

"I know you do, my dear," she said pleasantly. "You just need a little reminding from time to time."

So he took her to the bed and gave her a good hard rubdown, slipping his hands under her leotards. She arched her back and raised herself up on her knees, supporting her weight with her forehead and pulling aside the band between her legs. The light brown hair between her legs was already wet and curled. Coming toward her, he thought of how nursing her newborns, she'd had to buy pads because her tiny breasts sprayed out milk in spurts. *I want*—she started to say, then said it again, *I want*—and though he didn't know what that wanting was, it made him only want her more.

Afterwards she lay quietly quivering at him, seeming to look beyond him, at some distant point in the future, or perhaps it was the past. She had never been so beautiful as then and there, her back soaked with sweat, the skin under her eyes tinted with circles in lilac and mauve.

15

march 2003

A HUSH came over the city. Some new disease, some plague, was in the air. Or in the pipes and drains, because the very streets seemed to have trouble breathing, said the *South China Morning Post*, not normally inclined to metaphor. Sitting on her terrace, eating a cold orange for breakfast because, coming home last night from Kowloon, she had given Mina the day off, Jessica turned the page for more news. And that was when she saw it.

A name for it. Severe Acute Respiratory Syndrome, or SARS for short.

And some facts. One dead, one hundred and twenty-nine hospitalized, a building quarantined somewhere in Kowloon.

Jessica put down the paper and took out her phone. The signal was a little weak; two lines out of five. Her first call was to Elaine Kwan, who, knowing where she had been yesterday, had already left five messages. But for some reason she did not answer. Then she scrolled down the menu, pushing *husband* when she saw it.

"Jessica?" Dr. Sinden said, picking up, seeing her number come up on his screen.

"Edward!"

"It doesn't sound like you."

"I saw the paper, Edward. That's why I'm calling. I want to know what's going on."

"I have no idea, really. It may be the same thing I'm seeing in Foshan. But so far in Hong Kong it's only confined to one place. It could simply be some kind of fungus growing in the pipes of one building. Like Legionnaire's Disease a few years back."

Jessica was silent.

"Well, at least you can be thankful we don't live in Amoy Gardens."

"What do you mean, *Amoy Gardens*?" she said, hoping he did not hear her voice breaking.

"It only just came out. There's been an outbreak of something, certainly, as in Foshan, but so far it's been confined to only one place. Almost all the known cases are coming out of Amoy. I was going to call home when you called. Simply to warn you."

"Warn me about what?"

"Not to go to Kowloon for the time being. It's in the area near the old airport, you know, on Ngau Tau Kok Road."

"I know where the old airport is, Edward," she said, calming herself. "And I've certainly passed Amoy Gardens."

Jessica hoped they had not been seen there, and not photographed, but she had no way of knowing.

"I'm surprised to hear it. I thought you didn't really like mixing with those kinds of people."

"I don't. But I do wish to be kept abreast of events."

"As you wish." He was blithe and detached. "By the way, could you tell Mina to look for my braces? The pair with the little blue elephants on them. They should have been on the far left shelf of my dresser, the second drawer down, but when I checked before I left, they were not there."

She wondered why he would possibly be concerned with his braces if this crisis was a serious as he said it was. She was oddly reassured, and said,

"Poppy has taken to wearing them."

"So there you have it," he said, not really caring at all what she did.

"When will you be back?" asked Jessica.

"That depends on the hospital. They put us," and here he paused, seeming to search for the right word, "on alert."

Then she heard some commotion on his end. Shouting; a scuffle perhaps.

"What was that?" Jessica asked.

"I'll tell you later," he said.

"Where are you now, anyway?"

"I'm still at the First Peoples Hospital."

"Are they bringing in people from Amoy Gardens?"

"I think we've got our hands full here, Jessica."

"I'm sure you do, Edward. I'll speak with you later," she said, hanging up.

Then she called Philip.

"I can't talk now," he told her, picking up. "Roma and I are having an argument."

"An argument?" Jessica found it hard to imagine him arguing with anyone.

"Yes. She wants to leave Hong Kong. She's very afraid."

She heard him breathe heavily.

"I'm afraid she's going to do something impulsive."

"Did you tell her where we were yesterday?"

"No. But I may have to."

"Surely she knows—"

"Yes, yes! She knows I'm fond of industrial archeology. Now I'm afraid I might have exposed her to *this*—"

Jessica had not thought that far. But she had to get off the phone. She had her children to think of. Poppy and Tristan would have to be moved to safety. Sai Kung was out. You had to pass through east Kowloon to get there. The nearest accessible expat colony was Discovery Bay. Oh God, the Bennings. They were the only people she knew there. She would have to act quickly. Get them there before they had a chance to be exposed to her for long. Edward could take care of himself, and was well aware of any risks he might take, having made his peace with the consequences well in advance. He was a doctor, after all, and had taken the Hippocratic Oath, which he often made light of, calling it the Hypocritic Oath, but he was capable, on occasion, of taking it very seriously. To be fair, she would also offer Mina a one-way flight to the Philippines, which she would decline, of course, knowing full well what one-way meant.

"I'll call you when I can," said Philip.

"Yes, good. But are you all right?"

"Physically I'm fine. I doubt whether we were there long enough to be exposed."

"But we ate in the restaurant."

"True." He paused. "We can only hope." He paused again. "Be well, Jessica."

"Philip—"

"Yes?"

"Never mind," she said, sad but keeping off an encroaching feeling of resignation. "Go to Roma. She needs you now."

She needs you now. A few months ago it would have been an impossible statement for Jessica Sinden to make. And yet with Philip, it came so easily to her tongue. In no way did she feel that Roma was her enemy. In fact, she rather liked her. Her style of severity was different from hers, but it was no less severe. She hoped that Philip would manage to spirit her out of the country if that was what she wanted. She could help. Regular flights in and out might be curtailed or canceled. If Cathay Pacific, partly owned by one of Simpson's cousins, had no seats, the airline might still make a place for Roma, once Simpson, prompted by Elaine Kwan, made the necessary calls.

But first: Poppy was in her room.

She went in without knocking.

Poppy was on her back, her arms over her head, her hair fanned out behind her, looking at the ceiling. She had become rather slovenly lately about shaving her legs, which seemed to drift on the surface of the comforter. She used to look like this in the pool when she was a little girl, floating on her back, wearing red inflatable arm bands. Even with them, she never left the shallow end. She would kick her legs without managing to propel herself anywhere. The kicking tired her out, that was all. When she was tired out she was happy. Felicity once told her happiness was a form of exhaustion, but then again, that was Felicity.

Poppy should do something about her hair. It was limp and stringy. Perhaps she could wear it on top of her head, coiled in a bun.

"Mama!" Poppy exclaimed, happy to have an excuse to remonstrate with her mother. "I would appreciate it if you would do me the courtesy of knocking before you enter my room. These are my premises, after all."

The way she spoke startled Jessica. Her daughter sounded so much like *her*.

"Poppy," she began.

"Mama," said Poppy, trying to look solemn. "I insist on an apology. This is simply not acceptable."

Under normal circumstances she would claim the parental prerogative of entry. But these were not normal circumstances.

"Poppy. Where is Tristan?"

"I don't know," she said sullenly, giving up on forcing an apology out of her mother, who would never apologize. "Probably off with Aspidistra somewhere."

"Was he here last night?"

"You mean *you* don't know?"

It was Poppy's turn to be caught off guard. Her mother was nothing if not vigilant about the head count before bed. Jessica Sinden so loved sleeping faces, even when they were only pretending to be asleep.

"I want to know where he is," said Jessica, almost speaking over her daughter.

"In Discovery Bay," said Poppy. "He said he'd be back tonight. So," she said, indifferently, "probably he will."

Jessica spotted her daughter's open drawers. Instinctively, she moved to the top drawer and began folding Poppy's panties, stacking them neatly in serried rows.

"Mama, what are you doing?"

"You will need ten, perhaps twelve pair of fresh—underthings."

Poppy widened her eyes. What new punishment had her mother devised for her? Rules, for her mother, had a possible infinity of infractions.

"Why are you sending me away?" she whined.

"I want you to go to Discovery Bay. We will have to pack carefully. There is no telling when you can come back."

'But Mama," she pleaded, "what have I done?"

'You might as well ask what the birds have done. It's that flu or plague or syndrome or whatever they call it."

'Oh, that," said Poppy. "If it's a Chinese disease, I'm sure they'll use acupuncture. The thick needles are for the serious ones."

Jessica shook her head. She could not believe how dim her uncommonly bright daughter could be at times. But this was no time to apply a corrective. It would not be any better if she did. If anything, Poppy would probably be pleased to have a catastrophe to get excited about.

"I need you to get out of your bed and pack your bag," she told her.

Poppy gripped the edge of her comforter, trying to wipe away a couple of needles stuck in her skirt before her mother saw them (it was a fine black muslin and they stood out so). The day was going so well, with only a distant sighting of her mother just before breakfast. But perhaps there was a silver lining here. Discovery Bay was beyond her mother's oversight. And she liked Aspidistra, who, she was sure, would be a willing manikin for her little acupuncture experiments.

"You can bring your needles," she heard now, her mother's voice channeling itself, in that uncanny way she had, into the stream of her own thoughts.

Jessica squinted at an open box of needles labeled in Chinese.

"Don't they come with a pin cushion or something?"

Poppy wanted to tell her that wasn't sanitary, but she did not want to push her luck. She had already corrected her mother once today. Twice was simply too much to hope for.

"Oh. And one more thing. I want you to bring your own bedding."

"Mama, I think they have—"

"You may be there for quite a while, Poppy. A good guest does not obtrude."

Obtrude. Another one of her mother's specialty words. It meant to become noticeable in an unwelcome or intrusive way. But really it meant not to interfere with her, especially when she had something specific in mind.

The comforters were upstairs. Jessica went into the hallway and began to go slowly upstairs, her hand on the railing, tracing her way as she had so many times before, knowing that the stairs were one of the few places where, faced with what she still called this thing (because calling it by its name, a cerebrospinal fluid leak, ceded too much to it), she let herself go, where she let herself fully feel the tiredness in her body, all fifty-nine years of it, the ache it took to move one leg up one stair, the other leg up another. Wooden staircases were gray old places, creaky and tired, and there were so few of them here in Hong Kong. At the top of the stairs was a chest with her comforters in it. Above the chest were shelves in the narrow hallway leading to Poppy's old bedroom and her study, nearly always locked, where she kept Felicity's things. Jessica checked to make sure everything was in its carefully-apportioned place. Straw hats set on racks, paints on shelves with easels folded under them, a pile of skimpy plastic sandals, flannels (who knew why, here, so near the Tropic of Cancer) stacked in cubbyholes under the staircase, a glass vase, ossuary of the skulls of small marsupials, rescued for a season before dying in captivity, shabby summer books nobody ever finished, their covers swollen with dampness, and pinned to the wall, a calendar with dates circled, stopping sometime back in September of 1999, when Poppy moved downstairs.

Taking the comforter from the chest, she opened the door to Poppy's old bedroom just a crack. The sheets were clean, stretched tightly across the bed, the blankets, hardly needed here, folded neatly in a pile at the foot. The last time Poppy was here (for she still came up here sometimes), she was reading, what was it, something about the Spanish Armada, why Poppy of all people would take an interest in that was beyond her except that like her mother, she slept badly and needed some help to doze off, and only history was dry enough. Jessica felt a sudden pang for her, as though she had lost her too and was looking into the bedroom of a second dead child. But no, it was Poppy's childhood that was dead, and it was for that she felt such grief. Before she moved downstairs, at thirteen, a year after Felicity's death, she had been such a good girl, climbing these very stairs so cheerfully, chanting and stamping, *up up up with a tup tup tup*. So malleable then, trying not to think tractable, not about her, because recently she overheard Poppy telling Tristan that tractable was her favorite word.

Jessica closed the door gently and went back downstairs. Poppy was in her new room (for that was what they all called it in the family, *Poppy's new room*) waiting for her, her suitcase packed.

Poppy watched as her mother carefully inserted a fresh razor in the outer pocket. Perhaps, if she used it, when this was all over she would buy her a new dress cut low at the back. Something formal; that would do nicely.

16

late march 2003

THE WING, the lounge for the first class passengers of Elaine Kwan's personal airline (for that was how Roma Nye regarded Cathay Pacific), was behind tinted doors on the second floor of the secure area. From her table at the ledge, a fine travertine trimmed with bamboo, Roma had a good view of the big planes as they pulled into the Main Terminal at Chek Lap Kok.

It was getting dark. The beacons on the runways were lighted. There seemed to be more planes lining up to come in than there were people in the airport. It was the second week of March when the U.S. Consulate put out a red warning, but it took another week for Simpson to make an arrangement. And that was just what he called it, an arrangement. When she asked for a reservation number he said he wasn't given one and probably couldn't get one. She tried asking Jessica Sinden about the possibility of being tagged for medical evacuation, but Jessica said her husband was off with a team of doctors in Foshan, and was quarantined in an old hospital there. He could not do anything.

Philip tried the Consulate first. They were useless. American planes had been taking trips from Hong Kong almost everywhere, to St. Petersburg, to Manila, to Guam, to Honolulu and Los Angeles. But they were not coming back. That left Cathay Pacific, Hong Kong's biggest airline. When their planes flew home, they flew back to Chep Lak Kok. The problem, Simpson said, was that they were all staying here. They had planes and people who wanted to take them, but no airports anywhere in the world that would let them land. Philip said that a few days ago he saw an American C-5A in the air, preparing to land on some distant runway. But those were medical supplies coming in, and test kits going out. One of her friends at Baker Nicholson tried slipping her an expired box of Tamiflu. The white cards containing the blister pack of pills had already begun to turn brown. Even if she got sick, she would be afraid to take them.

But if anyone could move heaven and earth, it was Elaine Kwan.

So that afternoon, their last together in their flat on the Peak, Roma pleaded with Philip to leave Hong Kong with her. If Simpson thought he could get her out, he could probably get Philip out too, and maybe even throw in a ticket for his girlfriend, who was Elaine Kwan's best friend. But Philip was adamant. He wanted to stay. Roma reached out with nervous quickness to take his hand. She tried to assume a position of authority with him, the way she always used to, with rigid, stubborn arms, strong shoulders, and a stern chin. But it didn't work. Really it never had, so there they were at *The Wing*, waiting with Elaine and Jessica, who were talking quietly but intently at the next table.

A Cathay Pacific counter was just on the other side of the tinted partition in back.

A door opened, and Simpson Kwan came out.

Simpson came up to her, still looking quite smart in his Zegna jacket and Ferragamo loafers, even in the middle of an emergency.

"They're recommending you not to go," he began.

"What do you mean, *recommending*?" said Roma.

"They're not sure where they can take you, and they don't think it's wise to go to some of the airports that are still open."

"Will they let me go if I want to?"

Simpson hesitated. "I think you should listen to them, Roma."

"I said, *Will they let me go?*"

"Yes," he answered. "But you'd have to sign a release."

He paused.

"And they're not sure where you would be going yet. It might even not be a regular airport."

"At this point," said Roma, "I'd settle for a landing strip in Africa."

Philip turned to his ex-wife. "Roma, this isn't *Casablanca*. Those big planes can't land in small places."

"And anyway, they're afraid they might be turned away," added Simpson. "With no place to let them land, and not enough fuel to make it back to Hong Kong."

Roma sucked her lips over her teeth. She always did this in the middle of tough negotiations. Roma Nye was used to getting what exactly she wanted out of the people she wanted it from. Wood, iron, oil, steel, stock, bonds—it didn't matter what—she was sure she could get it.

"Can't I promise them something?" Roma pressed.

"There's only one thing in the world you could offer them to get those planes up in the air."

"What's that?" said Roma, brightening.

"A vaccine," said Simpson.

Elaine, who had been holding back, now spoke:

"Roma, sometimes things can't be done. Sometimes you can move heaven and earth. But only if you can move *both* heaven and earth. Move one and not the other and—"

"That's not what *I* hear," Roma said, thinking of her staging of the inquest for Felicity Sinden, an event still widely admired among those in the know in Hong Kong.

"Don't go there," said Philip, stepping in. His eyes met Jessica's. She had teared up and turned away. She liked Roma. Though she was not one to panic, she could certainly recognize it when she saw it.

"No, no," said Elaine. "Let her be. It's perfectly reasonable to assume that under normal conditions, Simpson's cousin Geoffrey could secure you a fight on Cathay to almost any major city in the world. But that does not change the fact that right now, there are simply no flights."

"No flights?" said Roma. "But I see two listed on the board. Look: Peshawar, and Iranamadu."

But even as they were looking at the big black board, the word CANCELLED flashed in red next to the flight to Peshawar.

That left Iranamadu.

"Okay," said Roma. Iranamadu it is."

"There's an airport there," said Simpson, "but I don't think anyone on earth could give you a release to go there."

"Is it big enough?" pressed Roma.

"Well, yes. Just barely."

"Then tell them. I want to sign on the line."

"If you go there, Roma, you might well be alone on that plane."

"Fine by me," said Roma.

So Simpson went off for a few minutes, then came back carrying some papers and a couple of boxes.

"You'd better sit down," he told her.

Roma sat. Simpson, folding his arms, began slowly to tell her what he knew. He spoke wearily, as a seasoned traveler. She would be flying into the middle of an insurrection. The Tamil Eelam held most of the north and east of the island of Sri Lanka. They had only just started building their own airport at Iranamadu. One, maybe two, runways were already operational. Usually Cathay flew to Colombo, but in this one instance, the airline was willing to make an exception. She should also know that when she landed, she would be passing over the front lines. During her approach, she would see a circle of bright specks around the airport. They were small skirmishes, but Cathay was pretty sure the Liberation Tigers would still be holding the airport when she landed. And once she was on the ground, she should make sure to do only what they told her to do, not moving a step unless she was asked to. Customs there knew to expect a Kwan.

"Roma—don't," pleaded Philip once last time.

"Philip," she said, sweeping her hair to one side with the back of her hand. "You *promised* me you wouldn't say anything once we were here."

Roma started moving, jerking her wheeled suitcase in front of her toward the gate, passing a double row of stainless-steel aquariums. A couple of the fish had died and were bobbing on the surface.

Then she turned around. Philip, Elaine, Jessica, and Simpson still hadn't moved.

"So, let's get a move on it!"

The others followed her quietly until they came to the north gate.

"What about my bags?" asked Roma.

"Just give them to me," said Simpson. "I'll bring them round."

"Where are the other passengers?"

"I don't know. Maybe they're already on the plane, or maybe it'll be just you."

Roma glanced at the clock. "Sure I'll make it in time? I mean, it says the plane leaves in ten minutes. I still have to take that little train to the gate, don't I?"

"The train will be empty," said Simpson, "and the plane will wait."

Hearing this, Jessica supposed, accurately it turned out, that Simpson had somehow managed to delay the flight to Iranamadu so Roma could take it. She wasn't even sure if Cathay Pacific ordinarily flew to Iranamadu. She certainly had never heard of the place.

Simpson then handed her a small plastic bag. "This is a box of N95 masks. You're going to be in a pressurized environment with circulating air, so you'll need to change them ever two hours. Sit as far from everyone else as you can."

"And— Simpson?" Elaine said to her husband.

"Yes, yes. There's this, too."

He reached into a manila envelope, pulling out a thin blue passport:

HONG KONG

SPECIAL ADMINISTRATIVE REGION

PEOPLE'S REPUBLIC OF CHINA

"Just in case," he said, handing it to her.

"How did you—"

"Don't ask."

"If anyone asks," put in Elaine, smiling with quiet satisfaction, "you're Chinese."

Roma's eyes widened.

"Yes, Chinese," said Simpson. "The insurgency is Communist. That makes us allies."

"But Hong Kong is—"

"Yes yes, I know, capitalist. But don't worry about what Hong Kong is for you. Think about what it is for them." He opened the passport. "This is your name now."

"Kwan Li Na Roma," she said, reading the name on the passport.

"I chose it," explained Elaine. "Li Na means 'elegant.'"

Roma smiled.

Simpson continued. "There are Kwans up and down the Asian subcontinent ready to vouch for you. A Kwan will be meeting you at the airport."

"Really?"

"Well, kind of a made-up Kwan. But he's Chinese and he's from the Mainland. He'll be considered an ally too, so they won't bother about him either."

"And—one more thing—take *this*."

He proceeded to hand her a box the size of a hat box.

Roma opened it. Inside, wrapped in white tissue, was a fitted wig with long straight black hair.

"Turn to the picture page," Simpson told her.

Roma did. Her regular passport photo had been doctored. Her long straight yellow hair was black, and her eyes had been narrowed ever-so-slightly.

"Your father," Simpson went on, "was British. Your mother lives in Sha Tin."

Roma didn't know how she felt. She wanted to get out, but she was anxious about what she was getting into. She wanted to ask Simpson about her new parents, in case she was asked. For the first time, she tried to imagine Sri Lanka, but she only remembered a picture she'd once seen in the *Asian Wall Street Journal* of a small yellow house in Jaffna, open to the street, where they put on puppet shows. They were string-and-rod puppets, telling the story of a family caught in palace intrigues between local warlords and the British colonizers. A clown puppet would sing and dance and beat one of the colonists with a club. Oh, God—the Tamil Tigers—

"I think you will make a very good Kwan," she heard Simpson saying. "Still, don't take your wig off, whatever you do. They're going to try and get you to India as quickly as they can."

Roma felt tears coming on, thankful to be leaving the invisible threat of the virus but afraid of the unpredictable violence ahead.

She could only stammer, "Thank you."

"You don't have to," said Elaine. "Jessica is my friend of thirty years. *My oldest friend*," she added, and because Roma knew Mandarin, she had a sense of just how much that phrase meant to a Chinese person. It meant nothing less than everything.

"Roma Kwan," Roma tried saying out loud.

"So—put it on," said Simpson. "And wear these, too." He handed her a pair of brown tinted sunglasses. Chances are, you'll pass a cursory glance."

"But I'm so tall," she said weakly.

"The passport lists your birthplace as Harbin, Manchuria. There the Chinese are as tall as you are."

Roma gathered her hair, lifting it into a small bun, placing the wig on her head.

Jessica came over to her, turning the wig a few degrees, worriedly tucking in some stray strands of hair. Roma's eyes met Jessica's with fondness.

Then Roma turned to Simpson.

"How do I look?"

"Great," said Simpson, barely glancing at her. "Now you'd better go." He motioned toward the gate, with its empty maze of stanchions with retractable belts, leading to a row of metal detectors.

"Oh Philip, Jessica. Simpson, Elaine—"

Roma still had two passports in her hand, a light blue one and a dark blue one. Jessica reached out and touched the dark blue one with the American crest on it, saying, "Better save this one for later."

Roma quickly slipped it in her bag, closing the zipper.

"Okay," she said, steadying herself.

Then, without turning around, she strided through the sliding glass doors, disappearing into the vast secure interior of Chek Lap Kok airport.

Jessica quickly said her goodbyes to Elaine and Simpson. A car was waiting for them at the curb under the front portico. She watched them walk though the series of sliding doors that led to it.

Then she went back to Philip. He was absorbed in looking up—at the steel section roof, with its parallel vaults.

"It's a crypt," he said to her. "I bet that's where they got the design. And maybe that's why they put that wishbone pattern over it, too. You know how it is around here. The Chinese always want things to be *lucky.*"

Jessica knew that already. Edward often counted on it. *Everything is roulette here, Jessica,* though she knew him well enough to know that he saw some science in it. Jessica herself felt that Hong Kong was a big gamble. They had made a religion here out of the fall of the dice. Simpson always said the Hang Seng Index was not much more than the instruments of the old arts of Fortune—the cards, the strangely shaped stones, the bowls of sand, the gyrations of birds—set to new purposes. As a doctor, Edward was fascinated by all the sciences of prediction, and had his own ways of calculating chance. But he always said, *Jessica, Chance never addresses the individual instance,* and looking over at Philip, whom she loved, and whose eyes were still following the Gothic tracery of the suspended ceiling, Jessica knew that it was only the individual instance that mattered.

17

early april 2003

So now that Roma was off, they would have a Decameron of days together. Maybe even more than ten, if she pushed her luck, and Philip was one to let her push. Edward was stuck in Foshan. Roma made it to Sri Lanka, where, so far as she knew, she was being spirited away to India and then to Connecticut, where she would be staying with her mother. Poppy and Tristan were with Jill and Aspidistra in Discovery Bay. Mina had the week off. For the duration of the quarantine, certainly well into April, she and Philip would have the Peak to themselves. It could be a time of make-believe, partly because she felt ready at last to tell Philip stories about herself, partly because it seemed unreal that a plague was here at last, lapping at their high rampart above the city. Plagues were for others, after all, and she would let others deal with them until the all-clear was sounded. She would of course do what she was told; she would wear one of Edward's surgical masks if she went out; she would have Mina pick up the free bottles of bleach they were handing out in the Post Office in the basement of the Peak Tower, and instruct her to scrub the flat with bleach, which whitened everything in sight.

Usually Philip drove to her building. Today he put on a mask, one of Edward's Jessica had given him, and walked down. He leashed up Wylie, taking a path only the maids took that connected all the buildings on the street and ended at a little clearing on top of Mount Kellett, where the maids had a gathering place they went to after work.

Jessica was hunched over the *South China Morning Post*. Seeing him come in from the kitchen, she slid the paper across the dining room table. Philip read:

SARS CRISIS CENTRE.

IF HELP IS NEEDED, WE ARE HERE.

CALL—

And it gave a number.

"Fools!" she said. "As if that will help."

"But talk is all we have, Jessica. It might help. Who knows?"

He struck her as very balanced, but still she said, "I would not want you to call this number and talk about me."

"Fair enough," he said. "But if it comes to that, I'd like you to call and talk about me."

"You would?"

Sometimes he deeply surprised her, but he always had something worth hearing out. Jessica readied herself.

"Yes," he began. "You remember when you met me walking the dogs in the fog. You were willing to talk to me because you didn't see me. Because you didn't know who I was. This number would be like that. I wish everyone had a call-in number with a blankness on the other end. Life would be so much easier."

He folded the paper and tore out the notice along the lines.

"Here," he said. "Just in case."

Jessica stood up. Her face was drawn. Talking about him was acceptable, though just barely. She did not want to ask him anything more about what that meant because she feared he might ask her, in addition to talking about *him*, to talk about *her*. It was just at the limit of possibility for Jessica to imagine telling someone about Philip, especially if he was safely dead and no confidences currently active could possibly be violated. But to talk about herself? No, never.

"So," she said, ignoring the notice, but folding it and putting it on a shelf. "Let's go to Central."

"Really?"

"Yes. I want to see it. It's said to be quite empty. Mina will take care of the dogs."

"Then why go?"

"For the fun of it, Philip. Even if all we can get to eat is a bowl of Chinese soup, and some dried fish."

"Why don't we eat at the Helena May?"

"I think that's closed, too."

They went down to Jessica's car. The silver Mercedes was a little less shiny than usual because she had become rather lax with Mina about washing it every day. But inside the car smelled of bleach. Everything did nowadays. Bleach killed the virus. Free jugs of it were being handed out at post offices. The smell gave her a pleasant stinging feeling of alertness.

There was little traffic. Philip drove. Jessica rather assumed the city would be in complete catalepsy down the hill. But on the way down, the view from her window showed peach trees in bloom, clumps of white and purple bougainvillea hanging over iron fences, the road winding with arboreal calm under a canopy of trees. The sky was the usual lemon-colored sky of Hong Kong, the color, Jessica supposed, of mustard gas. In Central the big restaurants were closed but the little markets were open, selling their cakes of rice, honey and nuts, and speckled small eggs that might have been laid by sparrows and thrushes. They passed a half-built skyscraper with its bamboo palisades, the wicker baskets used by the workmen to haul up supplies piled neatly at the base. Really it seemed more like somebody's day off rather than a moment of national crisis.

They parked on a side street off Queen's Road Central.

"Why, it's old China," said Jessica, looking down the block.

She was right. It was as though the doors of the past had been flung open. Philip saw people eating behind painted glass screens, saw lacquered red chickens hanging in store windows, saw little altars lit everywhere, with odd stones, bowls of sand, browned mirrors and desiccated pieces of fruit. The alleys swayed with sheets covered with strange astrological signs, augury pivoting on the points of the human body, a kind of acupuncture of fate, Philip considered, thinking of Poppy and her needles. Hard by were Chinese doctors cupping their patients with round glass bulbs filled with blue smoke.

Only one stall on the street sold food. It was a single corner room, open on both sides to the street. An L-shaped counter enclosed it, stacked with large brown jars and tin vats of steaming tea, arranged with a ceremonial calm. The man behind the counter wore a brown smock and an old tweed hat. He had a wife with skin dry and wrinkled like an onion, and one demure daughter, who sat quietly on a stool behind the counter, smoothing her dress over her knees. Flies spiraled around the stall.

The stall-keeper squinted at her with oily brown eyes, the unsmiling smiling face you saw only on the poorest of the poor.

"You stay?" he asked Jessica, who came up to the counter first.

"Yes."

"You not go your family?"

"No," she said. "My family is here."

"Here China?"

"Here in Hong Kong."

"You not go back? England Denmark?"

He said it as though it were one place. *Englanddenmark.* She supposed that, for him at least, it was.

"No. This is our home."

"So you—you Hong Kong people now."

"Yes," she said, saying it his way, "we Hong Kong people now."

And he felt the force of it. Her speaking English his way—the Chinese way. It was as though she had reached over and said he would always be welcome as a guest in her home. He was a poor smiling man who, having something to smile at, stopped smiling because what he heard really moved him. This white woman was staying. She could have gone. So many did. But she stayed, along with this white man, who, reasonably enough, he supposed to be her husband.

"You many children?" he asked Philip.

"Two," said Philip, claiming them.

Jessica did not object.

Philip took the food he offered. But Jessica showed her acceptance of the food by touching one of the eggs. The man's lack of a smile deepened a little. Philip asked him how much he owed him, taking out a hundred dollar note. The old vendor pushed it away. Jessica winced. Philip so rarely got things wrong. It actually gratified her a little that he was a bit out of his element here.

The tea was perfect. Perhaps not what she would select in the Tea House in Hong Kong Garden, but it had a composed presence of herbs that felt soothing and medicinal.

"I'm a little surprised," she said, looking down the empty street, sipping tea from a paper cup. "Where are the police?"

"I think they're afraid, too," said Philip. "No one knows exactly what this is. The paper said some people think this is a ghost disease, and you know how they feel here about ghosts."

Poppy once said she might be interested in studying anthropology at college. But Jessica dissuaded her, saying it was a waste of time to make a profession of taking superstitions seriously. Really they just needed to be stamped out, by the local authorities if necessary.

"Well," she said, continuing her thought out loud, "I think at the very minimum there ought to be a greater police presence on this street, if only to maintain order."

Here she stopped, partly because the streets were empty, partly because Jessica's views on such subjects she generally kept to herself. Colonialism had such a bad name, but what was she, if not a colonist? Expatriate was such a bloodless word. No, in her twenty-seven years here she had joined in the effort to bring Britain to the East. On the whole it had gone well. The most prosperous countries in Asia were all former British colonies—Hong Kong, Singapore, Australia, New Zealand. Britain had brought order to them, and the semblance of law. Jessica did not like to think about law being a mere semblance in Hong Kong. Only on the Peak did she feel well sequestered by British law, which seemed to weaken with loss of elevation. The locals could be so restless downslope! One gave them gardens, parks, museums, and orchestras, of course, but what those could possibly mean to a dealer of shark's fins in Sai Ying Pun, she could not possibly fathom. Well, at least he had her to thank for his prosperity. Jessica might look down on him, but it was in both senses of that phrase, snobbery, to be sure, but also a mild suzerainty that redounded to his benefit, and hers too, because, after all, she had a fondness for shark's fin soup, which she felt, along with Elaine Kwan, to be a fine restorative.

Jessica said nothing of this to Philip, of course. But by now Philip had a good feel for what she was thinking. Though she often went a little further than he would like—Jessica once confessed she admired Pontius Pilate, a prudent colonial administrator much like many she had known—Philip did not mind her conservatism. In fact he rather relished it. It was such a curiosity it was actually comforting. In America, the conservatives were only a generation behind, near enough that it grated on him. But Jessica Sinden was at least a century, if not more, conservative. Really she often reminded him of Edmund Burke. Jessica took a dim view of the American Revolution, not because she disliked Americans, but because she disliked revolution. A revolution such as the revolution of the earth, more or less standing and spinning in place, was perfectly acceptable. It gave one day and night, and the seasons, which were her liturgy of the year in her little side garden, the daffodil and narcissus blooming in March, the Queen Anne's lace in August, the marigold and safflower rather late in September. But change did not sit well with Jessica Sinden. It could be so *untoward*. A plague would be like that for her, at least at first, until the government manifested itself somehow in a reassuring display of authority, though she feared it would only be a display, and a thin one at that.

"You're about to criticize me, aren't you?" she said to him now.

"Not really. I was just thinking about your reservations."

"I have so many," she admitted. "Things are so often not what I'd like."

"Yet you don't express them directly."

"The world is not as I would will it, Philip," she said, looking down the sere and empty street. "I would rather not have seen it."

Philip did not quite feel that way. He was glad they came down. For him some spell had lifted over the city. It was not dead down here. It was not even dying. The city had gone into a suspension of sorts. There was fear in the air that was prospective, a feeling not of fear fulfilled, but of fear waiting to pass. SARS was not the great high wind that would sweep the city clean. It was a ghost disease that seemed to haunt the city, not in large ways but in small, a haunting of trash cans knocked over and not picked up on Pedder Street, of old betting slips from the track tumbling in the sharp winds of Happy Valley, of white-clad buildings yellowing with dust drifting in freely from the Delta. And yet the city just kept right on, living the way it always did, ill at ease and yet perfectly at home, sequestered in its high towers, its ghosts just at bay.

⁓

The roads up were quiet. The parking lot was still empty. Her entire building, she presumed, was deserted. She unlocked her front door, then opened every door in the flat, checking every room on the first floor to see if the windows were still locked. Philip watched her touch the couch and chairs, so pale and elegant and not-new, to see if they had been moved. They had not been. Then she went out onto the back porch, going across the grass, reaching the hedge in her little garden. She found a couple of old lounge chairs in the shed. Philip pulled them together to make one large chair, and draped towels over them like a mattress. Together they settled in the shade for a long afternoon.

Jessica just knew she was going to enjoy being quarantined. The virus seemed distant. Seldom had she felt as gloriously awake as she did now. Quarantine gave her a vision of life free of impediments. Life off the Peak ceased to exist. Now not even tourists came up. There were no more tourists in Hong Kong. The World Health Organization was busy turning them away. It was so refreshing. For once the residents of the Peak had the place to themselves. Quarantine so suited the place. The Peak came to a point, a long ridge, really, and she had long liked that space up here was very limited. Possessions were almost beside the point. People had small houses. Living here was itself wealth. Her own little side garden was perhaps the largest private demesne in the area. With room for her body and, perhaps, one other. Now she knew for a certainty that was not Edward. Poppy and Tristan would seek her out infrequently, if only they could. Of course Elaine might stop by from time to time, but if there was a God, and if she could pray to Him, she might well have prayed that He clear out the Peak so she and Philip might have it to themselves for a while.

Well, He had. Roma was in Sri Lanka and Edward was in China. Tristan and Poppy were staying with the Bennings in Discovery Bay, a little island of expatriates that was thought to be safer, though for no rational reason she could think of, save that it was cordoned off from the creeping branches and fleshy leaves of the jungle. It was just what she had yearned for. Life with Philip, unimpeded. Almost too much to ask, given that she had never been one to yearn with impunity, and yet here it was.

Coming back inside after some hours in the shade of Jessica's garden, Philip had been looking forward to an evening with her. They had made love many times but he was curious about how Jessica slept in her own bed. He wanted, if he could, to stay up all night watching her, kissing her where he could from time to time, her forehead, her hands, her mouth. Did she breathe with her mouth open? Did she pull the comforter up to her chin? Or did she leave her arms outside, her hands clasped above her head—he was sure of it—her wrists tightening as she fell asleep? But tonight that was not what was going to keep him up.

It was the disease, and it was a presence for both of them.

Sitting on the bed next to him, she said, "Philip, I can't."

He knew she meant, *make love.*

"I know. Me neither." He glanced at the *South China Morning Post,* opened flat on the dining room table. "What did the paper say?"

"I don't know. I tried to read it but I couldn't. My mind is going in so many directions. I can't even begin to explain it. I just felt nauseous."

"They all have it there, don't they?"

The *there* was Amoy Gardens.

"Yes," she said. "Many of them."

Philip was silent.

"But some don't," she said tentatively.

"Yes, some. But they're not sure, are they? Because some people got away."

"Like us, Philip."

He raised his hand to his mouth to cough, needing to, but thinking the better of it.

"Yes. Like us."

Jessica shifted uncomfortably, trying not to notice the hoarseness in his voice.

"Had you been there before?"

"From time to time. I told you, it's the closest mall to Kai Tak. And there's a subway stop there."

"You actually take the subway?"

"It's not New York. There's no, well, Crosstown Bus."

"But this means you've been exposed at least several times."

"Yes," he said quietly.

"Oh, Philip," she said.

"I'm sorry, Jessica."

"I suppose you're exposing me now."

"Possibly. But you never get sick."

Jessica never talked about being sick. It was true though. She rarely got sick. She had only the thing she had always had. She felt odd about it. Over the years she had come to think of her meningitis as protective. It exacted its toll, but the toll went toward protecting her. It made her feel that having this one disease would keep all the others off. She never asked Edward if there was anything to her feeling. She was afraid of what he might say.

Philip faced her, still trying not to cough. He tightened his lips. He tried to breathe through his nose. He swallowed.

Then he coughed.

His raised his handkerchief just in time. But when he lowered it she saw the lines of red.

"Dear God," she said, making herself look down at the handkerchief. Such a light cough, and yet there was blood pooled in it.

Blood. Only a spot but there was more of it, because this was a blossom of blood on some fatal plant flowering inside him. In her garden it had flowered along with the sprigs of jasmine and wisteria coming up in the spring. In the spring of 1954 she too had coughed up blood, not a symptom of meningitis but her mother had taken her in, thinking TB, but instead they had found the swellings on her spine and when she came out of the hospital her one childhood friend, Judy, was dead and buried, leaving her to feel, as she felt now, death's spine tingling under the skin of life.

"What a thing," she said to Philip, gripping the stems of the flowers she had picked to give him.

"I was afraid of this," he said.

"I was even afraid to be afraid," she admitted.

"When we saw those people outside Amoy Gardens. We should have turned around and gotten out of there."

Regret was foreign to Jessica. She regarded him blankly, then said, "But you feel better now."

She was not sure what *now* meant. This second, this minute, this decade of minutes?

"Yes. A little."

"Then you would agree that we could hold off?"

Hold off meant her taking him to Queen Mary. It meant the isolation ward. It meant separation, for God knew how long.

"Just for tonight," said Philip.

"That's just what I meant. For one night only."

"I don't know if I want to go to sleep."

"I know you can," she said, running her hand along his forearm. "And I'll be there with you."

"Tonight," he said, "but what about tomorrow?"

For the first time she heard a trace of fear in his voice.

"They'll turn me away, you know, once I drop you off," she tried to say as matter-of-factly as she could.

"Perhaps they'll take you in, too."

"Possibly," she said. "But they can't do that with everyone. It depends on your degree of exposure, doesn't it?"

For once Philip did not answer.

"What will you tell them?" she pressed.

"I'm not sure. I've read the accounts. The deeper you go into that ward, the sicker the people are, and the worse your chances are of getting out."

"You mean—"

"You can actually get it worse in there."

Jessica paused. "Then stay here."

"No. You're already enough at risk. They said it seemed to take multiple exposures from multiple sources."

"But they're not sure."

"Nobody's sure of anything," said Philip. "They're just doing what they can."

What they can. Such an effort of will, and such weak results. She read that morning that two more doctors had died. When she tried looking up that doctor Edward mentioned over the phone last month, Ma Zhang Yong, she found that he died late in March in a hospital—perhaps this was what Edward was trying to tell her—where they treated only SARs patients, which must be, she realized for the first time, where Edward was. She also read how some of the patients were just being put in sealed rooms and left to die. They treated it as the worst possible end—a death alone—but if it came to that, it would not be so for Philip. If it came to dying, he would, like her, prefer to die alone. Death was so often a sham charade of sociability, when, after all, every death was the death of only one, a lonely walk into a dark empty hall and the feeling of something spent, gone, something that would never be again.

They took their time getting ready for bed. They showered together, washing each other off very carefully, holding each other for a long time under the pressure of the hot water.

Jessica lay awake in bed. Philip planned to watch her sleep all night; he often said he wished he could chase after her in her sleep. But compared to her, his will was weak. He fell asleep behind and alongside her, his hand holding one breast, gradually releasing it, his nose pressed against the nape of her neck. Philip's breathing dampened, his lips parting as he slipped more deeply into sleep.

Philip stiffened; jerked; relaxed. His breathing was raspy and staggered. Jessica stroked his cheek. She liked being soft with him even as she told him to be hard with her. His hair was still a light brown, a little longer now, falling over his ears, and she tucked it back over them. There. Better. He would have to get a haircut when he felt better. They would go together back to S/Z on Pottinger Street. They would sit in adjacent chairs, holding hands. She saw it quite distinctly. She would take a sprig of iris for him, too, to put in a buttonhole of his shirt afterwards, and he was the kind of man to let her do it.

Tomorrow she would take him to Queen Mary Hospital, though she didn't want to. Jessica tried to hold onto a hope that she would not have to take him in, at least not tomorrow, nor even the day after, but, looking at him now, his mouth a little ajar, she saw a light stippling of blood on his pillow. Oh, if he had *the thing*—for that was what she still called it to herself, the thing—he might die there. But he would most certainly die here. There would be no idyll for them here on the Peak.

18

april 2003

THE NEXT MORNING came, and Philip stayed. Then the morning after that, and then another after that. Every morning they lay in bed together, facing east, watching the sun slit up over the horizon, lightening the sky with the cold certainty of another day.

There was no question that Philip was getting worse. His breath felt strained. His cough was deepening. There was more blood, too, and less saliva. A box of tissues would not do. Jessica had to keep a roll of paper towels by their bed. When he started coughing he would leave the bedroom and go onto the terrace. The days were growing warmer with the coming of spring. There was more light and less fog. Somehow it made him feel better to feel sick outside, because, after all, the day was well. Perhaps the fine weather would make him a little better. The Peak had always seemed to her to be a kind of high sanatorium perched above the low massed buildings of Hong Kong.

Then he came back in, sitting weakly on the bed.

Jessica tried to turn his thoughts to the future. Any future would do. He had a little blood on his collar. She took him into the bathroom and turned on the faucet, trailing her hand in the water while it cooled down. She started to tell him how, when this was over, she would take him to Phuket. Her house was in the hills west of the city. The hills were not high but they afforded a good view of the bays and inlets along the coast of the Andaman Sea, and beyond it, the Indian Ocean. The house itself was very modest, not much bigger than a bungalow but in back she had a little stone-covered patio with a teak table. They could sit there in the morning and have iced tea.

"Stop, Jessica."

Then in the afternoon they could go to the beach. She knew a place on a boardwalk where there were a couple of restaurants with outdoor tables. She was not one to go into the water—her hair crinkled so when it dried—but they could watch the heat shimmer over the sea and the shadows flicker over the light gray sand.

"I said, stop."

But she kept talking, as though by the time she finished he would be feeling better and they could have another day together, a pleasant day in her side garden where the pergola would keep their skin from getting too pink in the sun. Did she not mention her patio in Phuket had a balustrade, a good old crumbling one in pink and white marble that put one in mind of Italy—

"Jessica," he said, wanting to put his hands on both sides of her head and squeeze. "*Stop*. You don't have to say anything."

"Yes, I do," she said.

Then she said, "No, I don't. I know I don't. But for the first time in my life I can't stop myself from talking because, really, I don't know what to say. I must sound like Poppy."

"Why don't we just have breakfast?" Philip said, trying to nudge her away from herself.

Jessica heard the bravery in what he said, heard how, even now, he was trying to help her.

"It's a disease," he tried to tell her. "And it's only a disease. Whatever it is, it acts entirely on its own. It will either take me, or not."

He exhaled a moist, raspy breath. He tried to smile, but his smile seemed heavy.

"It would be easier if they could treat it," he went on, "which they can't. Or," he said, tapping yesterday's copy of the *South China Morning Post*, unread on the edge of the bed except for the headlines, "at least it doesn't seem like it. So," he continued, "I suggest—"

"Yes?" Jessica said, looking at him intently, then leaning forward, her nose above the crest of his forehead, beginning to smell something new in him, something she did not like, a sour cream smell (just the kind of smell, she worried, that had an expiration date), and wanting, desperately, to hear what he had to say next.

Philip smiled again. "I suggest we have breakfast."

Jessica liked the feeling of laying out breakfast on the terrace. Two white plates, the porcelain the perfect color of cream (how she hated pure white), two fluted glasses, French with the flare of a petal to their facets, two woven napkins with the thickness of something you could never wear in the great heat of southern China. And a glass pitcher with a long yellow stirring stick in it, there not because the orange juice needed stirring, but for the sheer beauty of it, nestled in the lip of the spout.

She ate silently, chewing with neat little swallows. He did not eat at all, sipping his coffee and tapping his toast with his fork, glad at least that she had toasted it, for Jessica's bread was as expired as her marmite.

"I blame myself, you know," she said softly, finishing her coffee.

"For what?" Philip asked.

"Oh, I don't know," she said, tearing up. "For everything."

"It's her, isn't it?"

Jessica did not need to be told who *her* was. Her was Felicity. There were no substitutes, for Jessica Sinden was not one for shifting loyalties.

"I try not to think about her," said Jessica.

"You don't have to," said Philip. "Because she's always there, isn't she?"

"I don't talk about that."

"I know you don't," he said. "But maybe it's time."

Jessica took a deep breath, then stood up and went inside. Philip followed her into the kitchen. She opened a cabinet and took out a jar. She gripped the cap with the flat of her hand. This must have been one of the oldest unopened ones, a specimen five, maybe ten years old. But her hand kept slipping. The cap was gummed shut.

Philip hated that marmite. Poppy and Tristan and probably Felicity hated it too. It meant their mother was sealed shut. Philip tried looking

away from her, down at the cracks in the pink and green linoleum, but
then she handed it to him. Her hands were shaking and she was saying,

"Here. You open it. I can't."

He took it. It was not a jar of marmite, but something else she had
taken off the shelf. It was an old jar of Walkers English Plum Pudding.

"I have been saving it all these years," she said, adding, "Since that
Christmas Day."

———

Philip already knew about Christmas with the Sindens. He had seen
that picture of Poppy sitting on the floor in the living room next to the
Christmas tree, the wrapping paper torn open on her lap. The other pres-
ents were neatly stacked next to her. Her mother had just thrown away
the paper from the others, and she was reaching for the refuse from the
one she had just opened, the packaging for some doll. Poppy did not
care about the doll, which came tightly packed in a box the size of its
own coffin, and with that horrible white fluffy lining, too. She wanted
the paper. It was red and green and had bells on it. Everything in the
house was always so faded, even when it was new, except for that odd
reliquary. The paper was bright. Bright had been Felicity's middle name.
Felicity Bright Sinden. Jessica had been Jessica Bright. Poppy told Philip
her mother hated her maiden name. She once built a fire in the middle
of the summer to burn an old checkbook she had come across. The
top check was made out to Wycombe Abbey. The flames browned the
checks, singeing her name, *JESSICA BRIGHT SINDEN*, before they
crinkled into ash.

So Felicity had gone there, too. Or was to have gone there. Or was to
have gone there for the third time. Sitting in the living room, Jessica now
told him they had just had their final discussion about Wycombe Abbey.
They were in London for Christmas. "I went, you will go, and there is an
end to it." In many of their discussions they came close to arguing, but
they always stopped short. Felicity would simply not listen to reason. She
retreated into herself, drawing her napkin out on her nap and quartering
it neatly. Jessica worried that she might be thinking badly of her, so she

didn't press it. At least the question was out in the open. She was not about to drop it.

Felicity knew her mother had been unhappy at Wycombe. That she had hated the place. Her mother was not forthcoming about it. But Felicity had her own ideas as to why. All the walls there were painted white. The curtains were white too, and the floors had been sanded down to a kind of off-white. Her mother said the place hurt her eyes. Felicity knew about eyes hurting. When she was little she had a wandering eye and the doctors had to tighten the muscle behind it. Both her eyes were front and center now, but she squinted in the slightest sunlight. To shade them, Jessica made her wear bangs when she was little and let the bangs grow over her eyes. Her daughter never minded looking younger than she was because she liked looking at the world through a haze of hair.

The night they went—it would have been the first time Jessica visited there in years. But Felicity would have nothing of it.

"I didn't think you were serious," she told her mother. "I thought we were in England just for Christmas."

Jessica was *always* serious, so she said,

"I just want you to take a look at it."

"I don't mind looking," said Felicity, "as long as I don't have to go."

She had her there, Jessica thought with habitual honesty, but still she said, "Then it wouldn't be looking, would it?" Seeing her pick at her fingers, she added, "I want you to keep an open mind."

"What if I cut my finger?" Felicity asked. "Would I have to go?"

"*Felicity*," Jessica began with a sigh.

"I'd be cut," she said. "Bleeding."

"A minor thing like that would hardly get in our way," Jessica told her daughter. "You would have to know that."

"What if it wasn't minor?"

"I'm not going to listen to this," said Jessica. "You are going, you will see it, and even if you don't like what you see, you will learn to like it because you have to."

"What if I cut my finger off," said Felicity, "or threw myself out a window?"

Jessica confessed to Philip that, at the time, she only heard the first part, not the second. The threat was so exaggerated that it was not hard to dismiss. After all, Felicity was not even old enough to use the stove, nor even to light a match without her or Edward looking on. Besides, her daughter often said whatever came into her head on those nights when Jessica forced her to eat the shredded carrots in her salad, often relenting, though, when it came to the red-and-white radishes, so old coming out of the crisper they had begun to sprout. So Jessica worked for an hour or so in the garden, tying up winter orchids, then got ready to go. Edward was already in Hampstead, readying Christmas dinner with his mother and brother. He often went up there early to see them without her, sparing her any extended contact with them during these visits back from Hong Kong. His mother thought Jessica was shy, which was fine with her. Shyness was such good cover for scorn. Edward's family, last of this particular line of St. Johns, had dwindled to a low norm. A row house in Hampstead was a poor fate for a family that once been equerries to the King.

Jessica remembered the way Felicity hobbled her way out to the car through the snow, her coat blown open, her legs blue in the cold, a burst of red on both cheeks. She did not even tie her boots. Well, it did not matter. If she did not want to get out of the car she would at least drive her past it. In Fifth Form she and Judy and Sarah had shared a suite in Clarence House. She would show that to her first. It would give her something to aspire to while she was in the lower forms.

Finally underway, Felicity seemed a little light-headed in the car. Slumped in her seat, her high forehead perspiring in the close heat of the car, Felicity would not even look at her.

"Stop acting like this is a funeral," Jessica told her in the car. Her daughter shifted in her seat, putting herself in a half ball, one leg drawn up to her forehead.

"I have this taste in my mouth," said Felicity. "Maybe we can stop and I can spit it out or something."

Jessica shook her head before her daughter finished speaking, and she continued to shake it. She was trying to shake out of her head the very idea of her daughter spitting. Felicity took it as one of her mother's extended *nos*.

Jessica found herself driving faster than usual. She was beginning to think it might be wise to persuade Felicity to go to Wycombe Abbey. Her approach so far had been a bit like advertising, saying something, then repeating it again, then again and again, not changing it, but hoping it would sink in. Edward had gone up early because she was beginning this campaign with Felicity. *Your campaign against Felicity*, he called it, and perhaps it had gone on too long. He was in favor of letting her go to school back in China. Jessica was on the point of saying, Traffic is rather heavy dear. I would think we should postpone our visit to Wycombe Abbey, when she heard Felicity say, quietly,

"Maybe we should just go home."

"What did you say?"

I said, "*Maybe we should just turn around and go home.*" Adding, "To *Hong Kong*."

This was too much for Jessica.

"Felicity. Your grandmother will have been cooking all day. And your cousins are coming."

"I don't even know their names."

"Yes you do. There is Charles, the older one, and Pippa, which is short for—"

"Philippa," Felicity said sullenly.

"Yes, and—"

"You hate them, Mama. I know you hate them all."

What she said was so incontestably true that Jessica relaxed her head against the headrest. Yes. She hated them. She did not know why but she did.

"And I hate them, too," said Felicity.

"That," Jessica cautioned, "is no way to speak of your cousins."

"They just talk and talk," said Felicity. "And they never say anything."

Jessica was torn between agreeing with her and disapproving of what she said. Her hands gripped the wheel so tightly that her knuckles turned white.

"I don't know what you're talking about," she said finally, lowering her eyes.

"You hated it," she said.

The *it* was Wycombe Abbey. She never told her about the teasing, about her hands, about Judy's death. About the isolation that led her to achieve the highest marks in Sixth Form with nothing else to show for it but a room in Clarence House none of the other girls ever visited, a room covered with art prints from the V&A, including that Dali one showing the young woman folded over a wall like a garment.

She thought of trying to push her fingers through Felicity's. But Jessica did not like it when anyone tried to comfort her by touching her, and she supposed Felicity would not, either.

"They'll lock me in there, just like they did to you."

Jessica helplessly remembered the quilt folded at the foot of her bed at Wycombe. On cold days she used to cover her feet when she read. She would shut herself up in her room with her crackers and marmite, picking grains of salt off the crackers with the nail of her little finger. The world outside that door was cruel. Those girls were cruel. She could not even bring herself to remember the little ditty they made up about her. *Bones*, it began. *Bones*.

"They didn't lock me in," she told her daughter.

"That's not what I mean," said Felicity. "You don't understand what I mean."

"Wycombe Abbey is a good school," she said, wanting to say, *you know there are others*, but leaving it off because it conceded too much too soon.

"And you have to share a bathroom, Mama! You have to share a bathroom!"

"This isn't like you," Jessica said, still calm. "You share one with me. Only your father has his own, you know that."

"That's because it has a lock on it."

"Aren't you curious about—other girls?" Jessica asked her daughter, desperately trying another tack. "You might make a friend or two, you know."

"How many friends do you have?" Felicity shot back.

Jessica tightened her lips. "Friends enough, I think."

"No you don't. Your only friend was that dead girl, and that school killed her, just like it'll kill me—"

"How dare you—" began Jessica.

"I read those letters in your drawer. The ones she wrote to you when she was in hospital—"

"How—*dare*—you—"

But Felicity came back at her, almost shouting, "You hated it. Hated it more than anything else in the world. That girl said she hated it too. Why would you want me to go there? Why? Why—"

Then the door was open and Felicity slipped out into the darkness.

The opening was momentary and the closing was quick. The wind slammed it shut. She heard a muffled sound like a sack of potatoes bouncing, but she was not sure. The car continued on, her seat empty, but everything of hers just where it had been, her small duffle bag, her fuzzy mittens, a dark blue wool scarf.

Jessica could not believe it. At first she thought she might be in the back seat. It took her a moment to even begin to slow down. Her foot hesitated over the brake. She was trying to remember what she had seen. She had not seen it directly. She felt a coldness and had a feeling of Felicity leaning into something. Was it death? Had she really wanted to die? Or was it *her*? A feeling that anything, even a cold rolling fall onto a highway shoulder, was preferable to another moment with her? Jessica was angry. Why couldn't Felicity think of the moment, just before bed, when she always brought her a cup of tea with a couple of biscuits on a plate? That too was a moment with her. She often wondered why Felicity couldn't always be the girl under the blankets, quiet and beautiful and so unaware of her own beauty, pliably falling into a gentle sleep instead of the stubborn silent girl who, so often, suborned her will.

Jessica turned the car around and went back. Felicity was stretched out on her side along the shoulder, her long brown hair blocking her face. She didn't need to look at her long to know she wasn't dead. There was almost no bruising. Felicity had run away from home the year before, and when she returned, she had bruises on her face. But her face was clear and her mouth was open, she was breathing lightly but regularly, opening her eyes at her and blinking, and Jessica kept thinking of her saying,

But you have to share a bathroom, Mama. You have to share a bathroom!

There was a quarter moon. The snow was dark. A stubbled field ran into the blurred distance. A wind came up, blowing a spray of snow into Felicity's face. Jessica stooped to rub it off. Felicity was wearing a Christmas sweater with stars on her shoulders and reindeer on the front. Oh she looked so like a sleeping caroler, taking a break from a serenade, as though she only needed shake her shoulders to free them of the snow settling on them. Her body had come to rest against a foot-wide crack in the concrete. She couldn't have intended this. Not—death. Jessica understood wanting to escape from life. But wanting to escape into death? Had she really wanted to kill herself? Or had she wanted to just escape being in the car with her? Had it been a moment's whim? Or had it been deliberated? Could she even deliberate at that age? She must have told herself *something*.

'I knew her death was coming after that," she admitted to Philip. "I just didn't know *when*."

They stayed another week in England then went back to Hong Kong.

Jessica was quiet. Philip extended his fingers, lightly touching the bone between her breasts. Her bones, and all that was left of Felicity. She sensed in him a flurry of feelings like snow turning into sleet, a sadness melting over him that was partly hers, partly his, partly theirs. His eyes were a little wet. She couldn't remember the last time he cried, or if he ever had with her. She reached out and took his hand.

"Philip," she said, sighing with resignation. "I don't want you to go there."

'I know," he said. "I don't want to go there either."

There was the hospital.

"Would you want to take anything?"

"They'd take it away from me, you know. They even take off your rings."

"You only have the one."

"I want you to have it, though."

"Really? It seems so much a part of you."

"Otherwise Roma will take it, you know, if it comes to that."

If it comes to that. The image of Roma taking the ring off his body—where would it be, in a hospital room, a morgue, or out of a plastic bag of personal effects, slid to her across the counter of some crematorium—was almost too much for her to bear (though only almost, for she knew her own strength).

So she led him into the kitchen. With Hong Kong heating up in the springtime, the wedding ring on Philip's finger had swollen into place. She could barely turn it. Philip suggested she try butter or oil. But she knew a better way. Edward had a box of surgical masks in the kitchen closet. She took one out and cut off its elastic strap. Then she tied the strap just over the ring and under his knuckle. Pulling it tight, she wound it upwards toward the tip of his finger, which swelled to a light purple. Finishing her little tourniquet with a knot, she smiled, because it made his finger look like the foot of a ballerina dancing on pointe. So elegant, and so painful, slipping off the ring and putting it in the palm of his hand.

"Aren't you going to take that off, too?" he asked her, looking down at the little tourniquet she had wrapped around him.

"Not that I want to," she told him.

19

late april 2003

EARLY IN THE AFTERNOON a car drove up. A silver Mercedes. Two people were in it. Philip Nye could not see them but he could hear them. One got out.

Philip lay awake in the bedroom. Jessica had a sofa across from her bed and he avoided the bed during the day; he did not want their refuge to be a sick bed; he felt how much her bed had become *their* bed. The sounds in the next room made him feel helpless. He heard Simpson Kwan's voice. Why would he come here? Philip, unlike Jessica, suspected that they were never quite in their own world here in Hong Kong. They were not watched, but somehow, nevertheless, they were seen and noted. He heard Jessica moving cutlery in the kitchen. Then the pouring of tea. He wasn't a connoisseur of teas, but then again, neither was she. She was just going through the motions of something. Making noise just because, Poppy always said.

Philip undid a bib Jessica put around his neck to keep the blood off his shirt. If anyone did come in, she would not want them to see it on him.

Then he heard snatches of Simpson's voice from the next room.

You know how hard it would be for me to—

Then a rustling, then:

I'm sorry, Jessica, said the voice, but very firmly. *But there's nothing that can be done about it.*

Then a door opened and closed. Simpson was walking back to the Mercedes.

Philip heard steps in the hallway. He withdrew into himself, stifling an impulse to lay on his side, turning to the wall. He felt a tightness in his lungs. The disease, perhaps, but he felt he was going to be smothered. He tried to sit up higher to breathe. To his surprise, he drew in a breath so deep it seemed he would faint from inhalation. Inhaling was white, pure. Exhaling was red, dirty. He coughed, and wiped the blood on the bottom of his bib, folding it over so it could not be seen.

Jessica came in, saying nothing. She laid a blanket arund him and kissed his shoulder.

"Elaine wants to see you."

"I don't think that's such a good idea—"

"She has something to tell you, Philip."

"It's not worth the risk."

"She came all this way."

Philip considered, then said:

"Let her come to the door, then. I can stand behind it."

Jessica went out, shutting the door behind her. He leaned back against the door and closed his eyes. Then he began to tuck his shirt into his pants.

Philip heard more shuffling, then he sensed Elaine was behind it.

"Philip?" he heard.

"Yes. Elaine."

"I tried. You know I tried."

Philip expected she had. They had been left alone on the Peak for almost ten days. Jessica did not like to think about why, but Philip felt all along that Simpson Kwan was behind it, as he had been behind the inquest, keeping the forces of the outer world at bay.

"I wanted to tell you myself. I can't stop them coming for you any more."

He heard the *any more*, and thought what a problem it had been for them, Simpson and Elaine, to keep the authorities appeased for so long.

"I don't expect you can."

"But I can tell you what will happen when they do. When they come they will put you in a kind of white tent and carry you out. Then they will seal up the house with Jessica inside it. They will let me bring food to her: it was their only concession. I can leave it at the top of the road and she can can take it in once I'm gone. I don't even knew how long they'll let me do this for."

"Do they know the incubation period of the disease?"

"Edward said two weeks but he also said no one's really sure."

"What about my things?"

"They said Jessica should burn them in the fireplace. Anything you touched. Towels, blankets, and all your clothes."

Philip smiled weakly. Jessica's working fireplace; she used to be so proud of it!

"And I brought bleach. She'll have to scrub down the house herself."

Elaine paused.

"I had to scrub down mine too. All the maids—I don't know where they went."

"Tell Simpson—" Philip began, but started coughing.

The coughing went on long—much too long. Not any longer than he had been coughing before, but somehow, with Elaine and Jessica listening, the cough didn't seem to stop, and this time, what came out was not red but yellow and green.

"You don't have to speak," said Elaine. "Save your strength. I just want you to know—"

And here she broke off. Philip heard Jessica quietly crying next to her. Philip tried to imagine Elaine taking her hand, but she had never seen her touch her friend.

More shuffling.

"Philip?"

Jessica's voice.

"Elaine said they are here."

"Here? Now?"

Tears in her eyes, Jessica couldn't think of what to say so she said nothing, finding herself thinking instead about what clothes to pack for Philip while he was in the hospital. She felt her instinctive neatness returning. She would line things up for him and put them in a small suitcase. Some azaleas, too, from her garden, could go in there, too, if they let her—

"Yes. At the top of the road."

Then it came in a blur.

The men in the white suits walked very fast into the house. They passed Jessica but didn't seem to see her. Philip was trembling behind the door. He was very thin. He hardly ate any more, only drank. He would just sit and look at the May mists that sat on the Peak and stare longingly at the sky. She knew he felt afraid. The men seemed to know it too. They talked to him in slow voices. He tried to twist his head away from them but his neck was stiff. She wondered how sharp his awareness was. Because she was always with him it was easy to think he was still the same old Philip. But he wasn't. He responded to the men in delayed, staggered motion. It was as though he was drunk with the disease.

She watched as they packed him up. He couldn't just be taken out. They slipped a mask over his face. A really thick one. He tried to say something to her but the mask muffled his voice. They took out a large plastic bag and for a sharp second she thought they were going to put him in it. But no: it was for his watch and his wallet and some clothes. Jessica was glad she had his ring. She noticed they took nothing that was porous. Did clothes carry the disease? The papers spoke of a second smallpox. She would have to burn everything he touched. She started making making a mental inventory: the curtains, the throw on the sofa, the lamp on his side of the bed. There was so much; it would be like trying to wipe Poppy's dirty fingerprints off everything.

Then she caught herself: Philip was still here. She was thinking of him as already gone, but he was still there.

But he was layers away from her now. They did not put him in one of those white padded suits they were wearing but wrapped him with some kind of crackly white textile that rustled like newspaper. They were very nice to him. They called him Mr. Nye. She heard them telling them what they were going to do to him just before they did it. *This is a bundle. It will feel a little warm.* Then they handed him a brown liquid in a paper cup. *It is bitter tasting.* He drank it quietly. She wondered if he was thinking about the hospital. Sometimes he could see things in advance of seeing them and know what they were going to be like. But somehow he never thought about events themselves. He just knew what the future was going to *feel* like.

Bundled in white, Philip turned the light off next to him, then touched the door to her bedroom, closing it quietly. He lingered there staring at Jessica, still in the hallway. The men stood a little off.

His gaze was a fixative. They had said their goodbyes.

"Jessica?" she heard.

Elaine again, from near the door. She was still here. She did not know how much later it was. Jessica had forgotten about her.

"I can stay here a little longer if you like."

Jessica said nothing; *likes* and *not-likes* meant nothing to her now.

"You know you can't leave the property," Elaine continued. "But it's okay for you to go to the top of the road. I'll leave your meals there around five o'clock." She paused. "Gilles from Riposte on Arbuthnot Road volunteered to cook for you. He asked for a list of your favorite dishes. I really didn't have the heart to tell him that you're like me, that you eat only out of a sense of obligation. But I had to tell him something. So I told him you liked shark's fin soup."

Jessica tried to smile, but her friend might have been a thousand miles away. Philip was gone.

20

may 2003

DR. SINDEN, quite decently, though as inscrutably as ever, working the whole time from Foshan, did everything he could to get his wife in to see Philip Nye. The answer was always no. The protocols were strict, stricter in May than they had been in April. Jessica appreciated strictness but was willing to take the risk. They could put her in the hospital afterwards for all she cared, monitoring her with everything they had. But one more body incubating the disease was one too many for the authorities. The Chinese doctors were very polite. Dr. Sinden was welcome to continue his valuable work at the First Peoples Hospital, but they would appreciate it if he would cease his queries. Even the British Counsel, a friend, said as much to him over the phone.

Jessica expected no less. She had respect for a hard and fast keeping to rules. It was what had kept her alive all these years, wasn't it, and she supposed that other people, being what they were, probably could not do without their own little systems of rules. Never mind how arbitrary they sometimes turned out to be. They were little tropical islands of order. Edward had to abide by hospital procedures all these years, didn't he, and he never complained. The Second World War had been like that. Everybody had pitched in. Reading about it as a girl, she was often sorry she had missed it. She would have had the presence of mind to defuse bombs wedged in the tight, dark corners of London basements. Others might balk at the task, but Jessica's hands would be steady.

And yet, and yet! They were sometimes less steady than she supposed. She found herself running over conversations with Philip, recalling them, not with satisfaction, as she usually did, but with doubt verging on regret.

"It seems that whenever I call you," she said to him one time, "you're asleep."

"Hmh," he said vaguely. "Yes. Often."

"I didn't know this about you. That you sleep all the time."

"Well," he said laughing, "not all the time."

"Aren't you afraid of missing something?"

"No," he said, pushing his fingers through hers. "I'm more afraid of not missing something."

"I'm afraid I don't understand," she said pointedly, sweeping her bangs back from her face in a way that reminded him of Roma.

"Why not?" he asked.

"I fall asleep fighting it," said Jessica. "I dislike acquiescence. There seems to be no will in it."

"There isn't," said Philip. "It's just a kind of play."

Jessica frowned. *Play* was one word she was sure she did not like. Playing, nearly all the other girls detested her as a child. They had tiny hands and little feet. She had large hands, a high bony forehead, and thin pale cheeks. Her hands always seemed moist to her. She hated sitting down to tea as a school girl at Wycombe Abbey. She dreaded her turn pouring from the Brown Betty. They laughed at her hands. Even when they weren't laughing she felt them wanting to. She used to wonder, Is there anywhere on earth where there are no people? And that nickname they gave her. Bones! Oh, God.

> *Bones, bones,*
> *She's all bones,*
> *Not a grave*
> *Where she's not at home.*

She learned to hold her lips tightly while they teased her. She had one friend in those years, Judy Royce-Chapman. But she died of the meningitis she herself barely survived. After that she really was alone, except for Judy's grave on a Sussex down, which she visited on weekends. Her own Felicity was buried there now, two or three rows down. Jessica liked to think that Judy was now a second mother to her, for she imagined that Judy, though dead at fourteen, had somehow aged alongside her, looking in on her from time to time.

Perhaps Philip would rather like being in the hospital. Perhaps he could sleep freely there. She often had a feeling about him that, everything being equal, he would really rather be asleep. Perhaps, not much liking the world—who knew why, perhaps its general ugliness (nearly every building on the Peak), or perhaps the general low average of its denizens (her Tristan), he prolonged his sleep to cover as much of the day as possible with a shroud. It was an odd exercise of will, and it had to have been characteristic of all the Nyes. They had, after all, willed themselves to sleep during the Revolutionary War, and again during the Civil War. She wondered what the waking up had been like for them. He was from that very place, perhaps the same bend on the same river, where that man in the story by Washington Irving fell asleep and woke up to find that everything had changed. He had a funny name. Rip Van Winkle. What was Rip? R.I.P., rest in peace, quite possibly. The Nyes were always resting. She tried to remember the line he had quoted her from the story. *He was one of those mortals who took the world easy.* Yes, that was it, Philip's undoing was taking the world easy. He lacked the thing all the Nyes lacked. A will to live—no—a will to *risk* living as fully as he might have. She knew he considered himself a failure. He never excused it in himself by blaming his agoraphobia. She had often wanted to ask him about it, but it was too closely held a flaw, like a birth defect that could never be mentioned. She was sure he would answer her if she asked, but he would not want to be asked. She was sorry to have even touched on it.

She checked the clock in the living room. So little time had passed since last she checked.

This was not going to be easy. Nothing ever was, of course, but waiting gave one so little latitude to be busy. Jessica went outside to her little garden. Her trees seemed dry. So she started snapping off branch after branch, collecting them in little bundles until, looking up, she realized she had completely denuded several trees of their branches. They looked like dried-out Christmas trees. One Christmas, then another, then another, all gone awry. It was true. Though she certainly did not know about Felicity, Poppy never let her forget all the wrong things she did every Christmas. The cheap gifts. Fires even on hot days. The family made to sing those cloying carols. Why was she sentimental only about this one thing? Oh, but the holiday gave that girl such license to say whatever she wanted, and she brazenly took full advantage of it, knowing, somehow, that her mother would let it pass, at least at that one moment. Any of her mother's little punishments would have to wait until after the New Year. Poppy never thought that far ahead.

The phone rang. Jessica flinched. Whoever it was, Edward, Elaine, or Aspidistra, who seemed, quite remarkably, to take to her, she tried to get off the line as quickly as possible so as to return to her garden.

And still the girls circled her.

> *Bones, bones,*
> *She's all bones,*
> *Not a grave*
> *Where she's not at home.*

Putting down the receiver, Jessica gripped the edge of her dining room table.

Edward had been kind on the phone from China, though he knew almost nothing. Philip Nye might have died yesterday. Or it might have been the day before. The authorities were not very forthcoming. Some army trucks from the base at Central Barracks had been seen parked along Pok Fu Lam Road. The only volunteers they were taking for duty in the isolation ward at Queen Mary were single men and women. Older staff with family were being sent home. That young doctor he knew in Foshan had also died at about the same time, and not in March, as had been reported. Edward said his wife could find out nothing other than that the doctor who had treated him was also sick, too. He was sorry. They were all in the same boat, it seemed.

But Jessica had no consciousness of other people, other deaths. Just herself and her one death. One death was more than all the deaths in the world. And yet, in all this plague, she had not seen any bodies. Not even one. Not even, now, Philip's. Men padded in white took him away to Queen Mary. All this death, and still no dead. Nothing definite marked it. Would they stack and burn them as they did in the Middle Ages? She surveyed the other buildings on the Peak. No signs of life in them. A few palms drooped over their roofs. Maybe there were people in there. Or maybe the people on the mountain were so rich they had expected their servants to die for them. Mina first; that would be very much like the Peak. Elaine Kwan used to joke about what would happen to them up there if a tidal wave ever hit Hong Kong. Nothing, she said. No wave would dare touch them. But still, it would be very interesting to watch the world below them disappearing, if only from a distance.

She needed to talk to her now. Edward said he was supposedly free to leave, but that he was under quarantine in Foshan and really had no idea when they would let him come home. But she had a hard time calling Elaine. The signal was weak. Parts of the system were down, but, turning on the computer, she read that no one knew which parts or where.

Her best chance was at the top of Mount Kellett. Going out along a path from her garden, Bovary, leashless, leading the way, she made her way through the trees, past an area of general dereliction below the concrete retaining walls behind them, full of old tires, bits and pieces of worn clothing, lengths of rusted iron, and plastic barrels full of sticks and dirt, to a little clearing where four or five paths led into the woods. Then she realized she was still in her underwear. Picking around, she found an odd piece of cloth, a batik of some sort, and wrapped it around her hips. Then she took the path that promised the most elevation.

The path went from house to house, right up to them, not around them, the way they would back in England. It reminded Jessica of very old

houses, where there were no hallways and you had to go through every
room to get from one side of the house to the other. She crept around
the tiled boxy mansions as best she could. They were dark and she could
just barely see in. Thankfully most of them seemed to be empty. Their
occupants had fled the country, to safe havens, though she did not know
how they could be certain that they weren't carrying the disease with
them. Maybe they were all dead now, too.

Then she heard a noise in one of them, a sort of creaking swivel. She
stopped at a sill, just to make sure. She looked in. And there she was—
Felicity! Her Felicity, dead these many years! Felicity stood in the middle
of the room under a turning fan. She seemed to Jessica to be swaying
a little, but in small circles timed with the fan. She wore a long cotton
dress. She was older than she was when she died, her hair very long and
a little less blonde, but that alone wouldn't account for the cut of the
dress, which fell below her feet and wound around them in a coil. She
was not looking at Jessica with her gray eyes. Jessica was not sure she was
looking at anything. Her expression was flat and unseeing. She tapped
her fingertips on her thigh. She never did that. Perhaps she was not
tapping them nervously but touching herself to see if she was there, but
the moment Jessica had this thought, the thought of her not being there,
she blinked and then Felicity wasn't. The room was empty and the fan
was spinning overhead as though to humor it in its emptiness.

Everyone has weaknesses, Jessica said out loud to herself, touching the
frame of the window to steady herself. Jessica had loved Felicity more
than any of her other children. And she would never see her ghost again—
until, perhaps, she would see Philip's. Perhaps now he was standing
somewhere under some fan, expressionless, too, with the gray eyes she
supposed all the dead had, for Felicity's had been green, like hers.

Jessica picked up Bovary and continued walking. Looking back, she
could see nothing of the rest of the Peak, let alone the coast some ways
below it. Bovary breathed lightly on her shoulder. The dog seemed less
disoriented than she was. Perhaps she knew her way around from all her
walks. She wished she could talk to her. She was a small dog in a big

world. She would have to have an instinct for how large and dangerous it was. She wondered if Bovary remembered the cobra. She had no leash with her. Bovary balanced herself contentedly on her shoulder, gripping her with just enough bite to stay in place, but not enough to hurt her. She was a companionable dog, though she took care not to turn and look her in the eyes. Animals disliked staring as much as she did.

The top of the hill was crowded. A lot of maids had gone up there. So this was where they met! She hadn't the remotest idea. They sat packed in small groups near the top, wearing gaudy branded clothing, cheap Chinese copies of famous brands with the names stamped on them in big letters, *FENDI, MASSIMO DUTTI, RALPH LAUREN.* Some of the maids looked at her as though they had seen a ghost. Well, she had, even though in some way Felicity had always been her familiar. Others stared at Bovary. *These whites and their animals,* she could see them thinking. *They care about them more than us.* There were no other whites there. They must not have known where their maids were, or even cared. Most were probably out of the country by now. She was glad the maids had each other. Mina this, Mina that, she heard them say in Tagalog, knowing perfectly well who she was, even though Jessica barely recognized the small brown faces she had seen almost daily around her for years. Most of them, unless they had animals to walk, had little idea where they were outside the gates of their employers' homes. The few who made it up here must have found that they were completely on their own. Again she was glad they had each other, and tried to smile at them, but they would not meet her eyes.

She turned around. She expected to see some kind of devastation, but at this distance, Hong Kong was just as it was. The coastline was a placid line of green fringed with steady blue water, lapping peaceably. A few of the high trees loomed a bit more crooked than usual, but she had always been struck by the high stooping trees of the Peak. So very ungothic, Philip might have said. He was so recently dead that it was easy to imagine him there with her now, not as Felicity had been, turning in a still circle, but next to her, talking to her. He would be alive to all the little details that were passing her by, and for his sake she pressed herself to try and see them, the light bending through the trees, the damp bark, the light trilling of the insects, pitched, he might have said, a little higher than those back home.

She took out her phone. The signal was weak but there was some signal. Elaine she still could not reach. So she tried the Benning's land line, thinking the connection might be stronger.

She got Tristan. Jessica always sighed when she got Tristan. He was inevitably vague. But when he picked up she found she could say nothing.

"Mother?"

Still Jessica said nothing.

"Is that you, Mother?"

"I should say so," she said.

"Are you all right?"

The last bit was lost in the chortling of Jill Benning's high-pitched laughter. "I'll tell you all about it when I get back!" she was saying excitedly. Jessica could also make out Aspidistra's somewhat lower voice, saying to her, "Mummy if you're going out could you buy me a pint of vanilla ice cream? You know, the kind with the pink swirls in it—"

"Pardon me?" asked Jessica over the din.

"I said," asked Tristan, "Are you all right?

"The flat is in good order. There have been no burglaries, as I feared."

"Well, at least that's a blessing," he said. "But are you all right?"

"Your father is still in China," said his mother, almost speaking over him. "He was invited to remain."

"Invited? Well," sighed Tristan, giving a little laugh, "I can't imagine he was in any position to refuse the invitation."

"Tristan," she said sternly, "this is no time for frivolity."

Tristan felt the heaviness of life with his mother returning in full force. Jill Benning might often sound to him like a greeting card, but she was really quite convivial.

"That's not what I mean," he tried to say, but weakly. "I mean, What about you, personally?"

"That is not why I am calling," she said. "I called to find out what I needed to know, and now that I have found out, we can get off the phone."

Tristan had no idea what that might be, but he knew from hard-won experience not to try to plumb his mother's intentions. Her voice was never soft with concern. Hard with concern was more like it, and though he felt her voice was slightly off, he said nothing, for Poppy was at his side, waving a package of needles at him.

"Oh, and there's one other thing, Mother, before you go. Poppy said she has a package of acupuncture supplies waiting for her at home. She ordered them some time ago, before she talked to you. I think she is afraid you might see them and send them back. What shall I tell her?"

"Do we really need to talk about it now?"

"No," he said. "But Poppy is here. She wants to say something to you."

"I don't want to talk to her, Tristan."

"I'll put her on."

"*Tristan.*"

But the receiver was already down. She heard the microphone scratching. Then Poppy picked up.

"Mama I'm sorry I didn't tell you about—"

"I don't want to hear about it," said Jessica.

"What?"

"I said, I don't want to hear about it. Now hand the phone back to Tristan."

"I hope this won't—"

"*Poppy.*"

She heard some scraping, then some voices, then Tristan was back on the line.

"Poppy's very upset, Mother. She thinks you won't let her go to that school."

"Tell her she doesn't need my permission."

Now it was Tristan's turn to be surprised. "She doesn't?"

"Just tell her to expect a package from the Peak. That is, if the mails are still functioning properly." She heard sniffles in the background. Poppy was crying. "Tell her she picked the wrong time to talk to me," she added.

"When can we come back?" asked Tristan.

"That depends on your father. I'll let you know."

"Do you at least have some idea?"

"Tristan. I hope you have become worldly enough to see that some things do not depend on my mere willing of them. You can return when you can return. That is all there is to be said right now."

"What does Father say?"

"I don't know yet!" she said sharply, and left it at that.

That had not gone well. If she had intended to derive some comfort by calling Discovery Bay, to take the measure of something, her intention misfired. Well, intentions so often did. Philip, after all, had been so unintended, so unwilled by her. It was what had given him such freshness. An image of him lingered. They were in bed. He was gently circling the rim of her navel with his little finger, and she was smiling with half-shut eyes, her small thighs closed around one of his legs, thinking how strange it had been that she had gone through most of her life without knowing what this was like, this thrilling of her body, this feeling of sex. She had such a sense of life beginning again. But now—

Philip was dead. The flat was empty when she got back. His ring was in a drawer somewhere. She tried eating a dried pear but couldn't. There was a drop of sweat at the end of her nose. She hardly had the energy to wipe it off. So she went back to bed and, pulling pillows around her, tried to close her eyes. Philip, Philip, she said, pressing her cheek into her pillow. She could barely breathe.

—

Mina went out back. Mum Sinden's little side garden was dark. She never put lights there. She would just go out in the middle of the night and sit in the dark. She had to go though the back door, past the wood pile and the door to Mina's little room. Her room was so small that Mina kept the door open. So when Mum passed through the mudroom, she always heard her. Her steps were quiet, but there was sand on the concrete. She heard the crunching.

Mum would often be out back for hours at a time. On moonless nights, Mina would lift her head in bed, her ear turned to the mudroom, listening for her sandy steps. Mum liked the dark. She once made Mina put up blackout blinds in her bedroom to keep out the light. *They're always bombing us outside,* you know, she would say. Mina did not know what that meant until she said it again when Tristan was there. He told his mother Hong Kong wasn't London during the Blitz. But she shook her head. She said, *You just don't know what I mean.*

Mina did not know what the Blitz was. So she asked some other maids one Sunday at their prayer meeting on top of Mount Kellett. Fanny from Vivian Court, where her friend Mr. Nye used to live before they took him away, said the English fought a big war with the Germans while they were fighting their own war with the Japanese in the Philippines. Mina did not know much about that part of the war. Fanny said that when the Germans bombed London people had to put black shades over their windows so the Germans could not see in. Mum Sinden must have been bombed pretty badly when she lived in London.

That night Mum stayed out longer that usual. Mina heard sounds from the garden, the creak of a lid being opened and the rattle of tools. Then she heard Mum move out from the garden into the yard. It was quiet for a little bit but then she heard heavy breathing. Then small sobs. Then tiny cries. They started then stopped quickly.

Mina slipped on her robe. Her door was open. The mudroom was dark. She had to put a key in the metal door to open it, even from the inside. Mina winced at the scratching sounds the key made. Even the tumblers seemed loud and tinny.

Then she walked to the side of the building. Mum's garden and fountain and a few of her orchids was there. A little lawn spread out, leading to a row of cotton trees. Just under one of those trees Mum Sinden was lying on her side. Next to her were some chunks of sod, a pile of dirt, and a trowel.

Mum had been digging a hole. She wore a white nightgown. The nightgown was long like a wedding dress. She was curled around something.

Mina went up to her.

Seeing her, Mum Sinden almost jumped.

"Mina?"

"Mum?"

"Well!"

"I came out, Mum, because I heard you trying to open the toolbox."

"Yes. I was trying to find the key."

"Do you want me to bring a light out? For your gardening, I mean."

"I—wasn't gardening."

She pressed a piece of clothing into a dirty paper bag.

"Did you lose something?"

Mum Sinden said nothing.

"Oh, if it's dirty laundry I can add it to the wash."

Mum Sinden blinked at her, then said:

"It can't be washed away, Mina."

Fanny once told her the Sindens wanted to move but couldn't because nobody would buy a house where there had been a hanging. That was was Fanny called it, a hanging. Mina knew Mum Sinden had a daughter named Felicity who killed herself. Maybe it had been in this house. She wondered which room. Fanny said they took her to England afterwards. Fanny also said she would ask her employer when she got back if she would hire her if Mina was afraid to go back into the house.

But Mina was not afraid for herself. Father Ramos from St. Joseph's said that suicides went to hell.

Poor Mum! She always tried to remember that when Mum Sinden was cold with her. Maybe she was trying to throw cold water on the flames.

Mum turned to her.

"I don't want you to stay."

Mina flinched with fear. Was she being let go?

She worried about her little house back on Luzon. She was building it on a dirt road that led north to Dagupan. The road was lined for stretches with unfinished houses like hers, mostly grayish unpainted frames with many half-open rooms and canvas partitions. It would take two or three more contracts to finish it.

And what about her sister and brother? She gave Inez a U.S. dollar a week to go into town and buy those purple sweet potatoes she liked. And she was always lending money to Ramon, who was a young man now and needed nice clothes to sit for exams to go the Ateneo de Manila at Quezon City.

She tried to compose herself. "Pardon, Mum?"

"I mean, I just need to be alone for a while. Your friend, what is her name—"

"Fanny."

"Yes, Fanny. Can you stay with Fanny?"

"I think so, Mum. Her employers are back in California. She has a big flat."

"Take a week, no, a month. "

She saw Mina's worried face.

"Don't worry. I'm not letting you go. I will still honor your contract."

"Yes, Mum."

"Take everything you need. Use the extra suitcases in the mudroom. But don't come back down. I'll call you when I'm ready."

She raised her eyes to Mina for the first time.

"Do you understand, Mina?"

"Yes, Mum."

"Good. And one more thing. There is about three thousand dollars Hong Kong in a tray under the cutlery drawer. Take that. It should be—adequate."

"Yes. Mum."

Mina moved off.

And then Mum Sinden went back to her sweater. She held it very close to her head like a pillow.

21

late may 2003

ASPIDISTRA made her way through the underbrush to the back door of the Sinden flat. She tried not to make too much noise. Jessica probably thought she was still in Discovery Bay with Tristan and her mother. Jessica could get jumpy if she were surprised. But she had to be there. Tristan said Philip was dead and his mother was up here alone. Dr. Sinden was still in China. Elaine Kwan warned Tristan over the phone not to go near the Sinden flat, that his mother might have the virus. Aspidistra wondered why she had not been taken away, as Philip had been, but then she remembered what Elaine Kwan was capable of doing. She and her husband Simpson had probably been keeping the authorities off from Jessica, but just barely. She might be living in there, she might be dying, or she might be in some state in between. Aspidistra was determined to find out.

The Peak Tram was not running, so, reaching Central after getting off the ferry from Discovery Bay, she walked up to the Helena May and circled out back, to where the tracks began their long slope up to the Peak. Nobody could see her here but it was delicate walking. The spacing of the ties was so unlike her natural stride that she kept stumbling over them. She quickly dropped into the rut of the roadbed if she heard anything at all, a voice, a car, a thump. Above May Road it was pretty empty. The police were looking for people hiding out in the parks because they were afraid of being taken to the hospitals, where everyone seemed to die. If

Jessica was taken there she would die, too. Aspidistra had worked as a nurse in Vancouver and seen people die from drug-resistant TB. Most people couldn't bear seeing themselves hooked up to tubes in sterile white rooms. It made them *want* to die. If Jessica had the virus, Aspidistra was determined to keep her there on the Peak for as long as she could.

She left a note for Tristan telling him where she was going, knowing that he was enough of a sheep not to follow her. She might love him with all her heart, but she also knew he liked spending time with her only because he didn't like being alone. Her mother and Poppy would keep him busy enough, and if he showed them her note, they would make sure he didn't leave the flat.

Mount Kellett Road had roadblocks on both ends. Aspidistra kept to the underbrush. Reaching the house, she passed through Jessica's little garden. It seemed neglected, the grass uncut, the vines a little long, the surface of the small fountain covered with a film of moss.

The flat had an open back area where Mina lived and wood was stored. Mina's door was ajar and her light was off.

Aspidistra entered through the kitchen. Jessica was not in the living room. The long hallway was dark and disappeared into bedrooms and a staircase. Aspidistra kept the light off. One hand flat on the wall, she moved slowly from door to door. Poppy's room, piled with clothes. Tristan's room, full of unfinished projects, models, drawings and mock-ups with cardboard and balsa wood. Felicity's old room, always locked, so she made no effort to budge the door. And the end of the hallway, the bedroom of the Sindens.

Aspidistra was breathing lightly. Her heart was beating rapidly. She heard every creak under the carpet. With each sound, she would pause, listening for evidence that she had been heard. Nothing. Then she moved on until she reached the last bedroom door, which was a little ajar.

She paused and listened just behind the door. Then she went in. The bed was empty. She heard dank intermittent breathing. So she checked the other side of the bed.

Jessica was sleeping on the floor. She opened her eyes and let out a low moan. It must have been hard for her to do even that. Her lungs seemed to sink into her chest.

Aspidistra tried to take her in. Her neck had swollen a little. Her lips were a little plump too, and reddened—but no, that was not lipstick but a dab of blood.

One arm was around her pillow. Her left leg was straight and tangled in a sheet, her right leg bent at the knee. Her hair was short but matted with sweat.

She tried to smile, rubbing her foot against the back of the sheet.

"You don't have to talk," Aspidistra said, scanning the room. No plates or glasses.

"When was they last time you had something to eat or drink?"

It took some time for Jessica to say, so softly Aspidistra could barely hear her, "I—I don't know. It's so hot in here."

Aspidistra went into the bathroom and found a thermometer in the medicine cabinet and put it in her mouth. Jessica's green eyes flashed at her with gratitude, but really, it might have been just confusion.

"Where is Philip?" she asked.

"Don't talk," said Aspidistra. "Save your strength."

"I don't want to—please don't—"

"Don't worry. I'm not going to call anyone. And you're not going to the hospital. It's just going to be the two of us."

"But you—what if you—"

"Never mind me. Whatever it is, oh, I'll fight it off." Adding, "I'm a fighter, you know." Aspidistra leaned over her. "Is the floor too hard?"

Jessica had no answer. It came to Aspidistra that she did not even know she was on the floor.

"Okay, then."

And so she took Jessica Sinden, mother of Tristan and Poppy, wife of Edward and keeper of Felicity, all in her arms and, standing up, held her for a moment. She was thin but heavy, as though her lungs were shriveling up and losing their buoyancy, leaving only her bones.

Jessica let out a low moan as she came out of her half-sleep.

"Aspidistra!" she exclaimed, fully recognizing her at last.

"Yes. It's me."

"Where's Tristan?"

"He won't be coming."

"You mean you won't let him."

Aspidistra smiled; still sharp as ever.

"Don't talk," she said again, placing Jessica on the bed and propping up her torso with some pillows.

Then Jessica closed her eyes again.

Aspidistra used the quiet interval to get everything ready. Philip probably had a heavier dose of the virus. It was just possible he had already begun to develop antibodies by the time he gave it to Jessica. It gave her at least a fighting chance. Jessica certainly was having trouble breathing, but it was only a light raspiness so far, and though she had blood on her lips, there was very little blood in her mouth.

The virus won't kill us, thought Aspidistra, tightening her hands around the bunched edges of the sheets as she tidied up Jessica's bed. I won't let it.

———

Aspidistra contracted it, too, but it seemed to pass through her rapidly while it was passing out of Jessica slowly.

She didn't do anything special. She tended to Jessica. She made her drink four glasses of water a day, then five, then six, then seven. She fed her crackers and ginger ale. She put cold compresses on her. And she changed her clothes three times the day her fever broke.

It was then she saw the scars on her back. Unlike Philip, Aspidistra knew perfectly well what they were. Her eyes met Jessica's. She seemed grateful that Aspidistra said nothing about them.

Then Jessica began her long recovery, while Aspidistra found herself square in the middle of the Sinden household. She tried to add up everything that she saw. Jessica, Edward, Felicity, Poppy and Tristan, and now her. She began with Felicity. She was the unspoken presence in the house. The books on the shelves she had read (and only she would read!). The years of her childhood, which seemed to add old prints to the walls (a lot of them were from old numbers of the *Illustrated London News* Felicity had rifled through, looking for anything faintly medieval but really it all looked Victorian to Aspidistra). And then, last of all, every single bit of bric-a-brac in the house, the brocaded napkins, the candlesticks taken from some old church, and the faded samplers pinned up behind glass on the walls (THIS IS *FELICITY* HER WORK BORN APRIL 2, 1845)—and underneath a little poem, stitched in red:

> *This I have done*
> *To let you see*
> *What care my mother*
> *Took of me.*

Aspidistra did not know if it was it old or if it was just trying to look old. Had Felicity sewn it, or was there a Felicity born somewhere on April 2, 1845?

Jessica spoke haltingly about Felicity. But Aspidistra also saw how determined she was to hold nothing back. And the stories she told were so open-ended that they only seemed to lead into other stories. *She wasn't religious. She didn't like singing or praying. She liked concentrating on things. She also liked holding her breath. I'd ask her why and she'd say, Leave me alone, Mama, I'm practicing.* Practicing for what? Aspidistra wanted to ask, but by then Jessica had moved on to something else. Aspidistra never pressed her for the meaning. She actually felt relieved when Jessica would approach one mystery, give up on it, then move on to another. There just seemed to be so many things she didn't understand about her daughter, things she took for granted when she was alive, but which ate away at her endlessly after she was dead. Aspidistra felt she wasn't clever enough to put any of this together to help her, even though, after all, that was what she was always trying to do, to help her mother, to help Tristan, and now to help Tristan's mother—but that want of cleverness didn't seem to bother Jessica.

"Philip could listen, too, just like you," Jessica sometimes told her.

Aspidistra smiled gently. If she had to choose between speaking and listening, she would choose listening every time. She became a nurse, not because she cared for medicine, but because patients talked to nurses. Sick people let their guard down. She was used to her mother's openness, as bad as it was, with her emotions running down and spinning awkwardly like a top until it tumbled over the edge of a table. Her nickname as a girl had been *Toppy*. Over the years she came to know basically everything her mother was worried about, her brittle hair, her sagging breasts, her body that wanted to be fat, the second child she would never have, and above all, the money from the divorce that her deadbeat father never sent her, prompting a move to Hong Kong, where everyone said people were rolling in money.

But Jessica had one thing that her mother never had: a curiosity about *her*.

Jessica was slow about it. She began by telling her how she missed seeing everything in her life while it was actually going on. At first Aspidistra thought this was a kind of regret, but it was more than that. Jessica was determined not to miss anything that was square in front of her. So as soon as she began to get a little better, she began to ask Aspidistra about her own life.

Aspidistra had never been asked. Her mother shared her life but never asked about it. Tristan seemed to learn to recognize certain recurring details, that was all. But Jessica wanted to know what she was feeling. It did not occur to her then that Jessica was herself only learning how to want to know what somebody else was feeling, and she did not know until later how much this had to do with Philip Nye. But she asked, and kept asking in that grimly determined way she had when she had fixed her mind on some end or aim. She did not want to hear mere stories.

Long stories bored her the way they bored Tristan. No, she wanted to know only one thing:

Why Aspidistra was *happy*.

Aspidistra genuinely did not know. She lived in a kind of cloud of content. Jessica sensed that too, saying, *You always seem to have extra oxygen*, as though she believed the lungs were the seat of happiness.

But Aspidistra could only say, "I don't know. But I know I'm happy here with you."

"I don't think I'll ever be happy," Jessica confessed.

But Aspidistra also saw how, saying that, she pulled herself closer to her in bed. They never quite touched, but they slept together now. Perhaps happiness was hearing someone breathe. Lungs again: the SARS passing out of Jessica's chest made her breath audible again. Aspidistra knew Jessica was getting better when she started to hear her snore. She loved snores. They were so helpless and ugly, like little tadpoles flipping in the back of your throat. Or one of those flags flapping in the breeze. Jessica was sleeping now, but when she woke she would have to make sure to tell her she got her name not because of a plant with purple flowers, but because of a flag in a book by George Orwell. Aspidistra never read the book, *Keep the Aspidistra Flying*, but before she was born her father had a copy, and she had it from her mother how it was about a flag rather than a plant. Or maybe it was a plant rather than a flag. With her mother you never knew.

Oddly enough, it turned out Jessica knew for sure it was about a plant. Doubly odd, because Aspidistra already knew how suspicious Jessica Sinden was of reading.

⁓

Only after Jessica started to snore—why that was the line, and not another, Aspidistra did not know, but there it was—was she finally able to talk about herself, and not Felicity. And then she seemed to talk about everything at once. Her father, those days in Hyde Park, her fear of the Bible and of reading, her time at Wyncote Abbey, *Bones, bones, she's all bones*, Judy's death, her meningitis (but never her scars, though once, raising her top to just under her chin, she turned around and asked Aspidistra to put her hands on them and hold them steadily there for a few minutes, keeping up a steady light pressure), Edward when she first met him, their wedding, the birth of Felicity and their leaving for Hong Kong on BOAC in 1976. And then there were the children when they were young and she was nursing them, lactating madly, as she put it. Nor did she neglect to tell Aspidistra about the little treasures of their childhood she kept stored under the staircase.

And then there was her. The physical fact of Jessica Sinden. It was not something she talked easily about. But Aspidistra slept next to her, and was her nurse. So she confessed to her what only Philip knew: that she was a creature of the senses. It was why she covered herself so completely. Jessica liked the feeling of being insulated from the world, and felt that, if only once she felt the tease of the sun on her skin, she would never put on clothes again. The very follicles of the light brown hair on her arms seemed to rise, yearning, toward the sun when she rolled up her sleeves to garden in her side yard. She never wore sunscreen because she liked to savor the light tingling of the burn afterwards.

"I love it," said Aspidistra. "Have you tried—just taking it all off?"

"Whatever do you mean?"

"Just not wearing clothes."

"Really?"

"It's easy. Look."

In a quick second Aspidistra snapped off her top and slipped out of her pajama bottoms, or rather, Tristan's.

She put her arms over her head. There was a little light hair in her armpits. Her legs were long and her breasts were adolescent.

"You can ask me about things, too," she heard Aspidistra say.

"I can?"

"Like this scar under my arm. Here. You can touch it. See how stringy it is?"

Jessica touched it. "Yes. Like rope."

"I got it when I fell off a bike when I was seven. I stuck my arms out instead of my hands, so the bottom of my arm is what got scratched."

"Such a little scar," said Jessica.

"Yes, but it fades out in the sun, you know."

"But you'd have to take off your top."

"That's just what I do." She took a long breath. "You know you can sunbathe without your clothes on, Jessica. Tris and I do it all the time when we go to Peng Chau."

"I could never do that alone."

"Then we can do it *together*."

"You would do that with me?"

"Oh, I think it would be fun."

Quietly, shyly, Jessica said, "I've always wanted to try. I saw a picture in a German magazine once and thought it would be the best thing in the world."

"It is," said Aspidistra. But then she started to giggle. "Well, *just about* the best thing."

Opening herself up to her, Jessica did not confuse Aspidistra with Philip as she had earlier. But Jessica was well aware Philip had opened the portals of speech for her, and now she poured out her feelings to the gangly blonde girl in the peasant dress—when she could bother to put on a dress, because it turned out Aspidistra liked slouching around the flat wearing no clothes at all. And the dresses were actually Poppy's peasant dresses, because Aspidistra had brought nothing up with her, just a wallet with her Hong Kong identity card in it, ASPIDISTRA BENNING with Chinese characters underneath that actually, it turned out, meant *Aspidistra*.

"Ye Lan," said Mrs. Sinden, reading it. "You know, dear, it says Aspidistra."

Aspidistra barely heard what she said except for the word *dear*. Something inside Jessica Sinden was shifting.

"Is it a real Chinese name?" asked Jessica.

"I don't know. I think maybe someone made it up."

"Well! They did a proper job of it."

"I thought you didn't know Chinese," said Aspidistra. "Tristan said you only knew hello and goodbye."

Jessica hesitated (hesitation came so naturally to her, Aspidistra observed) then said:

"Elaine once took me to the Shaolin Monastery in Henan. I don't know why she did. I was miserable the whole time. They told me to stop fidgeting and not to say a word. They tried explaining it to me, something about stillness and light, but the best I could make of it was that they didn't want to hear any English at the Monastery. So I flummoxed them by picking up some Chinese."

"But you picked up more than a couple of words, didn't you?"

"Well!" said Jessica. "It turns out that there is only one kind of book that I like reading."

"Dictionaries?" ventured Aspidistra.

"Yes," said Jessica, continuing to marvel at the girl's feel for her. "I never quite got beyond the letter *A*, you know, but for *Aspidistra*, that was sufficient."

"I like cookbooks," offered Aspidistra, "but I can never seem to remember the titles or names of authors. Just the directions."

"Do you follow them, though?"

"I don't really follow anything. Those eggs I made for you this morning—"

Jessica suppressed a grimace.

"I mean, I didn't *mean* to burn them. It's like they were in the pan and then I started looking through this big pile of rags in the corner of the kitchen."

"Poppy's rags," said Jessica.

"Really? They're Poppy's? What does *she* need them for?"

"She needs them for *me*," said Jessica.

Aspidistra did not know exactly what she meant, but she was developing a good ear for Jessica Sinden. Somehow Poppy had appeased her mother with rags. There had to be a good story behind it, but she doubted that she could ever force it out of either of them. Some things were like that.

~

The days went on. Jessica slept and Aspidistra slept next to her. Well into May, one day seemed very much like the next, until the morning Jessica's cell phone started to buzz around the table like a fly.

It was Elaine Kwan texting her. Aspidistra almost jumped out of her skin when her handle came up on the screen: ELAINE KWAN HK SAR DEPT OF HEALTH.

Aspidistra I know you're there. My driver says he saw you in the garden. Stay inside from now on. AND PUT SOME CLOTHES ON. I am going to have to call you RIGHT NOW on Jessica's phone. I'll give you a few minutes to find it. She usually keeps it in her fanny pack. When I call, don't say anything unless I prompt you. Just follow my lead.

Ten minutes later Aspidistra heard Jessica's cell phone buzzing away.

"Hello?" she said, picking up.

"Is Jessica there?"

"She's taking a nap. May I take a message?"

"This is Elaine Kwan. I am calling as a courtesy to check on her status." She paused gravely. "If she is—not well—you know that would be a matter of concern to us."

"Oh, she's quite well," offered Aspidistra cheerfully. "She just took a Bovary out for a nice long walk on Peel Rise."

"Ah, that's suitably isolated. I hope she wore a mask."

"Why, yes. Dr. Sinden always has a good supply of them on hand."

"I'm glad to hear it," said Elaine. "Did you lay in the store of bleach?"

"Why, yes."

"So you must be the *maid*, Mina."

Aspidistra widened her eyes and quickly said, knowing the phrase, "Yes, Mum."

Aspidistra could have sworn she heard Elaine smiling over the phone.

"It's good of you to stay on with your employer, Mina. So many maids have fled for the Philippines. Your have your own quarters, I presume?"

"Yes, Mum."

"Suitably distanced?"

"In the back by the garden, Mum."

"Mina, I need to tell you that should Mrs. Sinden develop any of the following symptoms," and here she read off a long list, fever, cough, shortness of breath, chills, muscle pain, headache, sore throat, "you should call this number immediately and ask for me."

"Yes, Mum."

"And not panic."

"Yes, Mum."

"So. Do you have any questions for me?"

"No, Mum."

"Very good then. You should know I will call in to check from time to time. Goodbye for now, Mina."

Aspidistra heard two clicks at the end; Elaine, then a second listener hanging up.

22

july 1, 2003

EDWARD AND JESSICA were on the patio outside the bedroom. The patio faced east, toward Aberdeen, and to the north, Stanley. A moderate breeze came in over Aberdeen, a wind with a diesel tang. Edward was used to the smell, knowing that up here, on the Peak, a sudden updraft was liable at any moment to carry it out to sea. The air in Hong Kong was bad, but on the Peak it was intermittently fresh. It was one of those small blessings he was thankful for.

Dr. Sinden didn't spend his days with his wife any more. He took on more patients than he had to. He even started to develop a reputation as one of the very few Western doctors in Hong Kong who had responded to the call of the coronavirus. He received a medal from Tung Chee-Wah and a citation from the Hong Kong Medical Association. So, more than ever, he had a very full case load. He even began making house calls. He did not actually think of it as calling on patients, but as calling on households themselves, places where the household deities were other than Felicity Sinden, Judy Royce-Chapman, and more lately, Philip Nye.

He knew about his wife's affair fairly early. A colleague at Matilda asked if he needed a place to stay. The rest was more or less in plain view. He was jealous, but Nye was dead by the time he came back from China. Edward was inclined to leave well enough alone. He saw how, recovering from the coronavirus that killed her lover, the skin on his wife's thighs started to become loose. She also began to divest herself of her clothes. She used to wear sweaters made of oiled wool. Now she wore thin blouses with draw-string pants and sandals. Aspidistra also dressed this way, but there was little to see when his wife dressed lightly. It was as if she had decided clothing was pointless. Aspidistra often came over, to walk Bovary, or so she said, for Edward never once saw her out with the dog.

Jessica sat across from him. She was in her heavy white terry cloth robe She had already ordered breakfast. He heard the light clatter of Mina preparing it in the kitchen. His wife had begun to eat more of late, at long last putting on a little weight after recovering from the coronavirus. He watched her as Mina came out and put the coffee and milk on the table.

"The milk is rather tepid, Mina," she said, touching the creamer.

"I'll go reheat it, Mum."

"Use the temperature gauge the way I showed you."

"I will, Mum."

"To precisely 68 degrees Centigrade."

"Yes, Mum."

"Not Fahrenheit."

"I know, Mum."

"And Mina?"

Mina gazed at her, unblinking.

"You may bring out the hot milk when it's ready. Then we wish to be left alone."

"Yes, Mum. Should I get I Bovary's leash ready?"

"Yes. You will find her in my bedroom."

Mina winced out a smile, and withdrew.

Her husband poured her a fresh cup of coffee and Jessica, settling into her chair, took a sip.

Edward read the paper and she watched him reading. Jessica avoided reading herself, as she had when her father was alive, but she liked watching people read. It was, in fact, one of the very few things she liked watching people do. Books enforced a quiet and mannered solitude. They were the dead, after all.

"Mum, may I—"

"Yes, Mina—"

"You know about today?"

Edward lowered his paper. He seemed to know about today, though Jessica did not.

"There is a—march."

"So there's going to be a celebration?" asked Jessica. "For the anniversary of the Handover?"

"Not exactly," said Dr. Sinden, putting down his paper. "It's going to be a demonstration. Against certain changes to the Basic Law. I suppose you know who Regina Yip is."

His wife took him in blankly.

"Well, your friend Elaine certainly does." Edward pointed to a picture in the paper, where Regina Yip was giving a speech about Article 23. A number of people stood behind the podium of the former Secretary for Security. Elaine and Simpson were among them.

"It says here they are expecting half a million people." Adding, "I think Mina would like the afternoon off."

"Oh. Well, then. Off with you!" she said. "You'll be back for dinner, though, won't you?"

"Yes , Mum."

Mina went off. Jessica reached for the paper and tried to read it. The words were there, but she could barely take them in:

DEMOCRACY RALLY SET FOR JULY 1

Mina came back with her hot milk. She waited until her employer poured some into her coffee, took a sip and nodded lightly. Then she went back into the flat, sliding the door almost shut. Almost, but not quite, because however occupied she was with her husband outside, Jessica Sinden would also be listening for the sound of her busy at work.

Dr. Sinden put down his paper and reached for his coffee. "I've been meaning to tell you, Jessica. A developer wants to buy this building. Someone from Shanghai. It's said he'll be making us a very generous offer."

"What will happen if he does?" asked Jessica. "Can we refuse?"

"I'm afraid not. It will be far too lucrative."

"Then what will he do with it? The building, I mean."

"Why, I think he'll take it down and build another."

"Just for the sake of it?"

"Nearly," said Dr. Sinden. "The building is nearly forty years old. Quite ancient, in Hong Kong terms. But really I think it's the land around it. With all this abutting property they could build three or four times as many flats."

"It would fill it up the Peak, though."

"I think that's the point, Jessica. More people in the same space."

She made out the outline of Philip's building. Roma no longer lived there. She had seen a picture of her when she returned to Hong Kong early in June to claim his body. It was oddly unaffecting. Jessica had cared for him alive, not dead.

"Will they take down Vivian Court?" she asked.

"Not while Vivian Hollister is alive. But once the old dowager bites the dust—"

"The mites will gather."

"Exactly. I should think if we came back to the Peak in twenty years, we should find the place unrecognizable."

"The mountains will still be there. The paths."

"Possibly. But I think if they could take down a mountain and put up a building in its stead, they would."

"Would it still be the Peak?"

"Well, I suppose they could call it that. After all, they are as craven about that as the Americans are. Think of Madison Square Garden."

"It's just a big ugly building, isn't it?" ventured Jessica. "I must admit I've never been there."

"A very round and thick one. Rather like a large ventilation cap."

"It sounds dreadful."

"I'm afraid it's going that way here, Jessica. It can't be helped. A garden that is no longer a garden. A peak that is no longer a mountain."

"I suppose that's what they're celebrating down there," said Jessica.

Dr. Sinden glanced again at the paper, which said that the protestors planned to dress in black.

"Our expulsion," she added.

Jessica tried to add up everything she had done in Hong Kong. She began with her flat—an old colonial flat in a block of them, derelict years ago, its windows framed with iron rusted down to a brittle powder, its floor buckled with moisture and mold. Then her garden, which used to be a parking lot. Jessica did not try to count people; she knew so few; Elaine and her husband, and now, Aspidistra Benning. She concentrated on her little plot of Hong Kong, such as it was, which is what she always said when referring to the life she had scratched out for herself. Now her little world would be taken down to build another little world for someone else, but by then, she hoped, she would be miles away, across one, two, three oceans, tending to the only small plot of land she knew to be permanent, Felicity's grave.

"Perhaps it's time to move, then," said Dr. Sinden.

"To Discovery Bay? Or perhaps Clear Water Bay?"

"No."

"Surely you don't mean England?"

"We are *from* there, Edward. I think Elaine means to retire there."

"What about Poppy? Tristan?"

"Poppy will follow us once she finishes her program." She still could not bring herself to say *acupuncture*. The word was just too prurient.

"And Tristan?"

"I think Aspidistra would prefer Britain."

"What about the mother? Won't she follow? I took it you thought she was rather appalling."

"Oh, leave her to me," said Jessica, thinking of her Limoges. "She will go back to Canada soon enough. I will see to it."

She said it so forcefully that Edward let it pass. Jessica's tone was in itself a *fait accompli*. If she somehow presumed it was in her power singlehandedly to resettle Jill Benning back in Canada, he knew to take it on faith that it was. He saw it in her hard cold eyes, green as the north Atlantic on a winter's day.

Dr. Sinden rustled his newspaper. "Whatever happened to the wife of that American?"

"What American?" asked Jessica.

"You know, the wife of the one you used to walk the dogs with? The one you tried to visit before he died in the outbreak. I haven't seen her, since—well, that time she came to go out with you to Elaine's. Just before I was called to Foshan."

He rustled his paper again. The headline said something about the Hang Lung Group coming to an agreement with Baker Nicholson—Roma's firm.

Jessica composed herself. "Ah, her. I think she's left."

Dr. Sinden lowered his paper.

"Really?"

"Yes. For New York."

He sighed. "I didn't know she was gone, but why would I? I don't even remember her name. Do you?"

Jessica shook her head slowly, but said, "Yes."

"Pity. I remember hoping you'd befriend her. I know you took her once to a party at Elaine Kwan's. Impressive woman. I was a bit sorry you let her go after—well, the incident. The two of you seemed to have so much in common."

Jessica's mouth tightened at its edges.

"You know, Jessica, I often think we just bypassed that one. Several doctors died at the First Peoples Hospital; I knew one of them; he was a good man."

"A good man," she repeated, thinking of Philip.

"Still," he said, ignoring the slight tremor in his wife's voice, thinking rather of his old mental game of viral roulette. "It could have been either of us in some hospital as well. You were lucky Aspidistra decided to go looking for you."

He turned a page of his paper. "I see Baker Nicholson is expanding. They're opening a new office in Shanghai." He folded his copy of the *Post* to show her a group portrait of the Baker Nicholson office after the restructuring.

"I'm sure they were sad to lose her, though."

"I'm not so certain," she said quietly.

"I see what you mean," said Dr. Sinden, reading on. "It says here the firm is making an effort to hire more Mainland Chinese." He put the paper down. "I suppose that does seem to be the way it's going now."

"Rather," said Jessica.

"What?" he said, hearing something in her tone. "Do you actually not like it here any more?"

"No, well, yes, I mean, still, somewhat. But I must admit I have been thinking occasionally about going home."

"Back to England? I'm surprised to hear you say it again. Why, you were the one, only five months ago, who said that our little house was keeping, oh, how did you put it, the last watch of the Empire."

"I can still watch it from there."

"I dare say we can watch the Empire dribble away from anywhere. But if we went back, you'd have to give up your little room at the Helena May."

So he knew about that. What else he knew, he did not let on. He tended to ignore lines that refused to run exactly parallel. She carefully let it pass. She was still a member there. She had a perfect right to retain a room. It was a woman's club, a place where Hong Kong matrons could lunch with their friends and entertain guests. It had any number of conveniences, a lounge, a dining room, a small garden. It was the only place in Hong Kong, off the Peak, where she genuinely felt at home.

"The Helena May," said Jessica to her husband. "No, no, I'll never give that up, even if we go back to England. Not my room at the Helena May."

epilogue

july 1, 2007

TRISTAN MEANT to stay close to his mother and Aspidistra, but time went by, and after he had moved several times, he found himself in London. He knew very little of his daughter's life. Aspidistra liked to take her to the beach in Brighton, out to the end of a long Victorian pier where there was a carousel and a store selling sticky candies. Clover was a sticky little girl the way Poppy had been, and still was. Tristan disliked the way his sister still smacked her lips when she talked, and rarely visited her in Hampstead, where she had opened a small acupuncture practice that was never quite clean, and never quite patronized. If his father was still alive Tristan was sure he would say his acupuncturist daughter was *sticky*, though also in that Chinese sense of sticking people with needles for reasons that never seemed remotely clear to him.

His mother and Aspidistra lived in a horrible little cottage with the grand name of Pepys Hall, Moulsecoomb, Bevendean, East Sussex. Didn't they use numbers here in England? The house itself was more a hallway than a hall. The room his mother called The Great Room was actually the smallest room in the house. The walls were sandstone but seemed like sandpaper pasted to cement. The air was dusty and humid. The room was upholstered, curtained, and stocked with small blurry photographs dwarfed by their frames. The only thing the cottage had was land, but the land was all behind it, not in front. The cottage stood at an odd angle only a few feet from the nearest road.

That day he took the A23 from London to Brighton instead of taking the train. He left Cheng Li, the broker from Shanghai he lived with in Sloane Square behind in the their flat, and went along King's Road, through Eaton Square and past Grosvenor Garden, turning south after Waterloo Station, watching with envy the people waiting, on corner after corner, for buses taking them anywhere but to his mother's house.

What a place! Last time she made him water her garden. The hoses leaked, the soil was damp, and he spoiled a perfectly good pair of beautifully-faded pink pants for which his mother seemed to have a barely-concealed antipathy. Of course he had to visit his mother, daughter, and whatever it was Aspidistra was to him (for they had never married) from time to time. But because this was July 1st there would always be the danger of a visit to the East Sussex down where Felicity Sinden, and more lately, Edward Sinden, were buried. He would have to use his influence with Aspidistra to get out of whatever obligation his mother meant to impose on him, so he could stay behind and play super-market with Clover behind her toy cash register.

Tristan came in from the north. He passed a running stream and an old water-mill. A thin light came from the house through the leaves in the trees. Sighing, he pushed back his hair from his face, and got out of the car.

His mother was already at the door.

"Cheng Li," she began. "She never says a word to me."

Tristan always had to remember that his mother had no store of *hellos*, *goodbyes*, or even anything remotely pleasant. She merely picked up where she had left off last time she saw him.

"Funny," said Tristan, adjusting himself, "that's just what she says about you."

They made their way to the living room. There was a single tray with some dry crackers on it.

"Why don't you put out some more marmite?" he asked his mother.

"Tris, haven't you ever seen her marmite?" asked Aspidistra from an overstuffed chair in the corner, seeming, as always, unafraid of what his mother might think.

And his mother was smiling at her. Odd how she liked to be needled by that girl!

Tristan wanted to tell Aspidistra how, one night last week, he woke up in a panic about his mother's marmite, thinking he had taken some home and it had exploded in his refrigerator. But he didn't, because he'd already told Poppy about it and they'd had a good laugh.

They were sitting in a room with the lights out; another of his mother's little economies. Aspidistra was wearing her hair in a long plait. Her eyes were sleepy. His mother's thin hair was tied back in a ribbon, and her green eyes, as always, were compulsively alert.

Jessica moved off toward the kitchen. Aspidistra called after her, "Mama, remember the tomatoes. I left them out on the table."

So she called her *Mama* now. She liked having more than one mother. Aspidistra was prurient about parenting, and if Clover could have more than one father she would probably be all right with that, too.

Jessica returned with a plate of stuffed tomatoes in her hand saying, "I want to go over to Deidre's. I'd like some of her rosemary."

"I was also thinking," said Aspidistra. She opened a drawer and took out a card case from the twenties made of iguana leather. She turned it over. "Do you think she might like it?"

"Whatever for?"

"It was her birthday yesterday. And you know how much she likes old things."

"I see." The case had belonged to her father but Jessica was not attached to it. Even Philip's ring she never took out of a locked drawer in her study. He lived on through Aspidistra, who kept channeling Philip's perceptions in that uncanny way she had. Just the other day it was to tell her she had very beautiful skin; not a freckle or mark of any kind on it. The day before it had been picture frames, saying that the windows were like pictures on easels, making the inside of the house into a museum of the outdoors. Jessica almost felt Philip there. But only almost: he was there, not as ghost, which was an image, but as a constant presence in and around her, a floater in her field of vision, there only if she didn't concentrate on it, and vanishing if she did.

She was glad to give the case away. Touching it made her want to wash her hands. It bothered her, not that the iguana had been killed, but that it had been chopped into little pieces. You never saw a whole iguana skin made into a coat or rug. Just these little bits made into bands for watches or trim for purses.

What on earth am I doing thinking about iguanas, she thought.

"Just give it to her," she told Aspidistra, turning away.

Tristan saw his mother was thinking something, but he had no idea what. She was bent over the table top, looking at how someone's glass had made a white ring on the mahogany finish. She frowned. She had five coasters out. She caught his eye as though he hadn't noticed. But she was wrong. He noticed *some* things.

Then he felt the graze of Aspidistra's touch.

"I was wondering if..." she began, trailing off.

He knew the last part. Aspidistra wanted him to spend the night.

Tristan wouldn't have thought at that moment there was an emotion he could feel stronger than exasperation with his mother, who never gave him credit for anything, but then he felt the sadness of Aspidistra's touch. She wanted him back. She was willing to take a little part of him, even for a night. She had little intimacies. Last time he stayed over she gave him a cheap greeting card, something displayed in one of the stands at the pavilion on the pier, with a picture of a woman on the outside. There was a tab at the bottom of the card, and when he pulled it, her clothes slid off. It was only then that he noticed the woman, a blonde with wavy hair and a half smile, looked a lot like Aspidistra. She wanted him to think of her naked. So like her, to take something generic and make it her own. His mother was ruthlessly selective in what she made her own; few things ever qualified, and if she lost them, she always seemed to get them back. But Aspidistra could take almost anything and fold it into her world. Cheng Li liked shopping for new things. Aspidistra found old things, strays, and adopted them.

He was one of those strays. So too, he supposed, was his mother. He watched her pass her hand over her forehead, sighing about something.

He watched Aspidistra watch her, too. She came up to his mother and stroked her hair. So intimate: he almost expected his mother to recoil, but instead, she took Aspidistra's hand and began to laugh.

"It's not funny," said Jessica, "but I can't help laughing about iguanas."

"Then maybe it is funny," said Aspidistra.

His mother lifted her eyebrows, a little startled.

"Well! Then perhaps it is."

The *it* was unclear to Tristan. The two of them had a private world of mutual reference. It bound them. Whenever he had a cut, his mother wound a crepe bandage round and round it, fastening it with a safety pin. She liked the ties that bind, only here she was not doing the binding. Aspidistra was.

Aspidistra caught his eye. Her skin was pretty in a peach-fuzz way, though her skin was not beautiful. He found himself thinking what the night would be like, how Aspidistra would wake up at two or three, pulling her knees under her chin and opening the window to look at the moonlight, sometimes glancing over at his face with a remote, wistful calm. There was a kind of courtship between them, but it was after the fact rather than before. She was willing to be something to him without defining just what that something was, just as she was willing to be something to his mother without ever saying what that was, either. That lack of definition was strangely satisfying.

Aspidistra picked up right away that Tristan was admiring something about her; she also knew it meant he wanted to stay the night.

⌣

Jill Benning had not meant to come that day, that week or even that month. She just got on a plane in Toronto, and when Tristan answered the door that afternoon, there she was.

She had a box under her arm. A bit of twine with a bell dangled from the bottom.

Tristan watched as she tiptoed into the house, going down the hall, looking from side to side, her yellow hair swaying stiffly.

"Is—*Mrs. Sinden*—in?"

Well might she call her that. His mother had paid a steep price to get rid of her. He watched while Jill Benning unbuttoned her coat, for it was a cool day in July—and said something or other, he couldn't make out whole sentences, just fragments, *here to, a thought I had, just a notion.* She didn't seem to have any luggage, just that big heavy box. He found himself thinking it was some ugly housewarming gift, probably made of plastic, wishing she could just give it to her mother and leave before his mother opened it and managed to say said something nasty.

He took her to the living room, where his mother was, then scuttled off to the next room to see if Aspidistra was back from Deidre's.

Jill had not seen Jessica Sinden in three years. Not, since, unaccountably, she pushed her reliquary on her a few days after Aspidistra found out she was pregnant. She wanted to run straight to her appraiser, an old man on Gough Street, who, seeing the snapshot Aspidistra had taken, said that the third of these 12th century pieces, long thought missing, must be worth several hundred thousand pounds, minimum.

In the parking lot, Jill sat in her Toyota and dialed the number of her appraiser over and over again. But she could not bring herself to push the call button. Jessica Sinden had given her something precious— something so full of meaning to her that Aspidistra, who she once asked about it, could not even begin to explain it. *It means—everything—to her, Mama. Nothing less than everything.* And yet Jessica Sinden had given it to her, of all people.

Jill was unable to sell it. The reliquary was a force that had arrived in her life. She took it home to Discovery Bay. Then she took it to Toronto. It was so beautiful it made everything else around it look ugly.

And now she was giving it back.

"Here, this is yours," she said, walking into the living room, a dark place with walls that seemed almost damp.

Jill didn't know where to put it, so she just shoved it toward Jessica Sinden.

Jessica felt the heft of it. She flinched with surprise. She was always one for knowing the weights and measures of things; she had handled her Limoges a thousand times. Her breath seemed to collect at the top of her lungs, as though the air had weight. Then she took the box and sat in a hard chair in a particularly lightless corner of the room.

Jessica looked down at the box, took a slow, deep breath, and then softly, as if the reliquary were a living thing, put her open hands over the box.

"I tried to sell it. Twice," Jill said over her, in a trembling voice. "No, three times. But I always changed my mind."

Jessica tried not to notice that Jill Benning was wearing turquoise shorts, yellow running shoes, and a white halter top.

"I'm so sorry to arrive unannounced," she continued. "I mean, I just kind of got on the plane. I took the reliquary as a carry-on. I was terrified they would find it on me coming through customs. But you know, the thing is so fancy it kind of looks like a fake. The woman in front of me was bringing in this gigantic gilded bird cage that looked like it was worth twice as much as this. They let her through with the damn thing anyway, and then they let me in. Just waved me through, think of that! I'm glad they didn't try lifting it, though. Gold is just—so heavy."

The longer she talked to Jessica Sinden, the more stupid Jill Benning felt.

"I'm not Aspidistra," said Jill after a long, awkward pause, seeing the rigidity of Jessica's face. "I'm clumsy. And I know I don't speak well. I'm always talking, well, out of turn."

Jessica's long fingers rested lightly on the box.

"I mean, almost the last time I saw you, you had this super complicated relationship with that man Philip Nye, and I all I could do was stand there making—insinuations."

"I well remember," said Jessica.

"It's just that I want to apologize. I don't know what you had with him. But it was none of my business to ask. I want to start again—if you'll let me."

Jessica said nothing.

"You don't have to think of me as a relative. Or even as a friend."

"You are Clover's grandmother," said Jessica, her voice softening.

"I suppose, but Aspidistra—she is sort of your daughter now, isn't she? I mean, I just kind of dropped out."

The statement was so incontestably true that Jessica felt compelled not to gainsay it.

"And I like that she is. I mean, I want her to be here. I don't have to visit much, you know, but I want you to know how glad I am—"

Tearing up, she broke off.

"They may never marry," said Jessica, quietly enough so that Tristan, who was in the other room, could not hear her.

Jill wiped her tears. "I know that. But still—I want to start again. If you'll let me."

"Very well," was all Jessica said. Then her green eyes seemed to sharpen.

"Where are your bags?" Jill heard her ask.

"I'm staying at a hotel," said Jill.

"I see," Jessica said flatly, looking into Jill's slightly frightened face. "Please call for them."

She said it without warmth, yet Jill Benning felt the fact of it rippling through her: it *was* warm. *You belong here,* she seemed to be saying. *As much as Aspidistra. You belong with us.* Jill Benning had never been further than three feet into her flat on the Peak in Hong Kong. Gad did they have money then! Where had it all gone? Dr. Sinden was dead. Perhaps they had been living beyond their means—expats so often did. She saw the dirty plaster on the walls. The house was old and so unlike what she expected. The wallpaper was grayish pink with a pattern of small rosebuds. The windows were dull with dust. On the sill was a single sickly plant with dark stemless leaves. The plant in its green-glazed pot looked somehow familiar to Jill. Maybe she used to have one, or maybe she just read about it somewhere. She just couldn't place it.

"Oh Mama!" cried Aspidistra, rushing into the room, having correctly divined, in that uncanny way of hers, what was in the box. "You are so good!"

Jill put her shoulder bag on the ground and began to rummage through it. "Honey, I brought you something, too. I know I have it in here, just give me a sec."

She started to turn the bag upside down, stopped, pored over at her daughter's face and said, "You're missing an earring, honey," then dumped the contents of the bag onto the floor. There were three brushes and several wallets, a flashlight, several packs of chewing gum, a couple of parking tickets, and some crumpled papers with lists on them.

"Here," she said. She handed Aspidistra an old picture of her daughter holding Wylie, Philip Nye's dog. I know you liked walking him so much, and now you've got Bovary—"

"Bovary is dead," said Jessica, without emotion.

"Oh, I'm sorry. It's me being me again. I'm always saying the wrong thing. I didn't know."

"How could you have? In any case the memory is legitimate."

Jill caught the word, *legitimate*, but had no idea what Jessica Sinden meant by it. Were there illegitimate memories?

"Well! In any case, come in out of the cold," continued Jessica. "Let me show you your room."

It was not cold. It was July in fact, and they were in the living room, not on the doorstep, but for Jessica Sinden everything was cold, no matter how warm it might seem to her.

Walking down the hallway, Jessica put her thin arm through hers. Jill felt a trembling in her left eye. Jessica still did not look at her directly. Jill tried not to look at her. If she met her eye, Jessica's mouth would immediately tighten. Jill found herself looking longingly out the casement window as they went up the stairs. Outside was the real warmth of a July day, the quiet green of a distant line of trees, a field in flower, a passing flock of birds.

"Come. Let me show you your room."

Jessica gave her a mild smile. Her voice was unmistakably accepting. Jill rushed to interpret it, then wondered why she couldn't. She felt a sweetness about her, but it was sad too, as though anything touching her turned partly into sorrow. Jessica Sinden was not about to start exchanging confidences with her. She still had that same face cut in stone, with colorless lips and exhausting green eyes, so unlike the wool of Aspidistra's soft blue eyes. And those hands with long branch-like fingers, while Aspidistra had such sweet plump hands. Aspidistra took Jessica's hand sometimes. She held it when they sat together on the sofa near the fire on winter days.

The arduous warmth of Jessica Sinden would take some getting used to. And yet Aspidistra seemed so at ease with her!

Jessica paused at the threshold to a bedroom.

"I thought we might go to the cemetery today, but Poppy doesn't want to. Elaine is also disinclined. But if I do go, you are welcome to accompany me."

"I would be happy to," Jill began, regretting right away that she said *happy*. Jill was always happy to do things, but she never visited cemeteries. She supposed there was some way of talking about them without mentioning happiness, if only she had a presence of mind she would never have.

⁓

Elaine Kwan meant, like Tristan, to see Jessica more often once she moved to England, but it rarely fell out that way. This time she made her promise not to take her to the cemetery where Edward and Felicity were buried. Edward's funeral had been hard enough. Congestive heart failure—at his age! She did not want to relive it.

Back in Hong Kong there would be celebrations on this day; ten years since the Handover. Here was nothing but the sense that something had gone into the past—what, she was not sure, the two Sindens, or perhaps old China as it was in Hong Kong when she was a young woman, the last redoubt of the British Empire.

Simpson rarely went there on these July 1sts. He said his wife was free to martyr herself, but no, thank you, that he would rather spend the day rolling down country roads north of London, top down, in his green

MG. He had seen the mold inside the marmite jar and did not like going to a dinner where there would be nothing to eat but canned tongue, hard boiled eggs, boiled beef and bitter herbs.

The last time Elaine went to the cemetery, she brought a bag of oranges and a couple of sticks of incense. She meant to leave an orange at each of the graves, a propitiatory orange like the ones she was used to seeing on the small street altars of Hong Kong, but Poppy got ahold of one of them for one of her little acupuncture demonstrations and made a pulpy mess of it. This time she considered bringing apples, grapefruit, pears, or even little boxes of Whitman's chocolates, but finally she just took a bag with her pajamas and toothbrush. Jessica might go or she might not, but either way, Elaine was not going.

Another car pulled up. Poppy in her Land Rover. She was wearing a yellow down jacket. Her hair was parted in the middle and carefully brushed in two distinct sections, probably a concession to her mother.

Elaine found herself wondering if men found Poppy attractive. Like her mother, she spoke in precise, clipped rhythms, and flapped around like a lopsided bird. Did she still like lying around in her room, red-faced in the stuffiness, staring at the ceiling, trying to balance a tennis ball on her chest?

"Well, what are we going to do?" she began, coming up to Elaine.

Seeing her mother was always a problem for Poppy. She spent years avoiding her in that flat in Hong Kong. Now she had all of England to avoid her in.

"You know what time it is?" Seeing Elaine shake her head, she added, "When I used to ask Felicity that she'd say, *Time enough, Poppy. Time enough.*"

Elaine rubbed her hand across the back of her neck. She tired easily of Poppy, just as her friend did.

"Your mother told me to expect an additional visitor. She said Jill Benning is here."

"Her? You've got to be kidding," said Poppy. "Mama hates her. She even paid her off to stay in Canada, you know."

Elaine supposed this was a family secret, but that Poppy was not sophisticated enough to know the difference between a concealed and an unconcealed secret.

Elaine started moving toward the house, Poppy following her.

"Maybe Aspidistra is pregnant again," Elaine heard Poppy saying from behind.

Another thing not to be spoken of, thought Elaine, who was relieved to reach the door and ring the bell.

Tristan answered the door. Poppy brushed past both of them.

"We were just talking about you," she said.

"That would be a first," Tristan said, calling after her. "Mother is in the kitchen."

He was putting on weight, just as Felicity had. Elaine felt sorry for him. His life was miserable, just as Felicity's was, but unlike Felicity, he was never going to figure out what he wanted in life. He didn't want Aspidistra's love, didn't want his daughter, didn't want to do a day's worth of decent work. He had a perfectly beautiful little flat near her in Sloane Square and lived there with Cheng Li, a perfectly beautiful woman. His hand shook when he brought a glass of water (or was it gin?) to his mouth. His eyes seemed dull and spiritless.

Jessica Sinden was sitting with her hands folded on the kitchen table. She asked how Elaine was, and Elaine asked how her friend was, both of them knowing they would find out later. She seemed a little surprised to see her, but then again, her friend was always a little surprised to see anyone.

Tristan came in. "The place next door is up for sale. I saw the sign."

"One would think they could advertise in the papers," said Jessica.

Elaine heard the *one*. Jessica hardened into formality in groups. Tristan sighed deeply and looked across that yard at the neighboring house, which, with its wattles and thatch, was perfectly beautiful, too.

"Maybe Mama could buy it," said Aspidistra, following him in.

Elaine almost jumped out of her skin at the statement—Jill Benning, living *here*—but she was even more surprised by how unsurprised Jessica Sinden was. This would be just the moment when their eyes might meet, sharing condolences at how easily good things—what few there were—could be ruined. But her friend let it pass.

"Perhaps you should leave your card with her," Elaine heard her tell Tristan.

This was already too much for Elaine Kwan. What had happened to her friend? Someone had left the top off a jar of marmite and stuck a knife in the brown paste. Three or four boxes of crackers lay open in the table. Aspidistra's cookbooks were all over the room, some open on the counters, some piled on a chair in the corner, a few on the floor. Elaine wanted to pull out a cigarette and light it in contempt right then and there, but her cigarettes were back in the car. She always assumed Jessica Sinden, living with Aspidistra, would in the end break her over a wheel and turn her into another Jessica Sinden, but look, just the opposite had happened! Her friend was not easy-going; she never could go that far; but here she was, mysteriously edgeless in a quiet, passive way.

Perhaps Phillip's death lingered in her, though she never spoke of it.

The phone rang; an old dial phone on the wall. They all looked at one another, Tristan, Poppy, Aspidistra, Jessica. It rang and rang then it stopped. Then Jessica turned to her son.

"Tristan, call Cheng Li when you have a chance."

The way she said it implied he wouldn't. How she knew who was calling was beyond Elaine, though, knowing her friend, it was possible that Cheng Li was the only person in the world who ever called this house, and that these people, in this room at this moment, were the only ones who had ever been in it. Come to think of it, she had never heard a phone ringing in Jessica's flat on the Peak in Hong Kong; not even once.

Elaine's eyes met Jessica's. Her friend had a limited store of patience, and her son and his new girlfriend were already beginning to exhaust it.

"I just want to see you for five minutes," she heard her say. She began to move off.

"Where you going?" asked Aspidistra.

"We'll be right back, dear," said Jessica.

Her friend took her by the elbow into the next room, a small study, quietly shutting the door behind them.

"How long are you staying?" Jessica asked her.

"It depends. Are you going to the cemetery this year?"

"I don't know. But I doubt it."

"Good," said Elaine. "I don't mind peeling potatoes for my supper."

"So you'll stay the night?"

"No cemetery?" pressed Elaine.

Jessica sighed. "Very well. No cemetery. I will set a place for you with the others."

Elaine heard the odd sound of *others*, then she heard her friend say:

"The others include Jill Benning, who is upstairs now, unpacking her things. She came for a very real purpose, and I must tell you that she is now welcome in my home."

"You don't mean Aspidistra's mother?"

Jessica gave her an unyielding look.

"The one who took your reliquary?" pressed Elaine.

"I did give it to her, you know."

Elaine frowned.

"Still. Why on earth is she here?"

"I suppose it's a form of repatriation," said Jessica.

"I was *wondering* what that box was in the hallway."

"As well you might," she said, pleased with her friend's quickness, for she rarely received packages; the last one had a baseball bat in it. "And, if you must know, she is a grandmother in at least one instance."

Elaine took *at least one instance* as her friend's way of announcing a prospective pregnancy, and left it at that. They were both high crumbling walls of themselves at this age, weren't they, and some breaches of their resistance to the general social madness of the world might well be resistant to repair.

"Just don't look at her," Jessica advised her friend, moving toward the door. "If you do, she'll start to talk."

"Heaven forfend," said Elaine, folding her arms in front of her.

Jessica smiled slightly, hearing this renewal of their little compact of old. Jessica would do her best to keep them apart for the rest of the day. But in some way her friend had left her. Elaine thought of her now as Aspidistra's mother, though *mother* would never describe who she was to Jessica Sinden. But she also thought, hearing the laughter spilling over from the next room—Tristan was telling a story about Poppy that Poppy, Aspidistra and Jill found uproariously funny—*and then with all those needles in it Elaine's orange just exploded*—that it hardly mattered to Jessica who was there, or what they said or did, because they would never be Philip Nye.

~

And so they came together around a long table in the kitchen. Jessica brushed down her apron and stood in the center, mixing flour into water, squinting, trying to decipher Aspidistra's handwriting on a recipe card. Elaine peeled potatoes and talked to Tristan about real estate in London. Poppy came in and started sticking needles in another orange. Jill was for once happy to say very little, seeing her daughter talk to Poppy about how squeamish English people could be about needles. Listening, Aspidistra laughed lightly, pulling a little gold barrette out of her hair and pushing it back in. Clover moved around under the table, talking to herself about how one day she would like to have a little sister.

"You'd have to share a bedroom," Aspidistra told her, but Clover did not hear her, moving away to snatch a cherry tomato that had dropped from the table.

Jessica felt contented. She could never remember feeling it before. Things always had content, didn't they, something placed inside else, a jar with marmite in it, a ring around its finger, a reliquary with its ashes, but then again, sometimes things were simply empty, and not in a bad way. Like now: this content was strangely contentless: seven people in one room, that was all, but strangely enough, it *was* all. Jessica looked around her and liked what she saw: the six acres of land behind their house and the arc of sky above it, Clover safe in her little booth in the kitchen with her toy cash register, Aspidistra looking over Tristan in that state she had, yearning for another state of pregnant self-sufficiency (she would make sure her son spent the night); Jill Benning here for the week, and perhaps much longer, back with her reliquary, which would always follow her around until she at last slipped into it. And the name *Sinden* prospectively, for once, in a state of increase rather than contraction.

The sun climbed higher in the sky. Outside she saw the dowdy brown ducks resting at the river's edge and the rows of willows with their long leaves drooping, swaying lightly in the wind. Jessica put on her apron. She sharpened a paring knife and went to the salt box and took out half a dozen onions. She set them down on the cutting board and began work, slicing them one way, then another, then chopping them until her eyes began to water. Aspidistra smiled gently at her, taking out her barrette again and letting her hair fall free.

She felt no happiness—happiness would be too much to ask from Jessica Sinden, but if this was peace, why, she could live with it.

A Note of Thanks

Many friends read this novel and helped me along the way.
I would like to thank Donald Ross, Athena Stockwell,
Bernd and Lilly Hagg, Susan Ginsburg, Julia Thacker,
Priya Doraswamy, and Curtis Key. Most of all
I would like to thank my wife, Elizabeth Kleber,
and my daughters, Rachel and Rebekah.